I REALLY HATED IT WHEN I LOOKED AT MY WA~~~ ~~~
realized it was 11:10.

"I have to get home," I said.

"Bummer," Jason said. "I bet we could talk all night."

"Yeah," I said.

He came up off the elbow he had been leaning on, and with just one finger brushed my hair off my cheek. "I'm not going to take you home unless you promise me we'll have more nights like this," he said.

I wasn't sure I could even breathe, much less answer. I just nodded.

He smiled, right at my mouth, and then kissed it—gingerly, the way you set somebody's grandmother's best china teacup on a saucer. I didn't even think about his smooth-shaven upper lip. That was way too mundane for the moment.

Dear Parent,

Thank you for considering Nancy Rue's book for your teen. We are pleased to publish her *Raise the Flag* series and believe these books are different than most you will find for teens.

Tragically, some of the things our teens face today are not easy to discuss. Nancy has created stories and characters that depict real kids, facing real-life issues with real faith. Our desire is to help you equip your children to act in a God-pleasing way no matter what they face.

Nancy has beautifully woven scriptural truth and direction into the choices and actions of her characters. She has worked hard to depict the issues in a sensitive way. However, I would recommend that you scan the book to determine if the subject matter is appropriate for your teen.

Sincerely,

Dan Rich
Publisher

Raise the Flag Series BOOK 5

FRIENDS DON'T
LET FRIENDS
DATE JASON

Nancy Rue

WaterBrook
PRESS

FRIENDS DON'T LET FRIENDS DATE JASON
PUBLISHED BY WATERBROOK PRESS
5446 North Academy Boulevard, Suite 200
Colorado Springs, Colorado 80918
A division of Random House, Inc.

Scripture quotations from *The Message.* Copyright © by Eugene H. Peterson
1993, 1994, 1995. Used by permission of NavPress Publishing Group. All
haiku poems except Marissa's are by Clark Strand, *Seeds from a Birch Tree* (New
York: Hyperion, 1997). Used by permission.

ISBN 1-57856-087-X

Published in association with the literary agency of Alive Communications, Inc.,
1465 Kelly Johnson Blvd., Suite 320, Colorado Springs, Colorado 80920

Rue, Nancy N.
     Friends don't let friends date Jason / Nancy Rue. —1st ed.
          p.   cm.—(Raise the flag series : bk. 5)
     Summary: Marissa's prayer group, the Flagpole Girls, lends support
when Marissa's relationship with her first boyfriend becomes complicated and
she has trouble communicating with God.
      ISBN 1-57856-087-X (pbk.)
      [1. Dating (Social customs)—Fiction. 2. Interpersonal relations—Fiction.
3. Hispanic Americans—Fiction. 4. Christian life—Fiction.] I. Title. II.
Series: Rue, Nancy N. Raise the flag series : bk. 5.
PZ7.R88515Fr 1999
[Fic]--dc21   99-10708
                                                                        CIP

Printed in the United States of America
1999—First Edition

10 9 8 7 6 5 4 3 2 1

To Jim, the true love I waited for

"WE'RE SUPPOSED TO BE BASKING," TOBEY SAID. "I'M NOT sure I even know how anymore."

"Know *how*?" Cheyenne said. She raised up on one elbow in the grass and scrunched up her forehead. "I don't even know what it *means*. I always thought it was some Spanish thing."

"No, Chey," I said to her. "That's *Basque*."

"It means to expose oneself pleasantly to warmth." All five of us looked at Norie. Leaning against the lone tree in the park, she opened one eye and gave us a Norie Vandenberger square grin. "I'm studying for the SATs so I know these things."

Brianna grunted. "How, girl? Readin' the dictionary?"

"Practically."

Cheyenne cocked her thick head of Indian-black hair. "I thought you weren't all freaked out about going to Harvard anymore."

"I'm not. But you don't get into Northwestern with slacker scores either."

"See, that's the problem." Tobey rose up on her knees on the one patch of Nevada grass we had managed to find and gave her strawberry-blond hair a toss. It draped like a silk curtain over her forehead for a shiny second and then fell into place, leaving her brown eyes in full, serious view. "We all have so much stuff going on, we hardly spend any time together, just us. Norie has the SATs and the newspaper. I have the SATs, plus Honor Council and the speech contest—"

"You guys have the prom," Cheyenne said, looking at Brianna, Norie, and Tobey.

"Not me, girl. I have enough going on just trying to graduate in two months," Brianna said. "Besides, I don't feel like hauling Ira into the prom on a stretcher. Isn't a tux in town that's going to fit over that neck brace either."

We all laughed because she did. Personally, I found it a little hard to yuck it up over somebody's broken neck. But as I watched Brianna lean back on her elbows in the grass and close her eyes peacefully to the sun, I realized that since Ira's "accident" and everything she had gone through because of it, she was a lot calmer. Like she was so centered on something, nobody could tear her loose.

"Speaking of prom," Tobey said, "are you going, Marissa?"

I sat up straight over my Doritos bag, already feeling the surprised red coming up on my cheeks. I shook my head. "Not that *I'm* aware of!" I said. "I'm just a sophomore, remember?"

Brianna grunted and gave me one of those intense, black-eyed looks that had been known in the past to shrivel my soul—before I learned to understand her, that is. She put both long-fingered hands up to the sides of her almost-not-there African-American fuzz.

"You don't think some little ol' junior or senior boy could ask you tomorrow?" she said.

I laughed aloud.

"What's so funny about that?" Norie said. "Babe, if I can get a date, anybody can." She glanced ruefully down at her squarish body. Tobey gave her a look, and Norie added quickly, "Especially you."

"You don't have a 'date,'" Cheyenne said to Norie. "You have Wyatt. It's just like me and Fletcher. If we were juniors, we would automatically go to prom together. So it's not like a date—"

"Girl, I think now would be a good time to close that mouth of yours," Brianna said.

Cheyenne did, of course. She was our freshman. Lovable as a pup and twice as loyal, but prone to talk herself into corners without even knowing it.

Now Shannon, on the other hand, wasn't talking at all. As the conversation rambled on around us, I looked at her.

She was sitting cross-legged beside me, but her mind was

nowhere near, that was obvious. The tension in her body was like a brick wall, and I couldn't even see her face because she had her head ducked so low over her sandwich. Her corn-silk blond hair almost met itself over her nose, shutting the rest of us out and her inside.

Shannon was always quiet. Brianna called her and me the Timid and the Shy, respectively. But usually Shannon was listening, taking everything in with her pale eyes and smiling a sunny smile that lit up both her and us.

That day she wasn't smiling, and she wasn't listening. She also wasn't eating that sandwich she was clutching. She had squeezed through the bread so hard she had mustard under her fingernails.

"Hey," I whispered to her, "anybody home?"

She tossed the sandwich on top of her crumpled lunch bag and peeked through her hiding place of hair. "Sorry."

"For what?" I said.

"I'm just kind of out of it today."

I nodded. "Family stuff?"

She didn't really need to answer, and she didn't as she rolled the uneaten-but-massacred sandwich up in the bag. Ever since I had met her at See You at the Pole in September, Shannon had had "family stuff" going on. She had a sister who was every parent's nightmare. Even though they had sent her away to a Christian boarding school, she had a trouble radius of several hundred miles. Shannon absorbed her parents' anguish like a sponge; only she never seemed to squeeze any of it out.

"Anything I can do?" I said.

She shook her head until her hair went over her face again. "You have to be sick of hearing about it."

"Come on, what's a best friend for if you can't make her sick?"

She finally pulled back her hair with one hand and gave me a weak smile. Speaking of sick, she looked it. The circles under her eyes were green.

"Seriously," I said. "Are you all right?"

She looked over her shoulder. "Is there a rest room here?"

I pointed, and she shot up and went for it. I'd have gone after her if her back hadn't given off stiff, please-stay-away signals. I forced myself back to the conversation.

"Let's settle this so we can 'bask,'" Cheyenne giggled. "Now that I know what it is and since Ms. Race said we should take advantage of this gorgeous day to 'bask' in the sun. Only I can't be late getting back. Mr. Hopkins has a coronary if we're not there when the bell rings."

"What are we deciding?" I said.

"When we can get together and not have to worry about some absurd bell," Norie said. She glanced impatiently at her watch. "What about Saturday night? I'm free."

"That's good for me," Brianna said. "Pneumatic Diner?"

"Cool!" Cheyenne said. "We haven't been there in decades."

"You haven't been *alive* for decades," Norie said.

"I can come Saturday," I said. "I mean, if my parents will let me—and it can't be too late."

"Is that some kind of Mexican rule or something?" Cheyenne said. "You did just turn sixteen. Seems like they would cut you some slack. Okay, okay, I'll shut up." She dodged Norie's needle-stare.

Tobey shook her head.

"What's wrong?" Norie said to Tobey.

"I can't do it Saturday night. I have to be at this big youth rally."

"What's that, two, three hundred people?" Norie said. "You think you'll be missed?"

"Uh, yeah. Our church is hosting it. We've invited all these other youth groups. I have to be there."

We all nodded. Tobey's father was a pastor. Tobey had a lot of have-to-be-theres. Not that she wouldn't have gone anyway. She was the strongest Christian of all of us. She had been at it since she was a baby while the rest of us had had to meet Christ along the way, except for Shannon whose parents had also raised her with the Lord. I glanced nervously toward the rest room, where she was just emerging, wiping off her mouth with a paper towel and hurrying toward us.

"Hey, D'Angelo!" Norie shouted to her. "You free to go to a rally Saturday night?" Norie shrugged at the rest of us. "Why don't we all go, and then we can do Pneumatic after."

"Really, you guys would come?" Tobey said.

"'Course we would come, girl," Brianna said. "All you have to do is ask."

"What do we wear?" Cheyenne said. "Am I going to have the right clothes?" As the others pounced on Cheyenne's poor-foster-child insecurities, I pulled back into a few insecurities of my own.

Like: *How many people are going to be there? Is it going to be like this huge crowd—a hundred new people I've never met before, all looking at me like "Who's she?"*

It had taken me all fall and most of the winter to feel comfortable with the rest of the Flagpole Girls. But a whole rally of kids…Mmm, I could feel myself pulling into my second, underneath, spare skin. With any luck, Mama and Papa wouldn't let me go, or my curfew would be too early, or…

"Marissa."

I felt the heat of Shannon's soft voice in my ear more than I heard her. She tossed her hair almost across both of us.

"What?" I whispered back.

"You're going, aren't you?"

I started to shrug, but she hurried on. "I'm not going if you don't."

I could have reminded her that Tobey was her other best friend, and that Norie would flunk the SATs before she would let Shannon get lost in the shuffle, and that, if nothing else, Cheyenne would make her laugh the whole time. Now that I think about it, I could have told myself that too.

But if anybody needed to get out of her house and get her mind off of her life, it was Shannon.

"I'm going," I whispered to her. "But not unless you are."

She looked up at Norie, who was waiting with her fingers spread out for counting, and nodded.

"That's if you feel okay," I said to her.

"What's the matter, girl, are you sick?" Brianna said.

"You sure look sick," Cheyenne said. "You're paler than ever. Look at her, Tobey. Should we take her to Ms. Race?"

I put my arm around Shannon's shoulders. Surprised as I was at how bony and frail they felt, I didn't let on. I shook my head at all of them. "It's just stuff."

"Oh, I hate 'stuff,'" Tobey said while Norie clapped her hand over Cheyenne's mouth and Brianna rolled her eyes.

Shannon put her lips close to my ear and said, "Thanks."

It's funny looking back. That day, as we ate lunch in the park and "basked" in the rare warm Nevada-in-April air, I thought I was going to the rally for Shannon. Very funny. Because it turned out to be all about me in a way that would change me forever.

CHAPTER ONE

AS IT TURNED OUT, MAMA AND PAPA SAID I COULD GO TO the rally. They didn't need me to watch the younger kids, cook dinner, or sit with Abuelo—that was my grandfather—and my Aunt Veronica said to them, "For heaven's sake, it's a church activity! Let her go."

She's only ten years older than I am, and I could see my parents saying to each other with their eyes, "Veronica turned out all right, didn't she? We could take her advice...you think?" The decision was a tooth-pulling, nerve-pinching one, but I finally made it out the door and into Brianna's car. She picked up a tote bag from the front seat and tossed it into the back so I could sit.

"What's that?" I said.

"Makeup. I just thought it would be fun since we're all dressing at Norie's."

"Shannon says she's bringing a whole bunch of clothes."

"Her mama makes her some cute outfits," Brianna said, although her own style was not "cute." Exotic was more like it, and she pulled it off. Cheyenne did the grunge thing—homemade jewelry, overalls, flannel shirts. Tobey was more flowy, and I think they call Norie's look "campy"—combat boots no matter what and funky hats. I, on the other hand, didn't have a look. I just hoped something would be at Norie's I could look decent in.

We picked up Cheyenne and headed into the exclusive Caughlin Ranch area where Norie lived with her call-the-caterer mother and her thoracic-surgeon father. Every time I went there I was afraid I was going to use the wrong fork for pizza or something.

I shouldn't have worried. Norie shooed us all upstairs right away, leaving Wyatt, who was Norie's boyfriend; and Fletcher, who was Tobey's brother and also Cheyenne's boyfriend; and Diesel, that was Cheyenne's foster brother, in the family room enduring Norie's father.

Shannon and Tobey were already up in Norie's suite of rooms. That's what I said, a suite. The Girls were spreading out skirts and pants outfits on the bed. Brianna headed for the bathroom with the double mirror and started clinking makeup containers.

"We can pick anything we want?" Cheyenne said.

"Yeah, except what I already have on," Tobey said.

"Cool," Cheyenne said. "I think I just died and went to heaven."

Norie picked up a Shannon dress, size six, and scowled at it. "Like anything here would fit me," she said. "Where are the tents?"

"Knock it off, Nor," Tobey said. "Here, I was thinking about this for you."

She produced a black embroidered top with fringe, but Norie shook her head. "Definitely not me. That's I-can-get-away-with-looking-like-the-sixties. I'm more a I'll-be-lucky-to-pull-off-the-nineties."

At least you know what you are, I thought. I gazed at the pile of clothes, which was now being gone through like it was a sale table at Macy's, and felt my protective skin taking over. Maybe I should just stick with the sweater set I had on. Aunt Veronica had bought it for me for my birthday…

"Isn't none of that going to jump off the bed and wrap itself on you, girl," Brianna said at my elbow.

I laughed. She didn't. She scrutinized the pile and then pulled out a black-and-white tweed-checked skirt I'd never seen anybody wear before. It looked microscopic.

"Whoever wants that skirt can have it," Tobey said. "I've outgrown it."

"Is there a red sweater in there?" Brianna said.

Norie yanked one out and tossed it to her. "I might be able to get that over my big toe."

"Enough with the I'm-so-fat thing," Tobey said. "You have a waist. You just hide it all the time."

"Girl, put these on," Brianna instructed me. "Where's a black T-shirt? Here."

I looked blankly at the outfit.

"That's cute," Shannon said. "You'll look good in that."

"She'll look fabulous, girl," Brianna said.

I didn't have much choice but to take it, although I wasn't counting on "fabulous." Now Aunt Veronica or my older sister Cecilia who was an L.A. model currently on a job in Italy, they could do fabulous. I couldn't.

"Go on now, girl," Brianna said.

I shrugged out of my sweater, still looking doubtfully at the startling flash of color Brianna had picked out for me. *Wonder what Mama would say,* I thought. Which, of course, nudged me like a reminding finger. We hadn't settled on a time for me to be home.

"Tobey?" I said.

She looked up from pulling a flowered thing over Cheyenne's head.

"What time's the rally going to be over?" I said.

"Nine. And don't forget Pneumatic after."

"Hey, where's the neck hole to this thing?" Cheyenne said, voice muffled in fabric.

Still carrying the skirt, sweater, and T-shirt, I went for the door. "I'm going to use the phone."

"I have a phone in here," Norie said.

Of course she did, complete with answering machine and probably fax, too. I pretended not to hear her as I slipped out into the hall and spotted one on a table on the landing. I'd just as soon not negotiate my curfew in front of everybody. Nobody else seemed to have the hassles I did over stuff like that.

I prayed for Mama to answer, but no such luck. My brother Anthony grabbed it on the first ring. He was thirteen and thought he owned the phone.

"Let me talk to Mama," I said.

"Who's this?" he said.

"Don't be stupid," I said. "Put Mama on."

"I couldn't be stupid if you paid me," he said. "Who made the straight-A honor roll this time—and who didn't?"

He cackled the way only too-smart thirteen-year-old brothers can and dropped the phone soundly on the kitchen counter. I held the receiver away from my ear and heard it being picked up and mangled, this time by my sister Irene. Eight years old, going on sixteen. She drove me nuttier than any of them.

"Who's this?" she said.

"It's me, Reney," I said.

"Why did you call me?"

"I didn't. I'm waiting for Mama."

"How come?"

"Because I need to talk to her."

"I thought you went out."

"I did—"

"Are any cute boys there?"

I could feel myself rolling my eyes. "What do you care?"

After another noisy exchange of the receiver, Mama's clipped voice came on. "Marissa?" she said. "What's wrong?"

"Nothing. I found out the rally's over at nine."

"You can be home by nine-thirty then."

"Um…remember…we're going out to eat after?"

"We?"

"The Girls, Fletcher, Diesel, and Wyatt. Remember? I told you?"

"I guess you did." Her voice had that end-of-the-week weary sound. I traced the banister with the tip of my finger and waited.

"Let me ask Papa," she said.

More phone covering and muffling. It was a wonder the receiver still functioned.

"Marissa?" Papa said into the phone. I pulled it away from my ear again. He always talked as if something was wrong with the connection and he had to yell.

"Hi," I said. "I just called to ask what time I have to be in."

"Ten-fifteen," he said.

I did a mental calculation. An hour and fifteen minutes to drive to Pneumatic, eat, get home. I had indigestion already.

"Did you hear?" he said.

"Yes," I said. "I was just hoping for eleven."

"Why?"

"They take a long time to serve at the Pneumatic," I said.

A crisp silence followed. I held my breath so he wouldn't think I was getting ready to argue.

"Eleven," he said finally. "Who's bringing you home?"

"Brianna. You've met her—"

"You just be sure."

"I will."

Yet again the phone bounced into other hands, and Mama said, "You come straight home, now, after you eat."

"I will."

"Nothing's changed just because you're sixteen."

"I know," I said.

"All right. Have a good time. Just…watch yourself."

"I will."

"All right."

Then she hung up, already halfway to the next thing she had to do. She did have a lot to do, I thought as I looked down the hall for a bathroom door. Even with Cecilia gone, six of us kids were at home, and Abuelo needed to be taken care of since his stroke. Plus Mama kept the books for Papa's brick business. All her responsibilities were always pinched in that space between her eyes.

"Ooh, that's going to be cute!"

I looked up in surprise to see Norie's mother coming toward me down the hall with a bucketful of ice and cans of soda. She was headed for Norie's bedroom.

"Pardon me?" I said.

"That outfit," she said. "You'll look adorable in that." She smiled and tossed her wedge of shiny hair. "I wish I could convince Norie to wear things like that, but I don't even suggest it. You know how it is; the minute your mother tells you something is great it's the last thing you're going to put on your body!"

I actually didn't know how that was. I just nodded, smiled, slipped into the hall bathroom, and started to change. I couldn't even imagine telling my mother that something she suggested for me was the last thing I'd put on. The fact was, Mama didn't suggest things to me. She just critiqued me after I dressed. "Marissa, that's too short. You'll disgrace yourself…Marissa, that's too wild.

People will think you're trying to show off...Marissa, that does not look good on you. Cecilia could wear that; she's tall."

I buttoned the red sweater partway over the snug little black T and smoothed my hands down over the skirt. I studied myself in the mirror. I could hear Mama now. "Marissa, what is this? This is not what you wear!"

I definitely looked different. I was shorter than all the Girls except Cheyenne, so I always felt young, but I didn't look young in this outfit. It had a classy flair to it; it was sophisticated. And I was neither of those things.

Someone rapped on the bathroom door.

"Marissa, are you almost ready?" Tobey said. "We have to go in about ten minutes, babe."

"Coming," I said.

Ten minutes. I could change back in that time. Except that Brianna's feelings would probably be hurt. I looked into the mirror. The outfit didn't looked trampy or anything. It might have been about the nicest thing I'd ever had on, actually.

Okay, I could do this—maybe. I balled up my other clothes and went back to Norie's room.

"Marissa, you look great," Tobey said. "Check her out, Nor."

"I'm checking. She disgusts me." Norie gave me her square grin and went after her boxy bob with a hairbrush.

"I like that top on you," I said.

Norie gave the fringe a bounce and rolled her eyes.

"Stand still, girl," Brianna said to me. "I just want to put a little blush on you. You don't need much else, not with that skin. Mmm, girl, you have some gorgeous skin. Now step back. Let me look."

I did, and she did, and so did everyone else. In a minute, they were in this admiring circle around me, oohing and nodding and saying stuff like, "I should ever look so good."

"Stop it," I said. My face was going against-my-will red, a sure sign that it was time to draw back in. I looked at Brianna. "I'm not sure," I said. "You don't think I look like I'm trying to be somebody else?"

Brianna's eyebrows knitted together. "Who, girl?" she said.

"I don't know. I just—"

She waved the blush brush at me like a pointing finger. "Girl, it's about time you started looking at yourself the way you really are."

"Ladies," Mrs. Vandenberger said from the doorway, "the guys say if you don't leave now Tobey's going to be in trouble, and the rally's going to be over."

"You really do look great," Shannon whispered to me as we followed everybody downstairs.

"So do you," I said. But then, she always did. She had on a flowing skirt and a cool vest that made her look thinner than ever. If she turned sideways she would disappear. Norie was always telling her that. Shannon was exquisite, except for those dark circles under her eyes. Even Brianna hadn't been able to cover them up.

"This is cool," Wyatt said, flipping the fringe on the bottom of Norie's top.

"Keep your paws off," she said to him. "This is a True Love Waits rally we're going to."

"True love waits," Cheyenne said. "For what?"

"For sex, Sherlock," Norie said.

"Oh. I knew that."

Everybody groaned and ragged good-naturedly on Cheyenne as we divided up into cars. I climbed in with Brianna, moaning to myself. *Like I really need this rally. Love? Sex? Oh yeah, that's real big in my life.*

It wasn't that guys hadn't ever asked me out. Guys had been hitting on me since eighth grade, but I hadn't been allowed to date until I turned sixteen. And Cecilia had reminded me daily that I was lucky; it had been seventeen for her. None of those guys had really appealed to me anyway. Some of them, early on, before I found the Flagpole Girls, were Latinos I used to hang around with. They weren't bad people. I mean, that's my heritage. I just thought if I was going to be interested in somebody, he was going to have to want to do something besides cruise around and brag. It was the same with the white guys. Right after Christmas Jerry Pavella had seemed to be everywhere I was, nagging at me to go out with him. I couldn't stand him. He and some others tried to get Norie in trouble back in the fall. He could have messed her up really bad.

No, I'd thought about it a lot. I wanted something special. A little like what Norie and Wyatt had. They were friends, had things in common, and joked around with each other. And a little of what Ira and Brianna had. They were loyal to each other, respected each other, and were so adult. Even a little of what Cheyenne and Fletcher had. There was all this wonder between them, like they thought each other was magic or something. I could do without the giggling and the way Cheyenne smacked the kid every time he teased her, but each of my friends had boys who were Christians and were making the Girls' lives better, not tangling them up like you saw couples do all the time. The chances of that happening for me didn't seem good. Like Tobey sometimes said, Norie, Cheyenne, and Brianna probably had gotten the last of the good guys.

"Where are you, girl?" Brianna said to me, as she pulled up to Tobey's church and creaked on the emergency brake.

"I'm here," I said.

"Uh-huh. So's Shannon. It's been real nice talkin' with you two."

I realized neither of us had said a word all the way, and I could feel my face turn red. Shannon muttered "Sorry" as she climbed out of the car.

"You two blow my mind," Brianna said.

I wasn't sure if that was good or not. Probably not. I moved in close to Shannon and followed the group to the door. I had other stuff to worry about anyway. Like whether I was going to be able to breathe with all those new people in there. What had Norie said? Two or three hundred?

Actually it looked more like a hundred and fifty, and most of them were in their little groups, talking too loud and laughing too loud and looking around to see if anybody noticed.

"I have to go, guys," Tobey said. "Just mingle and save me a seat."

"Mingle?" Cheyenne said. "Is that like basking?"

"'Mingling' means go up to somebody and say, 'Hi, I'm Cheyenne. Want to be best friends?'" Norie said.

Cheyenne stared at her, and Norie immediately grabbed Cheyenne's arm. "I'm kidding, okay? You would do it, wouldn't you?"

"I wouldn't!" I whispered to Shannon.

But she wasn't listening. I followed her gaze to a knot of kids a few yards away. She jabbed me in the ribs and hissed, "Don't look!"

"Why?" I said.

"Because," she said, "that guy's been staring at you ever since you walked in the door."

CHAPTER TWO

"NO WAY!" I SAID.

"Yes, way!" Shannon laughed like a little silver bell. "He's about to look a hole right through you."

Brianna nudged me on the other side. "That boy ought to go on ahead and take a picture. It would last longer."

"Look now," Shannon said. "He's turned the other way. Look now!"

In spite of myself I did, and I knew right off who she was talking about. Only one boy was in the group. The rest were girls, who were either hanging on him or looking like they wanted to hang on him.

"Look at that," Brianna said. "He's got himself a harem."

It was easy to see why. He stood like a soccer goalie. You know how they stand? All sort of put together real compact? He wasn't tall; he didn't have to be for all those girls to look up to him, and he looked right back out of eyes that were just close enough together to make him look intense. Only he was smiling, with the kind of lips that are sort of round and ripe looking.

While I was watching, he pulled his hand through his straight brown hair and laughed at the girl who was tugging at his left arm. I couldn't hear the laugh, but I could see it. In his shoulders shaking, in his jaw line all close-shaved and gleaming.

"And I thought *he* was staring," Brianna said to me.

I jerked my eyes away and covered my mouth. But I couldn't do anything to keep my face from turning red.

"I don't blame you. He's cute!" Shannon whispered.

"I believe the word is 'hot,'" Brianna said.

"I don't care!" I said.

"Uh-huh. And I'm gonna win the Nobel Prize this year."

"We ought to find some seats," Wyatt said. "They just opened the doors."

I shoved past Brianna with Shannon in tow and positioned us right behind big Diesel. He was six foot six if he was an inch and made a great block for my getting-redder-by-the-minute face.

"He's still looking," Shannon whispered to me.

"Stop it!" I said.

I forced myself not to glance back as we pressed into the crowd moving toward the sanctuary. They were already playing music and people were starting to sing as we went in so nobody could rib me anymore. I made a point to sit next to Diesel where I could hide.

"You know what's really a bummer?" Shannon said from my other side.

"What?" I said.

"The cute guys are never the ones worth having."

"Why do you say that?" I said.

"Because they always know they're cute. Why would they tie themselves down to one girl when they could have anybody?"

"Oh," I said. "I guess you're right."

She laughed her silvery little laugh. "Not that any of them would look at me twice anyway. But he sure was looking at you."

I showed her my teeth. "Maybe I have broccoli or something."

By then we were in the sanctuary, and a screech from the sound equipment heralded, "May I have your attention please?" Tobey was at the microphone. We all whistled and stomped, and the rally started.

I have to admit I didn't hear much of it. It wasn't that I was thinking about Cute Boy—really. Like Shannon said, what was the point? She had confirmed something I'd already thought: It was going to be a long time before love and sex had anything to do with me.

I did catch a couple of things from the rally though. Obviously the talks were about waiting until you're married to have sex—duh. And they kept mentioning something about going through the roof.

But mostly I sat there wondering, *What does this have to do with me? I'm unattached. And likely to remain so.*

Like a lot of my thoughts, it ended up a poem, and I started to play with it.

> *What's this got to do with me?*
> *I am, unfortunately, free,*
> *And likely to remain so.*
>
> *What's this say about my life?*
> *I may never be someone's wife*
> *Or even someone's trial run.*

Suddenly Cheyenne was waving her hand in the air, and so were about three-fourths of the kids in the room. Mama would have said, "Marissa, you are always going off in your own little world," which was true. I didn't have any idea what was going on.

"You want a card, Marissa?" Norie said to me across three people.

I said, "I don't know" so she handed me one, and I read it.

"Believing that true love waits," it said, "I make a commitment to God, myself, my family, my friends, my future mate, and my future children to be sexually abstinent from this day until the day I enter a biblical marriage relationship."

I almost laughed out loud. My future mate? My future children? Marriage? Me?

"Are you going to sign it?" Shannon whispered to me.

"Sign it?" I said.

"It's a pledge card," she said. "We're supposed to sign it."

"They're going to stack them up in the church hall," Cheyenne said. "If everybody signs, it could go to the ceiling!"

"Well, ours plus those they've brought from all over the state," Wyatt said. "Except they haven't done Las Vegas yet."

"Let me borrow your pen," Cheyenne said.

"Just swear you'll be in my group," Shannon said.

"What group?" I said.

She blinked her blue eyes at me. "Did you hear a word they said? We're splitting up into small groups for discussion after this."

"I hate that," I said. "I can never think of anything to say!"

"I know," she said. "And when you don't say anything, they call on you."

"Maybe we could hide in the bathroom," I said. "Don't you have to throw up again?"

I grinned at her, but it took her a second to grin back.

"I'm sorry," I said. "Are you still feeling yucky?"

"No, I just…who said I threw up?"

I was confused, and I was grateful for Diesel grunting at me to give him the pledge card. Quickly I scrawled my name on the line and handed it to him.

"I ought to keep this and give it to Ma," he said, grunting again. His mother was Tassie, Cheyenne's foster mother. Diesel was a good kid, but Tassie always kept a close eye on him. He grunted once more at the cards and passed them on. I grabbed Shannon's hand.

"Let's find the girls' bathroom," I said.

"I'm there."

We stood up, under Brianna's riveting gaze. "Where do you two think you're going?"

"Potty," I said.

"I want you two in my group," Brianna said. "I'll wait for you outside the bathroom."

"Who died and made her the mother?" Shannon muttered as we charged up the aisle.

"She knows we're trying to cut out."

"I really hate this, Marissa," Shannon said. "I have other stuff to worry about right now."

And I have no stuff to worry about, I thought. I didn't know which of us was worse off.

True to her word, Brianna was waiting outside the bathroom door, arms folded.

"Where's everybody else?" I said.

"In their groups. Come on. We're in room five."

"Which room?" said a voice behind us.

We turned around like some tandem trio. Another trio faced us. Cute Boy, with a girl on each arm.

"Who wants to know?" Brianna said. She still had a lot of her Oakland upbringing in her.

"We do," he said, although the two girls looked less than thrilled that he had stopped to talk to three *more* girls.

Brianna gave him another long look while Shannon and I stood there like stone statues.

"Five," she said finally. "You know where it is?"

"Right this way!" he said. "I come here a lot."

We followed him, with Shannon whispering in my ear, "Tobey must know him then."

I wasn't sure what her point was, but I nodded. It annoyed me that my heart was thumping.

About nine people were in the room already, and a sparkly-eyed guy about college age was standing up, tossing a dry-erase marker from hand to hand and champing to start a discussion. I looked for a seat in the back, but the chairs were in a circle. Brianna plopped us all down right in it. Before I could even put my hand on the seat next to me, Cute Boy had dropped into it. He smiled at me.

From close up, I could see that his eyes were green. Well, more than green. They were that combination of gold and green that looks so rich. The curly eyelashes didn't hurt his looks any either. I noticed again how obviously he shaved, close, every day.

What does a shaved upper lip feel like to kiss?

Ha! I will never get the answer to this!

I flipped my face to Brianna so I wouldn't turn red right in front of the guy. She was smothering a smile, I could tell.

"Isn't it just weird sometimes how things work out?" she said under her breath.

"What things?" I said.

But the guy up front said, "All right, I think that's everybody! Why don't we go around the circle and get everybody's name!"

He said each sentence like it ended with an exclamation point. I, however, was not excited. Say my name? In front of all these people?

"Matt."

"Carly."

"Vanessa."

They were getting closer. I started to lick my lips. I hated this kind of thing.

"Bonnie."

"Jason," said Cute Boy.

Jason. It definitely fit him. Half the guys in school had that name, and all of them were popular. It was a strong name, sure of itself. You didn't see many poor little waifs named Jason.

"And you are?"

Startled, I glanced up at the group leader, who was looking at me with eyebrows raised.

"Me?" I said.

The whole room laughed.

"You!" the leader said.

I nodded.

"Your name, hon," he said.

"Oh! Marissa. Marissa Martinez."

Then I realized I was the only one who had given her last name so I said, "Just Marissa."

The guy looked a little baffled, shook his head, and looked at Brianna. She could have said her name was Uma Thurman, for all I heard. I was busy hoping I'd slip into a coma.

"Cool name," said the voice beside me. "Is it Mexican?"

"No," I said—barely. "Venezuelan."

"What would Jason be in Venezuelan?"

I blinked at him.

"And I'm Charlie!" said our group leader. "Okay, let's get started! Who thinks this whole thing is unrealistic?"

Jason's eyes flickered from me to Charlie. "What, True Love Waits?" he said. "No way!"

"But you have to admit now...Jason, was it?"

"Yes," said the girl on Jason's other side. Bonnie or something. She said it with possessiveness. I moved another inch away from him, up against Brianna.

"You have to admit now, Jason, that most of society is laughing at us for being old-fashioned about sex."

"So?" Jason said. "Let them laugh. Why should we care?"

"You really don't care if people laugh at you?" Brianna said. "You just blow it right off?"

"He does," said another girl, whose voice was as possessive as Bonnie's. "He doesn't follow what's in at our school; he decides it."

"I'm impressed," the only other guy muttered.

"Did you say something, Matt?" Charlie said enthusiastically.

"No," Matt said. "Well, okay, yeah, I'm sorry I'm not Mr. Trendsetter, but it is, like, weird when everybody else is saying, 'Hey, did you get any?' and I'm all, 'No, I signed a pledge card.' They look at you like you're some kind of loser."

"Yeah, but they know they're the losers," Jason said. "They might be telling you how good it is and all that, but I've had guys tell me it isn't what it's talked up to be. I mean, once the chase is over—"

There was a burst of laughter, which didn't even color Jason's cheeks pink. I would have been crawling under my chair.

"Jason?" one of the other girls—Carly? Vanessa?—said, "Are you talking from personal experience?"

Everybody giggled except Brianna, who was rolling her eyes, and Shannon, who was hiding behind her hair. I found myself waiting for an answer.

"I'm a virgin; I'm not ashamed of it," Jason said. "What? Is that something that isn't in anymore so we have to hurry up and lose it?"

The Matt guy was muttering again.

Charlie was on him like a mosquito. "Did you want to address that?" he said.

"I don't know," Matt said. "I just think it's unrealistic."

"Why?" Jason said. "Is it unrealistic to decide you aren't going to go out and rob convenience stores?"

"No, man, armed robbery isn't a natural instinct. Your hormones don't tell you to hold up a clerk. But they sure tell you to…you know…"

"Well?" Charlie said to Jason.

Jason shrugged. "I don't mean to be rude or anything…"

"You couldn't be rude if you tried!" Bonnie said.

"Try," Matt said. "I've probably heard it before."

Jason looked right at him. His eyes weren't rude at all. They were sure of themselves and firm, and I was wishing he were looking at *me* that way.

"Okay," Jason said. "I'd just hate to have to admit that I was being controlled by my hormones."

Matt grunted, and Charlie was beaming like we had just discovered some universal truth. Brianna poked me. "Look at that Bonnie girl," she whispered.

I did. Bonnie, blue-eyed and pixie-faced, was gazing at Jason in rapt adoration.

"Hand her a Kleenex," Brianna whispered. "She's about to drool."

I held back a giggle. Brianna grunted. Even Shannon laughed. Charlie looked enormously pleased.

By the time Jason had given us a half-dozen more insights into avoiding Demon Sex, our time was up. Shannon dove gratefully for the door, and I was following when Jason said, "They're giving out food when they stack the cards. In the church hall."

"That's where we're supposed to meet Tobey and them," Brianna said. She took me protectively by the elbow. "Come on, girl, before they eat all the cookies."

I chanced a glance over my shoulder as we left. Jason was right on my heels, followed by Bonnie, Carly, Vanessa, and a few others who joined the entourage en route. It looked like one of those snake dances.

"Hey, over here!" Diesel called from the cookie table. He reached across to the center, scooped up a handful, and passed them out to us.

"Don't eat too much," Tobey said. "Don't forget, Pneumatic Diner after this."

"I want a smoothie so bad," Cheyenne said. "Fletch, let's buy one with two straws and share it."

"Careful now," Wyatt said. "True love waits."

A sudden cheer went up, and we all looked at the stage where somebody on a ladder was putting on the last of the cards. The stack missed the ceiling by about a yard, but the place thundered as if we had just taken the gold.

"They still have another rally to do in Vegas," somebody said.

"Oh, they'll have a *lot* of abstainers down there," Norie said, voice dripping sarcasm.

"Is anybody else starving?" Tobey said.

We all bolted. Outside, I gulped a big breath of fresh air.

"You two survived," Brianna said dryly.

"It wasn't that bad," Shannon said. "That Jason guy made it kind of fun."

Brianna gave her signature grunt and looked at me as she started the car.

"What?" I said.

"He was performin' for you, girl."

"He was not! Fifteen people were in there. He was talking to everybody."

"He was talkin' to everybody, but he was performin' for you."

"You are so out of control," I said. "I bet if I walked up to him on the street tomorrow, he wouldn't even recognize me."

"Good thing I'm not a gambling woman, girl, 'cause I'd take you up on that," she said. She glanced in the rear-view mirror at Shannon, but her smile faded. "You all right back there?"

I turned around to look at Shannon. Her face was a ghastly green in the neon lights of the motels we were passing.

"Yeah," she said. "I just need some food."

"You sure do," Brianna said. "Gandhi ate more than you do."

"Jason liked you though, Marissa," Shannon said. "Brianna's right."

"Nice try at changing the subject," I said.

"No, I'm serious," Shannon said. "Isn't it true, Brianna? Wasn't he staring at her the whole time?"

"When he wasn't in there holdin' forth, yeah," Brianna said.

"You didn't like him?" Shannon said.

"I don't know anything about him." Brianna glanced at me. "But he was cute—as white boys go. You two would make a right handsome pair."

"Good grief, I saw the guy for an hour and now we're a pair! There's no way! You saw how popular he was."

"Don't you start with me," Brianna said. Her face grew stormy. "You are every bit as good looking as any of those girls who were foaming at the mouth over him, and you have twice as much class. That one girl looked at him like she was ready to tear *up* his pledge card!"

"You are so evil!" Shannon said.

And Brianna wasn't the only one. I was no sooner out of the car in the parking lot at Pneumatic than Tobey was all over me.

"What's this I hear about Jason Oakman flirting with you?"

"He was not!"

"Oh, so I'm a liar," Norie said. "He followed you into the church hall like a little puppy dog."

"With fifteen girls hanging all over him!"

"They were hanging on *him*, not the other way around," Wyatt said. "There's a difference."

"You ever have that problem?" Fletcher said.

"Uh, no," Wyatt said.

Jason Oakman. That was a classy name. Oak tree strong. Tough but classic.

> *Jason Oakman, a real man's name.*
> *If I fell for him, who could I blame?*
> *Oh, Marissa, this poem is lame!*

"Hey, space queen."

I looked at Brianna as we trailed into the upstairs café toward our usual set of tables in the corner.

"What?" I said.

"Do not turn around like something's about to bite you, but do it real slow, and you'll see who just walked in behind us."

I, of course, bobbed my head around snakebite fashion—and whipped it right back around.

Brianna grunted. "You gonna pass out, or you gonna say hello?"

"He didn't come here to see me!" I said. In fact, I couldn't believe Jason Oakman was there at all. It was a figment of my imagination, surely.

But it wasn't a figment of everybody else's. Like they had rehearsed it, the whole group turned around and hissed to me, "He's here!"

I'd have crawled under the table, as opposed to into a chair, if Brianna hadn't given me a firm push. I could feel him breathing behind me before he even spoke. When he did, he said, "You guys mind if I join you?"

Every eye went to me, like it was my decision.

When I didn't answer, Tobey smiled at him and said, "No, come on. Do you remember me, Tobey L'Orange?"

Ah, so that was it. He already knew Tobey. She was definitely more his type. She was popular, a leader, and sure of herself. And boyfriendless at the moment. I smacked myself inwardly for letting my heart sink. I never had a reason to get my hopes up in the first place.

"Oh, yeah," Jason said. "Your dad's the pastor at that church."

"Right."

The others introduced themselves while I studied the menu like I didn't already know every entrée on it.

"So, Marissa, what's good?" he said.

"You've never been here before?" Wyatt said.

Jason shook his head.

"Then how did you find it?" Cheyenne said.

It wasn't exactly a major hangout. I couldn't even remember how we had found it. Tucked upstairs behind a hotel and next to a dance studio, the place held only about ten tables.

"I heard you guys saying you were coming here," he said. "So I invited myself." He looked at me, green-gold eyes sparkling. "I hope you don't mind."

I stared.

"You have to excuse her," Norie said. "She gets spontaneous laryngitis now and then."

"Really?" Jason said.

"Yeah, like every ten minutes."

"I do not," I said. I managed to smile at him, while making plans to pull out Norie's hair. "No, I don't mind. Just, it's okay. Have the potato bayard."

"It's a done deal." He slapped his menu closed and kept smiling at me. Everyone else looked at each other, then at me, then back at each other. I prayed for something to say. Anything. For once I was glad Cheyenne was never at a loss for words.

"So, which one of those girls who was hanging all over you is your girlfriend?"

"Chey-enne!" Tobey said.

"None of them," Jason said.

Really?

"I don't believe in, like, going steady."

"Wyatt wants to know what it's like having all those girls on you," Cheyenne went on.

"I do not!" Wyatt protested.

"It's all right, I guess," Jason said. "Except when you try to go to the bathroom."

"Gee," Brianna said, "that's too bad."

"I don't mean to sound, like, conceited. I don't lead anybody on or anything. I think I'm, like, safe for them."

"Safe?" Norie said.

"Yeah. I'm a guy they can have fun with, but they know I'm not going to try to get them into bed. Could we talk about something else? All we've done tonight is talk about sex."

"Really?" said our waiter. "I want to go where you guys were!"

I took that opportunity to glance at my watch. It was only 9:30. I couldn't help wishing Jason would stay for another hour and a half.

JASON DID STAY, AND I'M SURE THE WHOLE TIME I LOOKED like Bonnie What's-Her-Name, gaping at him with my lower lip hanging down. But he was amazing—and not just because the longer I looked at him the cuter he seemed. I think it was more the bracelet he was wearing.

Made with four pewter beads with a letter on each that spelled out WWJD, he wore the bracelet like it was part of him. Cheyenne, of course, asked him about it.

"Is that one of those What Would Jesus Do things?" she said.

"Yeah, friend of mine gave it to me."

Cheyenne grinned. "What was her name?"

Jason grinned back. "Actually, it was a guy, our youth-group leader. He gave one to everybody."

Diesel grunted. "I saw a guy wearing one the other day. I go, 'What's that mean?' just to see what he would say, and he goes, 'It means We Want Jack Daniels.'"

Jason shook his head. "Doesn't that just blow you away? Some people can't even talk about what they believe in."

"You do have to cut them some slack though," Norie said. "I mean, I'm not ashamed I'm a Christian, but half the time when I say I am, people roll their eyes, and you can see them thinking, 'Jesus Freak.'"

"Girl, we don't have time to be worryin' about what other people think," Brianna said.

I looked at Shannon. I knew she and I were thinking the same thing: *That's easy for you to say!*

Then I looked at Jason. He jangled his bracelet back into place over his sleeve and took a nice, easy drink of his raspberry smoothie. Here he was, sitting in the middle of a bunch of strangers, talking about Jesus, and he looked so comfortable. I could have watched him for hours.

As it was, I almost did. At a quarter to eleven, Tobey said, "Marissa, don't you have to be home?"

I about jerked off the chair. Jason was up as fast as I was, his hand almost touching my elbow.

"I'll take you home," he said.

I looked at him stupidly. "I came with Brianna," I said.

Brianna arched an eyebrow at me. "That's all right, girl. You aren't going to hurt my feelin's."

"No, it's just…" I shrugged and tried to untangle my purse strap from the back of the chair. "It's just…my parents…"

"The 'rents, yeah," Jason said. "You have to come home with the same people who took you or they go ballistic. I remember that. It's easier when you drive."

"Yeah," I said. I knew I was gaping again, but he had just offered to give me a ride home. *He had just offered to give me a ride home!*

Everyone sort of shuffled around us going for the door. I looked nervously at Brianna, but I just stood there as if I were drilled into the Pneumatic floor.

"Okay, so at least give me your phone number," Jason said.

"My phone number?"

He grinned. "Do your parents let you talk on the phone?"

"Oh, yeah! Yeah. It's 747—"

"Let me grab a pencil."

"I have one," I said. I took my little pad and pen thing out of my purse and handed it to him. Then I took it right back and wrote my number myself, all the time feeling the red seeping into my face like food coloring.

"There you go," I said.

He took the paper and stuck it in his jeans pocket. I couldn't help wondering how many other girls' phone numbers were jammed in there.

"At least he asked," Shannon said, as she, Brianna, and I headed out of the parking lot, going as fast as Brianna dared so I would arrive at home before curfew.

"Yeah," I said. "Even if he never calls."

"Why would he *ask* if he wasn't going to call?" Brianna said. "Mmm-mmm, girl, I never knew you were such a pessimist."

"I thought I was being realistic," I said. "My mother's always telling me I'm a dreamer."

"You weren't dreamin' that," Brianna said. She gave a half glance over her shoulder at Shannon. "Did you ever see that boy take his eyes off Marissa one time?"

"Nope," Shannon said.

"Did you see him watch her when she went to get more napkins and almost fall out of his chair?"

"Yep."

"He did not!" I said.

"You don't know; you were too busy dreamin'." Brianna said. "Now, am *I* dreamin', or is that your daddy lookin' out the front window of your house?"

That, unfortunately, was the real thing. Jason disappeared from my head as Brianna pulled into the driveway and I saw my father's silhouette.

Brianna glanced at her watch in the beam of my front porch light. "It isn't but two minutes after. You're not going to be in trouble for that?"

"Not that much," I said. "I'll see you guys Monday."

"Call me if he calls you!" Shannon said.

"Don't hold your breath," I said.

I was the one doing the breath holding as I took the two front steps and fumbled for my door key. Papa pulled open the door before I could even stick my hand down into my purse.

"You're late," he said.

"I'm sorry. I should have called."

"That wouldn't do you any good," he said. "I already extended you to eleven."

Papa reached over to snap off the lamp on the end table, and then he stopped to look at me. That was the first time I noticed how gray his black hair was growing around his temples and in his mustache. The light made the creases around his eyes look deep too. I'd figured out by the time I was about ten that he wasn't the tall, broad-shouldered man I'd thought he was when I was little, but just then, stooped over the lamp like that, he looked a little shriveled.

"I'm sorry," I said again. "What's my punishment?"

He snapped off the light and faced me in the dark. "It isn't that simple, Marissa," he said, rolling the r's. His accent only kicked in when he was really annoyed. "It's not, you stay out too late, you take your punishment, and it's over. I do this to protect you."

"I know, Papa," I said. "I didn't mean it like that."

"No phone tomorrow," he said with a backward wave of his hand. "You'll remember next time."

"I will," I said.

I think he stayed behind in the living room while I hurried on down the hall to the room I shared with Luisa, my four-year-old sister. She was already asleep in the other twin bed, breathing like a baby locomotive, one chubby foot sticking out from under her comforter.

I tucked the foot back in and sank down on my own bed with my little black-and-white-and-red outfit still on.

"That outfit did the job!" Tobey had said to me in the bathroom at the Pneumatic. "Of course, it helps to have a body like that to put in it."

Was that what it was? That I was wearing the right clothes, or that I was lucky enough to have a fairly decent figure?

"Meow?"

I looked up to see Sylvia picking her way across the pile of pillows I was lounging on, heading for my face.

"Hey, girl," I whispered to her.

She gave another Siamese "meow" and started her nightly routine. She purred loud enough to wake the dead, if not at least Luisa, and burrowed her face into my hair while she patted my neck with her paw.

"Could you get a little closer?" I whispered, giggling.

She gave my neck a lick with her sandpaper tongue and purred on. I absently patted her paw, sorting out the words in my head.

> Jason is the finest boy
> I may have ever met.
> He began to give me joy.

What rhymed with "met"? "Bet"? "Jet"?

> *Soaring like a jet—*

La-ame!

Far away in the kitchen, I heard the phone ringing and Papa shuffling after it in his bare feet across the linoleum.

> *He asked if he could call me.*
> *Of course I answered yes.*

Actually, he hadn't asked. He had just said, "Then give me your phone number." He was so confident, so sure of himself, so everything I wasn't—

"Marissa."

Papa was outside my door, tapping with his knuckles and whispering hoarsely. I got up and padded to it. He was standing in the hall with his arms folded and his mouth pressing his mustache in and out the way he did when he was irritated.

"Is something wrong?" I said.

"You know some boy named Jason?"

I didn't even have to answer. I could feel my eyes popping open like a frog's.

"He just called you on the telephone," Papa said. "I told him it was too late. You tell him, too, for the future."

"I will," I said.

He sighed and shuffled on down the hall to his and Mama's room. I shut the door very quietly—and then I hurled myself to the bed and squealed, facedown, into the pillow, sending Sylvia springing indignantly for the window sill.

> *He asked if he could call me.*
> *Of course I answered yes.*
> *Now I think in love I'll fall.*

I rolled onto my back and laughed at Sylvia, who was scowling at me over her whiskers.

"Now I think in love I'll fall," I said to her. "And probably make a mess!"

Sunday morning was still warm for April in Nevada. Papa had

already gone to work when I woke up. We didn't even question his working Sundays anymore. In the bricklaying business, he had to work on the good days as they came, especially when the ice and snow during the winter months put him so far behind.

Mama was also in her go-to-work clothes as she poured a bowl of cereal for Luisa in the kitchen.

"You're going in too?" I said. I silently took the milk from her and started fixing Luisa's breakfast while my little sister swung her legs at the table.

"I have to," Mama said. "I have a lot to catch up on. I was home all week with this one and her flu."

Mama gave Luisa a tight smile, but Luisa saw right through it. She took the bowl of Cheerios from me and wrinkled her nose at Mama, who wrinkled hers back. For a minute she almost looked young. Unlike with Papa, I'd thought for a long time that Mama was looking older. She was so thin—that was part of it—and so short. She was like the incredible shrinking woman these days. You could see more of the gray in her hair, too, since she wore it long and pulled back. When a wisp fell down over her forehead, she seemed softer, but most of the time she had a pinched look, like I said, between her eyes.

"You'll look after Luisa," she said.

"I'm taking her to church, if that's okay."

"Can I wear a pretty dress?" Luisa said, milk dripping from her chin.

"Veronica's picking you up?"

"At nine. Yes, Luisa, but you have to eat that first." I turned to Mama. "What about the rest of them?"

Mama just lifted an eyebrow as she poured some coffee into a carry-with-you mug. "Sleeping. All four of them. They'll still be sleeping when you get back. Ah, *buenos días, Abuelo.*"

She set down her mug and hurried across the room where my grandfather was just emerging from his little suite Papa had converted from what used to be the laundry room and pantry. It meant going out to the garage to the washing machine and going to the grocery store more often, but it didn't bother me. Sometimes Abuelo was the only person in the house who had time to listen.

He really couldn't do much else since his stroke. Right now, he moved with agonizing slowness behind his walker toward the table, refusing my mother's help with a patient nod of his crispy gray head. He was shorter and more gnarled than Papa, but other than that he was just an older version. Except that Abuelo smiled a lot more. Like, all the time.

"Buenos días, Abuelo," Luisa said matter-of-factly when he lowered himself into the chair next to her.

"Buenos días, Nieta," he said. His accent was still thick, even after a lifetime in the United States, but it was thickest when he talked to Luisa. He spent a lot of time teaching her Spanish. *Nieta*, for instance, was "granddaughter." Me he called *muchacha*, which is "girl" and sometimes "maidservant." He did that for my mother's benefit; he told her she worked me too hard around the house. Mama responded with a glare but not much else. You respect your elders in our culture.

"I'll be back around three," Mama said. "Marissa, you take care—"

"She will, Trini, she will," Abuelo said.

His eyes twinkled at me as Mama grabbed the lidded coffee mug, purse, and keys and left the kitchen muttering. Luisa smiled her tiny-toothed smile up at our grandfather.

"What was she saying?" Luisa asked.

"She was saying Abuelo was right as usual," he said.

"Oh," Luisa said. "Marissa, I'm full."

I glanced vaguely at the half-empty bowl of Cheerios and nodded. "Go pick out a pretty dress and put on socks to match. I'll be right there."

She scampered off, and Abuelo watched her softly.

"What can I get you?" I said. *"¿Huevos?"*

"No, no." He patted my hand. "You're going to church. I'll just have coffee, and Gabriela can fix me something when she wakes up."

I frowned. Gabriela was my ten-year-old sister. She was sweet—I mean, as compared to Reney who was not. But Gabriela tended to be scatterbrained. She forgot to eat her own breakfast half the time.

"You better let me," I said. "I can do it fast."

I went to the refrigerator for the eggs, and I could hear him sighing.

"You all right?" I said.

"An angel passed over the day you were born, Marissa," he said.

"No, I don't *think* so," I said. I smiled at him and clattered a pan onto the burner.

"I think so. You know things the angels know."

"Like what?"

"That nothing is more important than *la familia*."

"Uh-huh."

"That there is dignity in hard work."

"Right."

"We must respect and honor *los padres*."

I cracked an egg over the pan. "I didn't have to learn that from the angels, Abuelo. I learned that from you!"

He shook his head, but he was smiling. It was such a beautiful smile, like the dawn. He could look so stern, until he smiled.

He knew I was right, too, about learning all those things from him. When I was a little kid, I was like Luisa. I never tired of sitting beside him and listening to his stories. Gabriela and Reney thought it was dumb. They were always making excuses to run off, but like Luisa, I had listened by the hour.

I could tell you the whole history of how Abuelo came to the United States from Venezuela with his new wife when they were both nineteen. At first Abuelo was a *bracero*, a manual laborer, until World War II. He fought as an American and came back to start his brick business in Reno. He was patient and hard working and had been successful.

"Not in *dinero*," he always told me. "United States society is too materialistic. They measure a man's success by his bank account. I have found success *adentro y arriba*." Inside and above.

Currently, I was hearing noise, "inside and above." A banging came from the stairs that led to the add-on room over the kitchen, and Eduardo made his usual entrance, adorned in too-big jeans and a huge flannel, hair flopped over his eyes. Abuelo's favorite thing to say to him was, "Anyone home in there, *Nieto*?" Eddie never seemed to appreciate it.

"Look who just crawled out from under a rock, Abuelo," I said.

Eddie schlepped his twelve-year-old self over to the stove and peered at the omelet I was just flipping.

"I want mine with jalapeños," he said.

"You'll find them in the refrigerator," I said.

He tossed back his bangs and widened his already enormous brown eyes at me. "If I get them out, will you make it for me?" he said.

"No," I said. "I'm already late getting ready for church."

"Please? I won't pick on you for a whole week."

I put the omelet in front of my grandfather. "Anything else before I go?"

"If there's anything else I'll get it for him," said a voice from the back door. My Aunt Veronica swung open the screen and let herself in. Suddenly the kitchen seemed much prettier. She filled it with her Estée Lauder Pleasures, her head of massive dark curls, and her elfin smile, which she transformed into a pucker to kiss her father on the cheek.

"Get ready!" she said to me. "They won't let you in in pajamas."

"Where are you going?" said someone else from the hall doorway.

Gabriela stood there, rubbing her eyes and scratching her belly. I was amazed she could do both at once.

"I want to go!" she wailed.

"We're going to church, *pequeña*," Veronica said. "You're welcome to come."

Gabriela's brown eyes dropped at the corners. "Oh," she said. "No, I thought you were going someplace neat."

Whatever Veronica said to her, I'm sure it had something to do with, "Church *is* someplace neat." I didn't hear the whole thing as I dashed off down the hall to dress. So far, Luisa and I were the only ones Veronica had convinced to attend church. Why she turned out carrying on Abuelo's deep faith when Papa didn't, I didn't know. Somehow Papa and Mama had become too busy, even too busy to take the rest of us to church, until Veronica had intervened and started to take me a few years ago. She was also the one who had found out about See You at the Pole back in

September and told me I should go. It was one of the many things I had to be grateful to *Tía Verónica* for.

That we were best friends, even though we were ten years apart, was another. I was going to miss her so much when she and Gerald were married in a few weeks. Practically the minute the ceremony was over, they were going to be out of there—back to Costa Rica where Gerald was right now, doing missionary work.

She was, of course, glowing with wedding plans all the way to church. But after we had dropped off Luisa at the preschool class, Veronica put her face real close to mine and said, "All right, spill it."

"Spill what?"

"Something is going on in there. It's all over your face."

I giggled and pulled away from her. "I have to go to Sunday school. I'm already late."

"You're not off the hook!" she said. Her face twinkled at me. "I'll get it out of you!"

I was sure she would forget. I mean, she did have a few other things on her mind. But the minute I met her to go into the church, she was on me again, eyes laughing. "Since when do we keep secrets from each other?" She took a bulletin from the usher and smiled and then flashed her eyes back at me.

"I'm sure you tell me everything!" I said.

"I do." She blinked innocently. "Who was the first person I told that Gerald and I were engaged?"

"Not me!"

"Yes, you. Now, come on." She led us into a pew and lowered her voice to a whisper. "Tell me now, before the service starts."

If I hadn't really wanted to tell her, I wouldn't have. But suddenly it was out there, surrounded by giggles and eye rolling and sighs. Veronica listened to me as if we were two middle-schoolers at a slumber party.

"Your first crush!" she whispered.

"It's kind of pathetic. I'm sixteen!"

"It's exciting, but…" She tried to make her eyes darken, but I could still see the laughter in them.

"What?" I said.

"Are you sure you're ready for your life to become complicated?" she said.

"Complicated?"

"Oh, honey, that's all boys do is complicate your life. Trust me."

"Is yours complicated?"

"Hopelessly," she said.

I frowned at her. "Then why do it? Why become involved?"

She giggled her husky giggle and squeezed my hand. "That's what you're about to find out. But you had better pray, honey, starting right now."

Actually, starting right then we stood up to sing. But during the hymn, even though my mouth was saying the words, my head was spinning off in another direction.

Pray about Jason? Like, what would I say? God, please make sure Jason calls me again? Please, even though he doesn't believe in going steady, let him like me enough to…

Uh, no. It all seemed too silly for God. I prayed all the time, especially since I'd become involved with the Flagpole Girls—that was our biggest thing, but we didn't pray about dumb things. And this was dumb because it probably wasn't going to happen.

Nevertheless, I sat there during the sermon and made up a poem about it in my head.

> *Why this feeling of confusion*
> *Over a boy I barely know?*
> *Why these feelings in profusion*
> *About a place I cannot go?*

It was kind of a prayer, I decided. Some questions for God. Unfortunately, He didn't answer. As much as I prayed, I'd never heard Him send me a poem back.

I wrote my poem in my notebook that afternoon though, after I finished my homework and settled Luisa down for a nap and made sure Eddie and Reney and Gabriela all had their homework done. I didn't ask Anthony. He always got all testy when I asked him, Mr. Straight-A-Honor-Roll-Smart-Mouth. He thought *he* could teach the classes. And Eddie thought *he* was God's gift to middle-school girls. Where the two of them had gotten such egos, I wasn't sure. I knew I didn't get one like that.

Reney was the only one who hadn't done her schoolwork, and at about two o'clock I had her parked at the kitchen table with her math workbook. If she didn't have her problems done when Mama arrived home, both of us were going to be in trouble. I'd be worse than grounded from the phone.

"I hate this," Reney whined. "It's too hard!"

"That's because you haven't bothered to learn your multiplication tables," I said. "You wouldn't have to count on your fingers all the time if you would just learn them."

"It's boring," she said. She lifted her thin face—*hacha* face, Abuelo would have called it, for "hatchet"—and smiled at me. Poor baby, she had a mouthful of too-big teeth that she hadn't grown into yet. Giving her strings of light-brown hair a toss, she said, "So, were any cute boys there last night?"

I didn't answer right away. Big mistake. She raised up on her elbows so that her buns left the seat.

"There *were!*" she said. "I can tell!"

"Why does everyone in this family think they can read my mind?" I said. "Come on, finish these problems. You're poking."

"Tell me," she said. "I like to hear about cute boys."

"You don't need to hear about cute boys," I said. "You have enough problems."

She lowered her brows into a fierce scowl that made me want to laugh, but you didn't laugh at Reney. That was the one thing she hated most, and she could be spiteful.

I was glad when the phone rang. She, of course, leaped out of the chair to answer it before Anthony could rise out of a dead afternoon nap to claim his territory.

"I'll get it!" she said. "You can't. Papa grounded you!"

She smiled triumphantly and snatched up the receiver while I studied her tangle of numbers. Since when, I wondered, was four times four fifteen?

"She can't come to the phone," Reney said. "She's grounded from it. Can I take a message?"

I glared up at her, but she was twirling the phone cord importantly around her finger and looking up at the ceiling as she listened. "I'll tell her," she said. "By-ee." She took her time hanging the receiver back on the wall and arranging the cord.

"Who was it?" I said.

"It was for you, but I told him you were grounded from the phone."

"I *heard*. Who was it?"

"Who's Jason Oakman?" she said.

"That was Jason?"

"Yeah." Her eyes searched me and discovered at once that I was interested. She pounced. "Who is he? Is he cute? Do you like him?"

"Hush," I said. "What did he say?"

"Do you want me to hush or to tell you what he said?"

"Reney, don't be a brat! What did he say?"

Reney settled herself at the table and took a newfound interest in the multiplication tables.

"Reney, tell me *now!*"

"He said to tell you he called. I did."

"Why did you tell him I was grounded from the phone?"

"Because you are. What's three times six?"

I slapped my hands on the table and put my nose an inch from hers. "I wouldn't tell you if—"

"If what?" Her eyes dared me to threaten her. She liked to have things to hold over me for some future time when I wouldn't give her her way.

I backed off and sighed. It didn't matter anyway. Why would Jason Oakman, perfect Christian, want to talk to a girl who was grounded? It was over before it even started.

Desengaño, Abuelo would have said. Kind of like "a bummer."

CHAPTER FOUR

THE WAY I DRAGGED MYSELF TO SCHOOL THE NEXT DAY, you would have thought I was going to the orthodontist for a full set of braces.

You're being stupid, Marissa, I told myself, as I dumped my books behind the counter in the office and took my place to help with the absence slips before school. *You only met the guy once. You really can't miss what you've never had, so what's the big deal?*

I seemed to have plenty of questions but no answers. It felt like the day after Christmas or something.

Ms. Race saw my feelings on my face. "Bad day, Marissa?" She watched me as she fingered her thick auburn braid.

"I'm okay," I said.

"'Okay' is not an adjective I've ever understood," she said. "Especially from my friends." She put some admit slips on the counter. "Most of the time I think it really means, 'I don't want to bother you with my problems.'"

That was our Ms. Race. She was the secretary for Mr. Holden, the principal, but she had also become kind of the mentor for the Flagpole Girls. She seemed to understand everything, and what she didn't understand she worked at. Every time I talked about her to my aunt, Veronica said, "She sounds like the perfect role model."

Right now I wished I could be more like Ms. Race. She was sweeping around the office in her flowered wisp of a dress with matching sandals, earrings bouncing confidently against her neck as she smiled at everybody and acted as if she had it all together.

"I'm here whenever you want to talk," she said to me, opening the doors over the counter to let the swarms attack us. "You just say when."

What I would say to her I had no idea. I tried to busy myself with the admit slips for the hundred or so people who had been absent the Friday before, but the slightest comment or action stung me.

"It's Peterson, not Peters," this girl named Lana said to me as I wrote her last name on the slip. "Seems like you would know that by now; I'm absent enough."

"Sorry," I said.

Four more confrontations like that set me up for English first period. The *Mocosos* were in my class. That's Spanish for "sniffling brats." Why they had singled me out to pick on I had no idea. Well, I did know, actually. Brianna said I let them. Norie said people like that are so insecure they will ferret out people weaker than they are to pick on. Diesel offered to have a word with them. Usually I just tried to ignore the brats, but that day everything was sticking me so hard, I could barely ignore my own breathing.

Lana Peterson from the admit-slip line was one of the *Mocosos*. She sat on one side of me. Her best friend, Heidi, sat on the other, and Patrick was right behind me. I felt like I was in an elevator with people I couldn't get away from.

I didn't meet any of their eyes as they straggled in almost late, as usual, and made the routine racket settling in their seats.

"What's that smell?" Heidi said. "Did you just belch, Patrick?"

"I can't help it," he said. "I had a burrito for breakfast."

"That is so gross," Lana said. She sat to my left and caught my eye with her almost-too-big hazel ones. "What are you looking at?"

I just pasted my eyes to my notebook. On my right, I could see Heidi folding her tiny, skinny self up into her desk and working on pulling her chocolate-brown hair into a ponytail. It was way too short, and a bunch of it straggled down in back. Brianna would have been grunting all over the place. She hated messy hair.

"Give me a rubber band, Lana," Heidi said.

"What makes you think I have one? What am I, your supplier?"

"Yeah," Patrick said. He kicked my desk—that would be time number one for today. "Give me a pencil."

"What do you need a pencil for?" Lana said. "She hasn't even given us an assignment yet."

"She will, and if I don't have a pencil, she'll yell at me."

I could picture Patrick back there, freckles everywhere, including on his lips, with his shaved-up-the-sides red hair, making faces at Mrs. Abbey while the poor woman ran around the room trying to keep things under control. I watched her to keep my mind off of them.

At the moment she was pawing through a cabinet, hauling out stacks of books and blinking her eyes fast under her contact lenses. Norie, who worked with her all the time because Mrs. Abbey was the journalism advisor, said that the more stressed Mrs. Abbey was, the faster she blinked. To me, she always looked as if she was running from one place to another and couldn't have told you where she had just come from or where she was going.

"All right, gang," she sang out as she ran a hand over the tops of the books and looked at the dust on her palm. "All right, gang, let's settle in. We're starting a new unit today—"

"Goodie," Patrick muttered.

I sat there hoping what I always hoped when Mrs. Abbey said we were starting a new unit: that it would be something neat like what Shannon, Norie, and Tobey studied in their English classes. Shakespeare or something like that. Call me crazy, but I'd always wanted to study Shakespeare. They never did it in the classes I was in though. I think they thought we weren't bright enough.

"Now I don't want to hear a bunch of moaning and groaning," Mrs. Abbey was saying. "We're going to study some poetry."

Of course, an entire chorus of moans and groans started up. That probably would have gone on all period if she hadn't slammed the first stack of books onto her desk and given us a look that clearly said, "Knock it off, or I'll make your lives miserable for the next four weeks."

"Hey, Mrs. Abbey," Patrick said loudly.

She blinked at him. "Go ahead, Patrick."

"I don't think my dad's gonna let me do this poetry thing."

"Your dad?" she said. She licked her lips. "Pray tell why not?"

"He says poetry is for gays. He doesn't want me turning out gay."

"Yeah, mine, too," some other guy said from the back of the room.

Mrs. Abbey continued to plunk down poetry books on people's desks. "Anything else, Patrick?" she said.

"Okay, don't blame me if he hauls you in front of the school board," Patrick said.

"I'll look forward to that. I have a few things I'd like to say to the school board."

"Like what?" Lana said. She sat up straight in her seat, ready to do her job as the one in charge of keeping Mrs. Abbey off the track.

"Like why do I have to have little urchins in my class who think they hate poetry?" Mrs. Abbey said.

Lana's big eyes went into slits on her wide face, and she slumped her stocky self back down into the desk. It wasn't working today.

"All right, gang," Mrs. Abbey said. "Before you make a judgment, I want everyone to turn to page nineteen, and let's look at that form you see there."

"Good," Heidi hissed beside me. "It's short."

For once she was right. One poem was printed on page nineteen, and it had three lines. And, I noted, none of them rhymed.

I grunted to myself. All those hours I had spent staring at the ceiling, trying to find something to rhyme with "met."

"Poetry begs to be read aloud," Mrs. Abbey said. "We'll be doing a lot of that. I'm going to be the reader today since I hate to hear poetry butchered."

"Man, real nice," Patrick said.

Of course, he would have thrown himself against the wall before he would have read aloud, but he would buck her on anything, just to be doing it.

Mrs. Abbey read, "Chrysanthemums bloom / in a gap between the stones / of a stonecutter's yard."

I could hear pages flipping around me.

"That's it?" Lana said.

Heidi echoed her with a sniff.

"That's it," Mrs. Abbey said. "Think you can handle that?"

"What's to handle?" Lana said.

"We could turn to page one-fifty," Mrs. Abbey said. Her perm trembled as she flipped through the pages. Those of us who were still awake turned to it. Patrick cussed under his breath.

"What was that, Pat?" Mrs. Abbey said.

"This is, like, twenty pages long!"

"Walt Whitman does go on," she said dryly. "I'm giving you a choice."

"No, man, let's do that other stuff!" the kid in the back yelled.

"Like we're really going to read any of it anyway," Heidi whispered to Patrick.

"Wake me up if she calls on me," Patrick said.

Heidi snickered. Lana turned around and gave him a kick in the shin. He kicked my desk, time number two for the day.

"Hey, what was that for?" he said to Lana.

"Just wanted you to see how I'm going to wake you up," Lana said.

"What do we notice about this poem?" Mrs. Abbey said.

I honed in on the piece. Despite the kindergarten scene going on around me, the poem had kind of caught me. It had a sort of rhythm to it—I noticed that right away because I had trouble with rhythm in my poems. My lines just seemed to get longer and longer—

"Lana?" Mrs. Abbey said. "What do you notice about this poem?"

"It's short," Lana said dully.

"How many syllables?" Mrs. Abbey said.

Lana gave an exaggerated sigh.

"What was that for?"

"Here we go, count the syllables, tap out the beat things, whatever they're called—like this is ever gonna do me any good or make me a living."

While Mrs. Abbey launched into her lecture about education being more about training our minds than filling them with useable information, I counted the syllables. Five in the first line, seven in the second, five in the third. I turned the page, which had five more little poems on it. They were all the same way.

"These poems are called *haiku*," Mrs. Abbey said. "An educated person knows that, whether he expects it to show up on a job application or not."

"'Haiku,' sounds like some kind of martial art," Patrick said.

"Absolutely it does," Mrs. Abbey said, perm shivering, "because it's a Japanese word. Now..."

She whipped a transparency off her desk and floated it onto the overhead projector. Somebody dove for the lights. This, in some people's opinion, was the best part of class. With the lights out, it was easier to doze off and harder for Mrs. Abbey to notice.

She proceeded to count out the syllables, while Patrick's breathing grew heavy and even behind me. Heidi rearranged her ponytail, and Lana opened her notebook and furiously wrote a note. Any minute now she would ask me to give it to Heidi. I hated it when she did that.

"So, you ask," Mrs. Abbey said, though no one had, "is *any* poem with three lines, seventeen syllables arranged this way, considered a haiku? Heidi, what do you think?"

Heidi looked at Lana.

"All right, since Lana seems to be your source, Lana, what do you think?"

Lana looked up, unrattled. "My guess would be no."

"Lucky guess," Mrs. Abbey said. "To be true haiku, the poem has to be about nature, it must contain a season word or suggestion, and it must capture only a moment. In so doing, it creates a layer of meaning that is unstated but nevertheless important."

I was sure I heard Patrick snore. The room rustled for a few more minutes, and then lapsed into a telltale quiet. If the kids weren't asleep, they were doing something unrelated to poetry.

But I peered at the poem in the semidarkness. Layer of meaning, huh? I tried to picture it—these flowers poking up between stones—and not in a nice garden, but, like, well, like at Papa's shop, between the pieces of bricks. It would take some real will power on the flower's part to grow in there.

I felt a little chill. She was right. I did see a layer of meaning. I sniffed to myself. It would be like learning anything in this classroom with all these "stones" around me.

The lights went on, and people protested aloud as they rubbed their eyes. "Marissa," Mrs. Abbey said, "I believe I see some life in your face. What's your reaction to this poem? What do you think that other layer of meaning is?"

"What do I think?" I said.

"No, the other Marissa," Patrick said. He obviously was the type who was cranky when he didn't get to finish his nap.

"Well, tell us, Emily Dickens," Lana said to me.

"Lana, enough," Mrs. Abbey said. "Marissa, any ideas at all?"

I could feel Heidi and Lana looking at each other right over my head. It was like being under a bridge, hiding from a hailstorm.

"I don't know," I said.

"I do," Patrick said.

"Right, you do," Lana said.

"I do. The other level of meaning—"

"Layer—"

"Whatever. This guy's gay, and he's a stonecutter so nobody will suspect, only the flowers growing in the yard are a dead giveaway."

"That is so stupid," Lana said.

"Any other ideas, Lana?" Mrs. Abbey said.

Lana looked at Heidi and then leveled her eyes at Mrs. Abbey. "Uh, let me think about it…No," she said.

"Fine, then keep your comments to yourself." Mrs. Abbey turned back to the overhead, and then she flipped her perm in Lana's direction. "Oh, and Lana, it's Emily Dickinson, not Dickens."

I couldn't help it. I got this big ol' smile on my face.

"What are you laughing at?" Lana said to me.

Patrick kicked my desk—time number three. He was behind today.

Mrs. Abbey drove her way through the rest of the lecture and "discussion" on haiku, although thank goodness she didn't call on me again. I liked it all though. I was still absorbed in it when the bell rang and everybody else bolted out of there like money was waiting for them in second period. I was the last one out, and Mrs. Abbey caught me by the arm as she was leaving for the journalism room.

"Marissa," she said, "you're my one bright star in this class. I wish you wouldn't let those people intimidate you."

"Okay," I said.

She blinked at me for a moment and then went out.

Sure, I thought, as I watched her maneuver through the mob in the hall. *I'll come in tomorrow and be Little Miss Assertive.*

How many times a week did I hear that—Shannon and me both? *Don't let people walk on you. Stand up for yourself. Be yourself. Don't be afraid of what other people think.*

Oh, and move a couple of the Sierra Mountains, too, while you're at it, would you?

I shook my head and elbowed my way toward my second-period class. Shannon would appreciate this. Maybe she would be at her locker.

But she wasn't, and I didn't see her between second and third or between third and fourth either. I'd have to wait until lunch. Maybe she would show up in the theater lobby where the Flagpole Girls ate when they weren't off chasing after their hundred other activities. Fridays were sacred for us; the rest of the time it was whoever came.

When I arrived at the lobby, only Tobey had shown so far. As soon as she saw me, she came right up off the floor where she was already settled with her lunch.

"I have to talk to you!" she said. Her brown eyes were sizzling.

"Me?" I said.

"Yes, sit!"

She didn't give me a chance. She tugged me down onto the floor tiles and didn't even look up when Brianna and Norie joined us.

"Okay," Tobey said. "I get this call last night—from Jason."

My heart sank even lower. I'd been right. It *was* Tobey he wanted all along. Although I wouldn't have figured her for the type to gloat.

"And he says, 'Do you think Marissa is trying to blow me off?' And I go, 'Why?'"

"Blow him off?" I said. I could feel my cheeks simmering.

"He said he called your house yesterday, and some little girl told him you were grounded from the phone. He says, 'Do you think she really is, or is she just using her little sister to get rid of me?'"

"No!" I said.

Tobey laughed. "Well, yeah, that's what I told him. I said, 'Marissa is way too cool to pull anything like that.' I didn't, like, say, 'No, Jason, she's crazy about you,' but, I mean, was that okay that I said what I did?"

"Yeah!" I said. I was trying not to smile too big. This still seemed too good to be true. He had to be interested in Tobey. He was just using this to have an excuse to talk to her.

"So anyway," Tobey went on, "he's going to try to call you again tonight."

"Why?" I said.

"Why?" That came from Brianna, who set down her sandwich on its brown bag and wiped her fingers with a vengeance.

"Look out, Marissa," Norie said.

Brianna was winding up. "What do you mean, 'why,' girl?"

"Well, I just don't know why he would want to talk to me," I said. "We barely had a conversation the other night—"

"Who could with us girls all over the both of you? He obviously wants to know you better, and you're all, 'Why? Why me?'"

I could feel my underneath skin coming to my rescue. Brianna caught me just before I folded into myself.

"You need confidence in yourself, girl," she said. "After all we've been through—just you and me together alone is enough— you would think you would have figured out what you're worth by now."

"Um, here comes Shannon," Tobey said.

We all looked up at the tone in her voice. It had that she-doesn't-look-happy sound to it. Shannon didn't look at all pleased. She looked shaky, and as Cheyenne would have put it, "even paler than usual." You could practically see through her skin.

"Are you okay?" I said.

"Shannon, have you, like, gone to the doctor?" Norie said. "It seems like you're sick all the time."

Shannon shook her head, conveniently pulling some of her hair over her face in the process. "I'm okay," she said. "I just came to say hi. I have to go."

She left before anyone could say anything. Brianna put down her sandwich again. "I think we ought to pray for her," she said.

"Yeah," Tobey said. She stuck out her hands, and we all joined.

That was the way we always did it. Anytime, anywhere, no matter who was looking. It had been hard at first with people jeering from the sidelines, but most of us were used to it by now, and so were the people who passed through the lobby.

"Lord," Brianna said, "please let Shannon hear Your voice and know You're there. No matter what's going on with her."

I liked that, and I kept thinking about it after we were done praying and Tobey and Brianna had started to talk about possible "looks" for Norie for the prom. Hearing God's voice. I'd like to do that myself. I was still thinking about it on my way to the office to work fifth period when somebody grabbed my arm and said something very different. Something like, "Hey, snob, aren't we good enough for you anymore?"

JUST WHAT I NEEDED—ANOTHER STING.

I turned around and saw three faces leering at me, the *zonzas*, as we used to call each other—Francesca, Daniela, Roz, and me. *Zonza* is Spanish for "silly."

Daniela grabbed my arm and laughed so loud some guy turned in the hall to stare. "We're just messing with you," she said to me. "Don't start to cry or something."

She tossed her black, long hair over her shoulder and kept smiling at me. Daniela had the biggest smile on the planet. Also a Dolly Parton figure, which she couldn't hide if she tried, and she didn't. Which was probably why the guy was still gaping. Daniela ignored him. She was so comfortable in her body. But Francesca gave him the stare of death, and he hurried on.

Francesca was a big girl who liked to wear plaid and a lot of makeup. When she narrowed her black eyes and gave her to-the-waist, coal-colored hair a flip, it could be pretty scary. That was why, when we would get into a tight spot—the four of us—Daniela had done most of the talking, and Francesca had done most of the looking. I had done most of the crying, and Roz did most of the giggling. She was giggling even now.

"You guys are evil," I said. "You scared me to death!"

"So where have you been?" Daniela said. "We never see you."

"Just doing stuff," I said vaguely.

"Like what stuff?" Roz said. She was creamier colored than the other two, and unlike most Hispanic girls, she had a lanky look. Between the gangly arms and the constant giggling, nobody took

Roz seriously. She had long ago given up trying to prove she had a brain cell to call her own.

"Just…I don't know…school and everything."

Francesca gave Daniela a large nudge with her elbow. "See. Told you."

"Told you what?" I said.

"I told her you had those other girls now. You don't want to hang with us no more."

"Not if you keep using grammar like that," Daniela said. She flashed me one of her huge smiles. "I told her you weren't trying to dump us."

"I'm not!" I said.

"Okay. So what about this afternoon, after school?"

"Catch the bus," Francesca said. "Go to the mall."

I looked at Roz, who was doing what looked like the I-have-to-go-to-the-bathroom dance. Beside her, Francesca was just staring me down.

"Sure," I said. "I have to call home first, but I think I can, if somebody's there to watch Luisa."

"Cool," Francesca said.

"Meet us at the bus stop. One comes at 2:20," Daniela said. She hooked her arm around my neck and gave me a squeeze. "This will be a blast."

Roz giggled.

Francesca said, "You better not ditch."

"I won't," I said. I started to back away. "I have to get to the office. I'll see you guys at 2:20."

"Two-fifteen," Daniela said. "If the bus comes early, the driver could care less, you know? He'll just leave."

I nodded and kept backing up until they disappeared around the corner. Then I raced to reach the office before the bell rang.

Whoa, that had been a surprise. I'd noticed, of course, that I'd been drifting away from our little foursome since…well, since about the time the Flagpole Girls came into my life. I hadn't done it on purpose. I mean, Francesca, Daniela, Roz, and I had been inseparable since about fourth or fifth grade. It just seemed as if we had always been best friends, always at each other's houses, spending the night and whispering until all hours.

We had kept tabs on each other's puberty progress. Daniela, of course, had gotten the first bra. Francesca had been the first to start her period. Roz's claim had been the first zit, although you had to have a magnifying glass to see it. I'd been dead last in everything. When you shared that kind of stuff with other girls, you figure you're friends for life, and I still felt that way.

But they were right. We didn't spend much time with each other anymore. I was usually busy with my responsibilities at home or, now that I thought about it, doing something with Tobey, Cheyenne, or Shannon.

I stuck my books under the office counter, and when I stood up, I collided with a wall of flowers.

"I got a delivery," said a voice behind it.

I peeked around at a working-my-way-through-college-type guy.

"Who for?" I said.

He scrutinized the envelope. "E-nid Race," he said. "Is that really somebody's name? E-nid?"

"That would be me," Ms. Race said as she sailed toward us. She crinkled her nose at him. "I'm E-nid."

She tipped the guy and then opened the envelope that was attached to one of two dozen long-stemmed, American beauty roses. I hoped none of the secretaries would call me to do a job just yet so I could watch Ms. Race's face as she read the card. A soft smile stole across her lips.

"Are they from your boyfriend?" I whispered.

She nodded and tucked the card back into the envelope. "You saw him that day at my place. You might not remember him though. You all were a little upset."

I shivered just thinking about that day with Brianna and Cheyenne up in the hills. But I did remember the take-charge guy who had been at Ms. Race's when we had fled there for help.

"You two are still together then," I said.

Ms. Race stuck her face into the middle of the roses and said, "Get a whiff of these, Marissa. Isn't that an incredible smell?"

I didn't plunge my head in quite as far as she did, but I did get a noseful, and it *was* sweet. The kind of scent they write poems about. Haiku, maybe...

"What's the occasion, Enid?" one of the other secretaries called out from her desk. I shouldn't have worried about any of them giving me a job to do. They were all craning their necks.

"No occasion; just an apology," Ms. Race said breezily.

"Apology?" The vice principal's secretary had her mouth hanging open like a drawer. "What did he do, try to run you over with his car?"

To my surprise, Ms. Race didn't laugh. She just said, "I think I'll leave them up here so we can all enjoy them."

As I passed her desk, I heard one of the women mumble, "If someone sent me flowers like that, I'd have them on my *own* desk so everybody would know."

I didn't ask Ms. Race why she didn't want "everybody" to know.

Still, as I was making photocopies for her and doing some filing, I had to wonder what it must be like to receive that kind of attention from a guy. I tried to imagine the delivery boy running up the front walk to our house, smothered in roses. No, they would be orchids—I liked orchids better—ringing the bell and announcing he had a delivery for Marissa Martinez.

I tried *not* to imagine Eddie saying something like, "Hey, dude, this has got to be some kind of mistake," and Anthony chiming in with "Who died?"

No, my brothers wouldn't be home in my dream. It would just be me and maybe Luisa. I'd open the card and catch my breath at the writing: All my love, Jason.

Luisa and I would sit there on the couch, gazing at them, and she would look up at me with admiration shimmering in her big brown eyes and say, "I hope this happens to me when I'm grown up."

I had it all pretty much perfect in my head by the time fifth period was over. Once I was back out in the hall with the mob, though, it started tearing around the edges, like a photograph you've passed around too many times.

Still, in sixth hour, when we were watching a film on the fall of the Soviet Union, I felt myself wanting to hold on to it—my dream, not the USSR. I slipped out my notebook, the one I always kept my poetry in, and tried to count out some syllables.

> Armful of orchids
> carried to my own front door
> symbol of his love

Something was missing. I closed the notebook and looked back at the screen. Names like Yeltsin were not, I decided, the stuff you wrote poems about.

Francesca was already at the bus stop, practically tapping her foot when I arrived at 2:14 after a hurried phone call to Mama.

"You came," Francesca said.

"Well, yeah," I said. Like you would cross this girl.

She glanced around, I assumed to look for Daniela and Roz. Then she leaned in a little closer to me, blocking out the sun.

"So, did you, like, get religion?" she said.

I could feel my eyes popping open.

"What I'm sayin' is, do we have to, like, watch everything we say when we're around you now?"

"Why would you have to do that?" I said. "You guys don't talk dirty or anything."

"No, I guess not," she said.

I could have kissed Daniela for appearing just then. I had no idea where that conversation was going.

"Hey, girl!" Daniela said to me. She gave me a neck squeeze and dropped her backpack so she could dig in her pocket and pull out a mirror and a lipstick tube. She smiled her enormous smile at me, as she expertly applied another layer of Creamy Espresso.

"Where's Roz?" Francesca said.

"She's coming," Daniela answered. "Takes her fifteen minutes to decide what to take home out of her locker." She winked at me. Daniela had picked up winking in about the seventh grade. I always wished I could pull it off. In fact, I tried once, but Anthony said, "Hey, Mama, Marissa's getting a tic!"

"Not like she does any homework," Daniela was saying. "If that girl tried to study, she would probably blow a fuse. God, she's dumber than dust. Good thing she's cute."

"Cute?" Francesca said.

"Yeah." Daniela replaced the top on the lipstick tube and met

Francesca glare for glare. "She's kind of gawky now, but she'll grow out of that. She has potential."

"Potential don't get you a date to the prom," Francesca said. "Right, Marissa?"

I didn't know whether to nod, shake my head, or shrug. I was still reeling from what Daniela had said. "God" she had said. Had she always said that, like that?

Roz arrived just then, threw one shoestring arm around my shoulder and, naturally, giggled. "This is so cool," she said. "I have totally missed you. There's nobody to stick up for me. These two are, like, always on my case."

"Poor baby," Daniela said mildly. "Okay, there's the bus. Let's grab the whole back!"

I had to grin at that. We had always tried to claim the two seats that faced each other in the back of the bus. We had discovered as soon as we had been allowed to ride by ourselves that the louder we were, the farther away from us other people sat.

And we were loud that day—at least they were. I spent most of the ride to the mall laughing at the three of them. I'd forgotten how funny they were.

"Roz," Daniela said, "do your Mrs. Abbey imitation for Marissa."

Roz looked at me and started to blink her eyes at light speed and jerk her head around.

"Don't she look just like her?" Francesca said.

"Poor woman!" Daniela said. "First thing needs to happen is she needs a new stylist. My mama could do something with her hair."

"She could!" Roz said, gray eyes wide. "She's the best!"

"Is she still working at the Pink Puff?" I said.

Francesca snorted. "Can you believe that name? Sounds like a poodle-grooming parlor!"

"It's always been called that," Daniela said. "Remember when we used to go in there and play with the nail polish on the manicurist's day off?"

"I painted every nail a different color," Roz said, gazing nostalgically at her fingertips.

"You still do that half the time," Francesca said.

"I do not," Roz said. She looked at me. "Honest, I don't."

"I know," I said, patting her leg.

The mall was still pretty empty when we arrived at three, and we wandered through The Gap, the Sunglass Hut, and Victoria's Secret like four doctors' wives who had nothing to do but shop. At one point I stopped outside Waldenbooks and said, "Can we go in here?"

They all looked at me as if I'd suggested a cruise through a muffler shop.

"What for?" Francesca said.

"God, I hate bookstores," Daniela said. "They remind me too much of school."

There it was again—the "God." I barely heard Roz say, "I'll go in. I like the romance novels."

"You like to look at the covers," Francesca said. "What's that dude's name they always put on them?"

"Fabio," Daniela said. "He's too hunky for me. I like a guy with a little more character in his face, you know? Maybe a scar here and there, different nose, that kind of thing."

"Oh," Roz said.

I didn't say I thought I'd like to see if they had any collections of haiku. I just shrugged and followed them to Sam Goody's where we pooh-poohed the country music, turned up our noses at the classical, and generally laughed, snorted, and hooted.

When we had left our fingerprints on every CD in the place and were back out in the mall, Francesca sniffed loudly and said, "I smell cookies."

"Let's split a Mrs. Field's," Daniela said.

"Split one?" Francesca said. She looked so forlorn I laughed out loud.

"You'll live," Daniela said.

We bought the biggest chocolate, chocolate chip with walnuts cookie we could afford by pooling our funds and took it to a far corner of the food court to divide it up. I gave Francesca half of my piece, and she gratefully accepted it.

"No wonder you keep such a cute figure, Marissa," Daniela said. "You have a date to the prom yet?"

I shook my head slowly. Her face was gleaming.

"I do," she said.

From the loud "no way!" that burst from Francesca's lips, I assumed Daniela hadn't told either of them.

"You do?" Roz said when the announcement had registered. "You totally do? Really?"

Daniela was nodding happily. "I just got asked today."

"Who?" Francesca said.

"That same guy you went out with last weekend?" Roz said. She wriggled in the seat. "What was his name? Kevin? Keith?"

"No, not him," Daniela said. The gleam seemed to slide off her face. She put down her cookie and concentrated on blotting her lipstick with a napkin.

Francesca watched Daniela like a large—very large—eagle.

"What happened to that guy?" Francesca said. "You never did tell us about that date anyway."

Daniela shrugged.

"Well? What?" Roz said.

"Nothing," Daniela said.

But her face was full of "something," and whatever it was, she was trying to avoid telling it. I wished Roz would back off, and I even put my hand on her arm.

"What?" Roz said. She looked at Francesca. "She looks creeped out."

"She does," Francesca said. She hadn't taken her eyes off Daniela. "What happened? Did you have sex with him?"

I about choked on my cookie. Roz was blinking like Mrs. Abbey. And Daniela went back to blotting Creamy Espresso until there was none left on her lips.

Finally, she nodded.

"How come you didn't tell us?" Francesca demanded.

"What? Did you want me to pick up the phone the minute I got home and call you and say, 'Hey, Frannie, guess what'?"

"No," Francesca said. Her voice was sullen. "It's just that we've always told each other everything."

"Okay, I'm telling you," Daniela said.

Roz leaned in. "So, what was it like?"

"Uh, Roz," I said. "I don't think you can really ask somebody something like that."

"Why not?" Francesca said. Her eyes bored into me like a pair of drill bits. "This is us. I told you guys what it was like to have a period."

My voice fell to a mutter. "I think that's a little bit different."

"Okay, look, it was no big deal, if you really want to know," Daniela said. "We went to see a movie, and we sat in the back row and made out and then when it was over, we went parking and…finished it off."

She took a huge bite of her cookie and chewed slowly. That didn't stop Francesca and Roz from peppering her with questions.

Roz's ran from "Was it romantic" to "Why aren't you going to the prom with him?" Francesca was more interested in "Did he use a condom" and "Weren't you afraid you were going to get caught by the cops?"

All I could do was stare at Daniela. She looked suddenly cold—and old. The questions that were running through my head made me feel like I was about Luisa's age.

But you didn't love him, did you, Daniela? What about the wedding nights we used to all talk about, with the lacy lingerie and all that?

"Look," Daniela said, "all I can say is, it was weird. I don't know why everybody pants and groans in the movies. That's all acting. I didn't even feel like I was in my own body."

"What?" Roz said.

"It was like it was happening to somebody else, okay?" Daniela said. She looked so coldly at all of us that even Roz pressed her lips closed. Only Francesca had the nerve to say, "So, are you going out with him again?"

"No," Daniela said crisply. "He's a jerk. He hasn't even spoken to me since."

"Ouch," Francesca said.

Daniela shrugged elaborately. "It doesn't matter. Now do you want to hear about my prom date or not?"

"I do!" I said. I'd have listened to her lecture on the fall of the Soviet Union if we could just change the subject.

But my *mind* wouldn't change the subject, even after I got home and started to chop up stuff for fajitas and halfheartedly played a game of I Spy with Luisa and Abuelo in the kitchen. All

I could think of was how it felt being with the *zonzas* again, and I couldn't find the words to describe it. Words like "different" and "hardened" went in and out of my mind, and every one of them stung. I was beginning to feel as if I lived in a beehive.

"I spy *una nieta* who needs to bring a book in for her Abuelo to read to her," I heard Abuelo saying in the background.

Luisa scrambled down from her chair and took off down the hall toward our room where one whole wall was lined with all the kids' books our family had accumulated over the years. Choosing one would take her awhile. I had a feeling that was what Abuelo had in mind.

"Where are you today, *muchacha*?" he said.

"I'm right here."

"The body is, not the mind," he said. His old face crackled softly into a smile. "Sit for a minute. One minute won't make us late with dinner."

Reluctantly, I put down the knife and sank into the chair across from him. He pushed his gnarled hands over to mine and grabbed on, and I couldn't help but feel a little comforted by their warmth.

"Too many stings today, Abuelo," I said.

He nodded as if I'd just given him a whole paragraph explanation.

"And do you know what I hate?" I said.

He shook his head.

"I hate it that my life is so out of…oh, what's the word?"

"*No es el mismo,*" he said. "It's not the same."

"I don't want *their* lives!" I said.

He didn't ask whose.

"But I feel so…young! Like I don't even *have* a life!"

If it had been Mama or Papa or my sister Cecilia, they would have told me to stop being *la Marissa zonza* and be grateful for what I had. Not Abuelo. He sat nodding in that way he had that meant not only did he understand everything I'd just said—and hadn't said—but he also felt it. Maybe even more clearly than I did.

We sat in silence for a minute, and then he said, "You do have a life, you know, Marissa."

"I know," I said, "but where is it? In this kitchen? In school where people make fun of me because I care about something? With my old friends who are like strangers to me now?"

"Your life is in the details," he said.

Then he looked at me, still nodding, as if that was supposed to clear everything up. I didn't even get my mouth open to ask him to explain when the phone rang.

"That's probably your Aunt Veronica," Abuelo said. "She called for you before."

I picked it up on the second ring.

"Hi," I said. "I was hoping you'd call."

"That's cool," said a male voice on the other end. "Because I was hoping you'd answer."

I COULDN'T MAKE MY MOUTH FUNCTION. I STOOD THERE as if my lips were frostbitten until he said, "This is Jason Oakman."

"I know," I said. "Um, hi." Oh, man, *la zonza* didn't even begin to describe me.

But Jason was laughing on the other end, and even in my total befuddlement I could picture his clean-shaven jaw, his shoulders going up and down…It was too good a picture. I had to get hold of myself.

"I'm sorry," I said. "I thought it was my aunt."

"Oh, so you *weren't* hoping I'd call?"

"Yes, I was!"

Oh, now, how subtle was that? I might as well have said, "I've been pacing in front of the phone."

"I'm just glad you called," I said. "You know, because last time you phoned, my little sister—"

"Yeah, Tobey told me. I thought you were blowing me off."

"Oh no!" I said.

Good grief. I wanted to jump into the pan with the fajitas. Luisa skipped into the kitchen and gave me a second to try to recover.

"Just a minute," I said. "I have to tell my little sister something."

Abuelo looked up from the table and arched an eyebrow at me. "I'll tell her whatever she needs to know," he said. "Take the phone into my room."

I hesitated.

"¡Vete!" he said in a stage whisper.

I pulled the extra-long phone cord into Abuelo's room and

closed the door as far as it would go. Jason seemed to be waiting patiently. My heart slowed down some.

"Okay," I said. "I was so confused in there for a minute!"

"Hey, you know what?" he said.

I shook my head. Like he could see that.

"That's why I wanted to, like, get to know you better."

"Why?" I said.

"Because you're confused."

"Oh," I said. Wonderful. The boy had a thing for ditzes, and I fit the bill. Now isn't that every girl's dream?

"Don't get me wrong," he said. "I don't think you're a dumb blonde. I mean, you're not even blond. What I mean is, if you're confused, you don't try to act like you have it all together. I like that, that's all."

I sat down on the corner of Abuelo's bed, and for the first time, I started to relax. I even laughed.

"Then you've got the right girl," I said. "People tell me I show my feelings like they're printed on my forehead."

"Who tells you that?" he said.

"My mother, for one. My father. All my friends—"

"Those girls you were with at the diner," he said.

"Yeah," I said.

"You guys are like a group or something."

"They're the best," I said. It was a detail I hadn't considered when I was wailing about my life to Abuelo.

"Isn't it just, like, so obvious when you have Christian friends and then you hang with people who aren't, isn't it just like night and day?" he said.

I was startled.

"Were you reading my mind?" I said.

"No, why?"

"Because that just happened to me today."

"Tell me," he said.

Suddenly I was pouring out my whole background with Francesca, Daniela, and Roz, and how I'd drifted away from them. Whether I would have told him about Daniela and her last date I don't know. About then, my siblings clattered into the kitchen from wherever they had all been.

"Where's Marissa?" I heard Anthony say. His only reason for asking would be his next question, which came when he started banging on the door to Abuelo's room. "Hey, Marissa!" he yelled. "What's for dinner?"

"Who are you talking to?" Reney said. "Is it a boy?"

"Marissa doesn't talk to boys," Gabriela said.

"No, she's too ugly!" Eddie put in. He even pushed the door wide open and said, "I got all the looks in the family."

"What happened?" Jason said. "Is your house being invaded by aliens?"

"Yes," I said.

"Look, why don't I pick you up later? We'll get a Coke, and we can talk. Only don't bring any of them along. How many of them are there anyway?"

"Five," I said. My heart was sinking slowly into my stomach. "I would really like to. I really would. Only, I'm not allowed to date on school nights." I didn't go on to tell him I'd never been on a date on any night. I wasn't *that* confused.

"So, what about Friday night then?" he said.

"Uh, Friday?" I said. I'd heard him, of course. I was just having a hard time absorbing it. I felt like Roz must feel all the time.

"Yeah," he said. "We'll go…I don't know, somewhere. We can figure that out."

"Okay," I said. "I have to check with my parents."

"I kind of figured that out by now," he said. "I'll call you tomorrow then."

"Hey!" A fist pounded about six times on the door. "We're hungry out here!"

"Go before they eat you alive," Jason said.

I'm not sure if I said good-bye. I'm not sure I even finished cooking the fajitas or did my homework or got Luisa ready for bed. All I was sure of was Jason Oakman had asked me out, and I wanted to tell somebody bad.

Somebody besides Mama and Papa, who listened to my whole rendition of what a neat Christian boy Jason was and muttered to each other and then said all right, as long as I told them where I was going and came in by 11:30. I was good to go.

After that, it was time to squeal with somebody. I thought of

Roz, Francesca, and Daniela for a minute. But that felt so wrong I dove right on to the first real possibility. I dialed Shannon's number with my fingers shaking.

Luisa padded into the kitchen in her nightgown and climbed up onto a chair to watch me, wide-eyed. It was so much like my daydream I grinned at her and scooped her into my lap.

"Who are you going to talk to?" she said.

Nobody evidently. The phone rang endlessly in Shannon's house until the answering machine clicked on. I hung up, and Luisa was still staring up at me.

"Your eyes are sparkling, Marissa," she said.

"They are?"

She nodded and then pulled in her chin and crossed her eyes as if she were trying to see her own.

"What are you doing?" I said.

"Are mine sparkly?" she said.

I said yes and hugged her. I didn't add that hers weren't sparkly for the same reason.

When she was asleep and my jobs for the night were done, I turned on the little light above my bed and pulled out my poetry notebook. I sat there for a while, staring at the haiku I'd tried to write sixth period. It was lame, no doubt about that. I looked at the chrysanthemum poem we had read that morning and remembered what Mrs. Abbey had said. *It has another layer of meaning.*

I knew what it was, too, I thought.

If it hadn't been for the *mocosos,* I'd have said it, and she knew it. Only right now, I kind of felt like I had something they didn't. A date with Jason Oakman.

He wouldn't date Lana or Heidi. They aren't confused!

I turned to a clean page and wrote an explanation of the chrysanthemum poem for Mrs. Abbey. In the distance I could hear the phone ringing, and I hoped for a millisecond it was Jason again. But I could hear Mama talking too long for that, and then she tapped on my door, stuck in her head, and whispered, "Don't forget your fitting for your bridesmaid's dress tomorrow, Veronica says."

"Thank you," I said.

"Don't forget now," she said. "You know how you go off into your dream world and forget things."

"I won't forget," I said. No way. I couldn't wait to fill Veronica in on this development. Now *there* was a person who would squeal with me.

But I couldn't wait that long to squeal. The first thing I did when I arrived at school the next day was look for Shannon. I found Cheyenne, sitting on the floor with Fletcher outside her first-period classroom.

"You guys seen Shannon?" I said.

"About five minutes ago," Cheyenne said.

"She went whipping past us on her way to the bathroom," Fletcher said. "She must have had to go bad."

Cheyenne, of course, slugged him.

"Which bathroom?" I said.

But the words were no sooner out of my mouth than the warning bell rang. I couldn't look for her now unless I wanted to make like the *mocosos* and waltz into English late. I'd have to catch Shannon later. I just hoped she wasn't throwing up again. Norie was right. She needed to see a doctor.

I slid into my desk just in time and was ready to roll when Heidi, Lana, and Patrick arrived and took their time kicking my seat and doing their hair and all that. Mrs. Abbey wasn't in the mood for a lecture or a discussion. She told us all to open our books and study the five haiku on page twenty and fill in a worksheet about the second layer of meaning.

"Hey, Mrs. Abbey," Patrick said.

She blinked rapidly at him. "Yes?"

"I thought you said poetry was supposed to be read aloud."

"Do you want to read for us?" she said.

"No way!"

"Then I guess that answers that question, doesn't it?"

A deadline must be coming up. Mrs. Abbey always gave us seat work when she had a big school paper deadline on the horizon. Heidi immediately scratched out a note to Lana, and Patrick kicked my desk a couple of times and settled in for his nap. I opened to page twenty and was immersed up to my eyebrows right away.

> The cat fluffs his fur
> and tries to avoid the cold
> of his own shadow.

That's totally Sylvia! I thought. *She'll do about anything to keep warm.*

I turned to the worksheet. Second layer of meaning. *Well, who doesn't want to stay warm, away from the cold, away from the stings.* I glanced up at Heidi. She stuck a note at me. I tossed it over onto Lana's desk and went back to the page. *The cold of his own shadow. His own shadow.*

About then I wished *I* had some fur to fluff up. "You try to avoid the coldness of your own soul the most," I wrote on the worksheet. *Maybe that means loneliness.*

Whether that was right or not, I wasn't sure, but I was on a roll. I finished the worksheet and glanced at Mrs. Abbey. She showed no signs of stirring from the paperwork at her desk.

I pressed into the poems again, and then I looked at the one I'd tried to write yesterday. I put a huge *X* through it. It didn't have that second layer of meaning. You didn't have to be a rocket scientist to figure that out. But how did poems get that?

I went back to another one in the book.

> Summer afternoon
> the coolness of the newspaper
> from the grocery bag

It was so specific. Like one thing, one tiny, little thing.

Lana gave me a nudge, and I looked up at her. She was impatiently waving a note at me.

"Pass it," she hissed.

I did, and then I looked back at her. One thing. One tiny, little thing. If it was Lana I was writing about, what would that little thing be?

That was simple. She had such a wide face. Like a wall.

I started to write.

> The hardened wide face
> like a wall with mouth and nose
> Lana hides behind

That was closer, I decided. But maybe too obvious. I looked over at Heidi. She was fiddling as usual with her ponytail.

> Wisps too short to fit
> always straggle to your neck.
> Someone should tell her.

I wasn't sure what that meant, but it meant something, and I liked it. I tried another one. I didn't even have to look at Patrick for an idea.

> Patrick has freckles
> tossed like party confetti.

I stared up to think of the next line, just in time to see somebody go by the classroom door, dangling a big wooden bathroom pass. Shannon was moving as if she were about to miss a plane. I closed my notebook over my pencil, scooted out of my desk, and grabbed our pass off the hook by the door.

"Is it okay, Mrs. Abbey?" I whispered. She barely looked up to nod, and I took off down the hall. As soon as I opened the bathroom door, I could hear Shannon throwing up. I had to put my hand over my mouth to keep from gagging myself. I hate to throw up.

"Shannon?" I said. Like she was going to answer me in midregurgitation.

I moved closer to the stall door and waited until she was quiet. "Shannon," I said again, "are you okay?"

She opened the door and smiled, but she looked like a piece of asparagus as she brushed past to the sink. She leaned over to rinse out her mouth, and I put my hand on her back.

"This is happening a lot," I said. "Don't you want me to take you to the nurse?"

She spit into the sink and gave me a watery-eyed look. "It isn't happening a lot. I'm okay."

"Let me just take you to Ms. Race then. She always knows what to do."

Shannon stood up straight and went for the paper towels. I watched her dry off her mouth and thought, *Now would not be a good time to share my news. Sorry you just lost your breakfast, Shannon. Now, about Jason…*

"I'm really fine," Shannon said. "You know how you always feel better after you throw up?"

"I guess," I said. "But—"

Shannon glanced at her watch dangling from her wrist. "I have to go back to class. I'll see you at lunch."

She was out of there before I could say anything, and I started to feel that out-of-place thing again. I was so involved in thinking about that, I might not have noticed anything when I got back to my seat in class. Except it was so obvious.

My notebook was at a funny angle, and when I picked it up, the pencil was underneath it instead of inside it.

"All right, gang," Mrs. Abbey said. "Grab your worksheets and your books, and let's gather into groups of four."

I stifled a groan. I hated this, just like Shannon and I had talked about. In the first place, in this class I didn't feel comfortable with anybody so I always sat there until everybody else was in a group, and then I went with the leftovers.

Except suddenly three shadows were bearing down on my desk.

"Be in our group, Marissa," Lana said in a hard voice.

They pulled their desks up around mine and leaned in. From the looks on their faces, I knew it wasn't to talk about poetry.

CHAPTER SEVEN

AT LEAST THE *MOCOSOS* DIDN'T WANT TO TALK ABOUT the poetry Mrs. Abbey had in mind.

The second she finished telling us to be ready in fifteen minutes to present our layers of meaning, the *mocosos* shoved their books aside and came in on me like a trio of vultures landing on road kill.

"Just who do you think you are?" Lana said, wide face inches from mine.

"I don't know," I said. I was so rattled I *didn't* know who I was right then. I was definitely wishing I were someone else.

"Where do you get off writing trash about us?" Patrick said.

Heidi brought her skinny rear end up off the seat so she could get herself into my face. "No, what I want to know is what were you planning to do with that stuff?"

"Were you going to read it to the class?" Lana said. "You must have a death wish or something."

Patrick gave a most unattractive grunt. "She's not gonna read it in front of the class. She hardly says a word as it is."

"Then why did she write it?" Lana demanded. She honed her now-bulging, hazel eyes in on me. "Why did you write that stuff? It's like…slander or something!"

I finally got my jaws to work. "It isn't slander!" I said. "I didn't write anything bad. Look."

I opened my notebook, fingers shaking. When I saw the ragged remains of the torn-out page, Heidi held it up in front of my face.

"Looking for something?" she said.

I grabbed at it, but she snatched it out of my reach, and Patrick snapped it from her. "What do you call this, then?" he said. "'Patrick has freckles / tossed like party confetti.'"

Lana plucked the paper out of his hand. "You got off easy," she said. "I get—what did she say? Oh, a 'hardened wide face / like a wall with mouth and nose.'" Even as she read it, her face seemed to flatten into a piece of plywood. "You're going to find out how hard I can be."

"I wasn't putting you down," I said.

"Oh, right," Heidi said. "Like everybody wants to go down on paper as a wall. And while we're on the subject." She put up her hand and flipped at the blunt ends of my hair. "Your 'do is nothing to brag about."

I wasn't really writing about your hair, I wanted to say to her. *It was a whole other layer!*

But even if I'd been able to get together just what it was, mentally, I wouldn't have been able to speak it. My lips were frozen. My whole face was one big ice block of fear. I sat there and waited for it, and it finally happened. My safe, underneath layer of skin pulled itself over me, and I could draw back into myself. I closed my notebook and stared at the cover.

"You are such a freak," Lana said.

Now that I could agree with.

Although she didn't say so at lunch, I think Tobey did too, and Norie and Wyatt. Shannon was the only one who didn't seem to think I should have ripped the lips off of every one of them. I was just glad Brianna wasn't there, or she would have had a stroke.

I told them, of course. The minute I walked into the theater lobby, Tobey looked up at me, put down her bologna sandwich, and said, "What's wrong?"

After I'd spilled it, Wyatt said, "You should have told them it was their own fault for invading your privacy."

"Right," Norie said. "Like Marissa is really going to say that to somebody."

"I wish you could have said *something*," Tobey said. She put her hand on my arm, and her brown eyes were big and sorry. "Not that I'm criticizing you; I don't mean that. But didn't you just want to tell them to go—"

"Pick on somebody with their same IQ," Wyatt finished for her.

"I can never think of stuff like that," I said.

"This is the part of being a Christian I have trouble with," Norie said.

We all looked at her.

"We're supposed to pray for people like that, right? We're supposed to let them bring out the best in us, not the worst, all that."

"Yeah," Wyatt said. He looked at her blankly.

"So, do we all, like, do that?" Norie asked.

We looked at each other guiltily and then burst out laughing, even Shannon.

"Guess that answers the question," Tobey said. She squirmed like she was uncomfortable and pitched the crust of her sandwich into her lunch bag. "I just wish you could get them to stay out of your face," she said to me. "I know they're the ones who are wrong—"

"But they think you're easy prey," Norie said flatly. "I've told you that before."

I could feel myself pulling back. I think Tobey saw it because she suddenly made her face real bright and said, "Hey, did Jason ever call you?"

At last, I could tell somebody my good news, and doing it made the *mocosos* fade into the back of my brain. Life got even better that afternoon when I took the bus downtown and met Veronica at the bridal shop.

In the first place, the bridesmaids' dresses she had picked out made every prom dress I'd gazed at look like background material. I stood in the dressing room staring at mine for a good three minutes before Veronica tapped on the door and said, "Do you have it on yet?"

The dress was this incredible shade of teal blue. Mid-calf length in front, it was long in back. It came to a V at the waist in front while the back was cut in a V, and there was no big fanny bow like you see in all the brides' magazines. Veronica had already assured me that no girl needs a bow on her behind.

I found myself holding my breath as I slid into it—and "slid" is the word. The silk eased across my skin like lotion. I closed my eyes and felt its softness against me, and I think for the first time in my life I really felt feminine.

"You're making me crazy, *sobrina*," Veronica said.

I knew I had better hurry. When she started slipping into Spanish, that meant she was also tapping her foot and about to fling open the door herself.

I stepped out and read the verdict on her face. Her eyes lit up.

"Look at you!" she said. "You're gorgeous!"

Then one dainty little hand went to her chest, and she grabbed my arm with the other. "But do you like it? I mean, that's important because I know the day of the wedding I'm not going to even see any of you, I'm going to be so nervous, so you have to like it. It's your dress."

"I love it!" I said and threw my arms around her neck.

She hugged me hard, and then she pushed me away and scrutinized my face, like she was checking it for blackheads.

"What?" I said.

"It isn't just the dress," she said. Her eyes narrowed. "Has something happened with that boy?"

I nodded happily, and her face broke into her crinkle-eyed smile. "That's it," she said. "Take off the dress. We're going for coffee. I want to hear every detail."

Of course, a lady in the back came bustling out with a pincushion on her wrist and told us we weren't going anywhere until she made sure the dress fit. It seemed to take hours for her to finish tucking, pinning, and writing things down. But finally we got out of there and raced down the block to Java Jungle. Veronica ordered a latté, and I chose an Italian soda. Then she poked me toward a booth by the window and shook her mass of dark curls at me. "So, what? What's going on with Wonder Boy?"

"Jason," I said. Then I told her. I was already feeling like the lead role in a feature film anyway, so rolling out the whole story was a lot more delicious than it had been at lunch, when I'd still been reeling from the *mocosos'* inquisition. I spared no detail.

When I was finished, she just blinked at me.

"Aren't you excited for me?" I said.

"Yes, of course! This is your first date, Marissa; it's a big deal. A huge deal when you come from our family!" She cocked her head like some kind of beautiful, exotic bird. The way her hair fell just right over her shoulder made me wish I hadn't cut mine.

"So, what?" I said.

"I just don't see why you're surprised. Excited, yes, but you act like this is some kind of miracle. It was only a matter of time, you know."

"That's easy for you to say!"

"It should be easy for you to say too." She took a gulp of her latté and winced at the heat on her tongue. "Why shouldn't a nice, cute boy ask you out? You're beautiful, you're sweet, you're creative. If Tony weren't so strict, you would have been going out long before this."

"I don't think Papa had anything to do with it," I said.

She waved me off with her little hand and sipped thoughtfully at her mug. I drained half my soda and watched her. She wasn't finished with me yet.

"Okay, now," she said, "I know your mother hasn't talked to you about this, unless she's changed since Cecilia was your age, but what about the sex thing?"

I spewed raspberry soda all over the table. She calmly wiped it up with a napkin.

"You're like a cat, Marissa," she said. "Everything is a surprise to you."

I picked up the other napkin and dabbed at my chin. "What *about* the sex thing? This is only one date. I don't know if I'll ever see him again."

"That isn't the point. The point is, you're starting to date, and you can't wait until you're in some guy's car, breathing hard and loving it, to decide if you're going to have sex with him."

"I'm not going to have sex," I said quickly. This whole line of conversation was bringing me uncomfortably close to the one I'd had the day before with Francesca, Daniela, and Roz. I tried not to shudder too obviously.

"You think you're not going to like it," Veronica said. She hadn't missed a thing.

"It isn't that," I said. "I mean, I don't know. I've never even come close."

Veronica leaned in. "You've never been kissed?"

I shook my head.

"Now *that's* a surprise," she said. "But never mind; go on. Tell me why you know you're not going to have sex."

I ticked off reasons on my fingers. "I think you should be in love with someone if you're going to have sex with him. I'm not in love."

"Okay."

"I'd be so afraid the guy wouldn't respect me the next day."

"Would you really?" she said, "Or have you just heard that someplace?"

"Both," I said.

I was ready to stop talking about all this, I really was. Veronica wasn't. She waited.

"I'd be too embarrassed," I blurted out. "I wouldn't even know what to do!"

"You would learn," Veronica said dryly. "But at least you're honest. Anything else?"

"I don't want to get pregnant. Plus, the way guys are, I wouldn't want it broadcast to the whole school."

"Try the whole world," Veronica said. "They might as well wear a sign that says, 'Hey, I just got lucky!'"

I covered my face with both hands and giggled. I could hear Veronica's husky laugh. But when I pulled my hands down and tried again with the soda, she stopped laughing. She even stopped smiling. She ran her finger around the top of her latté mug.

"So, is that all?" she said.

"I think so," I said. "Isn't that enough?"

She looked me straight in the eyes. "Well, if it ever turns out that those aren't reason enough, you let me know."

"Okay," I said. I tried to make it sound like the discussion was over. She took the hint.

"I'm happy for you, Marissa," she said. "This calls for a cele-bration. You want to split one of those decadent-looking pastries with me?"

We pigged out and laughed, and it buoyed me right up, even over the *mocosos'* one big smear of the day. I got even higher when I talked to Jason on the phone that night. He called to see what I might like to do Friday night. I, of course, said whatever he wanted to do, and he was okay with that. He went on to tell me about his passion for old Humphrey Bogart movies, his collection of CDs, and the bike trips his family took every summer. I breathed it all in until I was about the consistency of a helium balloon.

I barely slept that night. Even Sylvia abandoned the bed because I was tossing and turning so much. She went to the window sill to wait for me to settle down.

"You just wait till some boy cat asks you out," I whispered to her. "Then let's see how you behave."

I knew I was behaving differently because Eddie sneaked an extra Hostess cupcake into his lunch the next morning, and I let him. Anthony acted like he was having a major heart attack when, at the breakfast table, I knew what some long word Abuelo used meant, and I didn't smack the kid. I didn't even roll my eyes when I noticed Reney had hair spray on her hair. I must have been feeling good because I exchanged knowing smiles with Gabriela across the table over that one.

What made it even better was the surprise at lunch. It was only Wednesday, but just about all the Flagpole Girls were in the theater lobby, including Ms. Race, Diesel, and Fletcher. A couple of minutes later Norie and Wyatt flew in with an ice-cream pizza from Baskin-Robbins and set it down square in front of me.

"I don't understand," I said.

"We didn't act very jazzed yesterday when you told us you were going out with Jason," Tobey said.

"Nah, we were too ready to bust some chops in your English class," Norie said.

Brianna cocked an eyebrow. "Whose chops? I was off on that field trip to see a play. What happened?"

"What play?' I said. "I want to see a live play so bad—"

"*Whose* chops?" Brianna said pointedly.

"So we're making it up to you, Marissa," Tobey cut in quickly.

"Yep," Cheyenne said, eyeing the ice cream hungrily. "And you know what's the best thing about this?"

"I bet you're going to tell us, girl," Brianna said. She reluctantly tore her eyes away from me.

"We have to eat the whole thing right now, before it melts all over the floor."

"Then let the grazing begin!" Ms. Race said.

Wyatt and Norie made a big thing out of figuring out how to cut every piece evenly, mathematically speaking, of course. While they were measuring, Shannon leaned over to me and whispered, "I'm really glad Jason asked you out."

"Me, too," I whispered back. "Duh!"

She laughed her silvery little laugh, and Cheyenne stuck a paper plate dripping with ice cream, chocolate chips, and Oreo crust in front of her.

Shannon's laughter disappeared. "Oh, no thanks," she said.

"What?" Norie said. "After all that, you're messing up the equation, D'Angelo!"

"Are you okay, Shannon?" Ms. Race said. "Any teenager who turns down ice cream is bound for the nurse's office as far as I'm concerned."

Shannon nodded, and I looked at her as closely as I dared without making it obvious I was looking for telltale signs of nausea on her face.

"I don't do well with sweets," she said.

"What happens to you?" Fletcher was looking at her as if he were afraid of catching whatever she had that would keep her away from Häagen-Dazs.

"I just get really hyper," she said.

Brianna grunted. "Now *that* I'd like to see."

"But you bake such wonderful cookies," Ms. Race said.

"Yeah, like for every occasion," Norie said. "I don't get it."

"So give me half of her share," I said.

"Yikes," Tobey said.

"Yeah, let her go for it," Cheyenne said. "It's her celebration."

It was, and I didn't want it spoiled by everybody getting on Shannon's case. Obviously, she didn't want everybody—well, anybody—knowing how sick she was. Nobody else seemed to remember the times Shannon had been the first one to pluck an oatmeal cookie from the platter.

At Cheyenne's instructions—like we needed prodding—we polished off the whole pizza. Diesel even licked the cardboard until Cheyenne told him he was disgusting and took it away from him. Then we prayed, a big prayer of thanksgiving that made me feel as if I'd already had the date, died, and gone to heaven. A funny thought crossed my mind as we were praying, *God, I hope You're excited about this too*.

From then until Friday nothing yucky in my life seemed to matter as much—not the *mocosos* icing me down with cold stares, not the day-to-day drudgery of making dinners and dealing with smart-aleck brothers and too-big-for-their britches sisters, not even the deepening sensation that I was drifting further and further away from Francesca, Daniela, and Roz. Even my phone conversation with Jason on Thursday night didn't bother me.

I was sitting in the kitchen on a stool, brushing Luisa's hair while I held the phone with the side of my face.

"You're going to have neck problems doing that," Mama said as she passed through.

I nodded vaguely at her and went back to listening to Jason.

"I have tomorrow night all planned," he said.

"Good," I said.

"Don't you want to hear what we're going to do?"

"Sure," I said. "Tell me."

"No."

I laughed.

"No, I want to surprise you," he said.

"Then why did you ask me?"

"Because I like to tease you. You're easy to tease."

"Is that good?" I said.

"It is," he said. "Most girls get ticked off and start to flip their hair and stuff."

"Oh," I said. "You've gone out a lot, I mean, with a lot of girls, haven't you?"

"Pretty many," he said. There was a funky silence. "Why do you ask?"

I really didn't know. His comment had just brought up a vision of this line of girls being checked off a list after a date because they had flipped their hair one too many times.

"I probably ought to tell you something," he said. "I mean, not that you, like, had any ideas or anything, but since we're on the subject…"

This had the sound of something serious. I tapped Luisa on

the shoulder and handed her the brush. "Go on to the room," I whispered. "I'll tuck you in in a minute."

"Okay!" she whispered back. It was no wonder she was my favorite of the brood.

But at the moment, I had a weird feeling in the pit of my stomach. What was he about to tell me? He really did have a girlfriend, and we were just going out as pals?

Good grief, Marissa, get a grip!

"I'm just not the type," Jason said finally, "to settle down and date one girl."

I was so relieved I almost laughed aloud. "Oh," I said. "I thought you were going to tell me…well, never mind. That's cool with me. I never thought you were."

And that was true. The only thing that mattered to me at the moment was that somebody like Jason even wanted to spend time with somebody like me. That was enough.

That was more than enough.

CHAPTER
EIGHT

I KNOW MOST GIRLS THESE DAYS DON'T MAKE A HUGE
deal out of going somewhere with a guy for the first time.
Cheyenne said she never actually had a first date with Fletcher.
They just kind of started to go out.

But for me it really was a big thing, especially since my parents
had made me wait until I was sixteen and even more so because I
was going out with somebody who seemed so perfect. The
Flagpole Girls seemed to understand that without my having to
tell them. That was the way it was with us. And they made it so
special for me, starting with Shannon.

She met me before school at my locker Friday morning, for
the first time all week, clutching this big shopping bag.

"What's that?" I said.

Her face grew pink. Shannon was so pale that when she
blushed she just looked like the rest of us—well, the rest of the
white girls anyway.

"Now I hope this doesn't make you mad," she said.

"At you?" I said. "Right."

"Well, I just wondered if you knew what you were going to
wear tonight."

I stopped with my hand still on the binding of my math book.
"No!" I said. "I forgot to even think about that!"

I looked down at the denim, overall-style jumper I was wearing with a striped T. "Oh, my gosh! I don't think I even have anything cool—I know I don't. I don't even know what cool is!"

Shannon was shaking her head patiently. "You're such a geek,
Marissa. You're the coolest person I know."

"Liar," I said.

"Would you be mad if I brought you some outfits to try on?"

I dropped my math book and threw both arms around her. It was like hugging air.

"Is that what's in the bag?" I said.

She nodded, still pinking up.

"You are so sweet!"

"Then you're not, like, offended? You don't think I think you have no taste?"

"I *don't* have any taste!" I said. "Why would I be offended?"

She looked reassured as she grabbed my arm. "Let's go in the bathroom. You can try on some of this stuff. If any of it fits you, you can have it. None of it fits me anymore."

I groaned. "Forget it, Shannon. If it's too small for you, I won't even get my little toe in it!"

"No," she said, "they're all too big. Not that I think you're way bigger than I am or anything."

"I'm Dumbo compared to you!" I said. "Did you go to the doctor yet?"

"Hurry," she said.

She shoved me into the girls' bathroom and pushed the bag into my hand. "I want to see how this top looks on you."

I hate to admit it, but the minute she pulled this short, flowered, sleeveless mock turtleneck with matching short sweater out of the bag, I forgot all about Shannon's health. "Put it on," she said.

I did, and it fit, and it looked amazingly great with the jeans she tossed to me. They were too long, but they were fun rolled up. They were also brand-new, as I noticed when she ripped off a tag.

"You've never even worn these!" I said.

"I know. I don't know why I bought them. They never did fit."

"Don't you want me to pay you for them?" I said.

"I want you to have the best time with Jason," she said. She shrugged. "I don't know, maybe because my mother is a seamstress and she's always made such a big deal about clothes for all us girls, I just think you have a better time when you know you look good." She smiled widely at me, and her blue eyes tried to sparkle. "And you do look good, Marissa. You are about the cutest girl in this school."

The Girls weren't finished. Cheyenne came charging into my first-period class just before the bell rang.

"What did you pick?" she said.

"Huh?"

"Which of Shannon's outfits did you pick?"

I pulled the top out of the bag, and she narrowed her eyes at it.

"What's wrong?" I said. "Do you hate it?"

She shook her head and darted out of the room. Patrick kicked my desk from behind, and I could feel his breath on my neck.

"Not only are you a freak," he said, "your friends are freaks too."

Not in my eyes. We had our usual Friday Flagpole Girls meeting at lunch, and everybody was all over me so much that Ms. Race had to remind us to pray. I've decided God understands stuff like that.

A lot of whispering was going on at the meeting, too, which didn't include me. I found out why about five o'clock when I was chopping tomatoes in the kitchen and the doorbell rang.

"Probably for me!" Eddie yelled from in front of the TV.

Abuelo looked up from the kitchen table where he was doing a puzzle with Luisa.

"Does he have girls coming over now?" he said. "I thought the telephone was bad enough."

To Eddie's disappointment, however, it wasn't a member of his admiring female public, but Norie and Wyatt with Cheyenne in tow.

"Hi, guys!" I said. I looked around to see if any horizontal plane was clear for them to sit on and yelled at Eddie to turn down the television. But they were too excited to sit, and they were practically shouting anyway.

"This is so cool, what they brought you," Cheyenne said.

"You brought me something?"

"You have no sense of the dramatic, Cheyenne," Norie said. She nudged Wyatt, and he produced a shiny gift bag from behind his back.

"For you," he said.

I reached in and pulled out a small book in telltale yellow and black. It was Cliffs Notes for *Twelfth Night* by Shakespeare.

"Gee," I said.

I looked at the three of them, and they all started to laugh and clutched at each other like they were about to be thrown off some speeding rowboat.

Abuelo craned his neck and muttered, "Funny play. I never thought it was *that* funny though."

"I don't understand," I said.

"You will," Norie said. "Just read it—at least the summary—before tonight."

"Time to shut up, Nor," Wyatt said.

"Right. We better go before I blab."

"Wait!" Cheyenne said. "I have to give her my present."

"You, too?" I said.

She dug into the pocket of her bib overalls and came out with a fist, which she thrust at me. "Open your hands."

"Is it alive?" I said.

Luisa gave a squeak and started to scramble up onto the chair.

"No, it isn't alive!" Cheyenne said. "Trust me; open your hands."

I did and felt something fragile fall into my palms. I looked down at a pair of earrings, the exact pinks, greens, and taupes of the flowers in Shannon's top.

"Did you make these?" I said.

Cheyenne nodded, grinning from one of her own earrings to the other. She could be so adorable.

"These are perfect!" I said.

"Isn't she amazing?' Norie said. "One time I tried to make myself a pair. Shades of Brownie Scouts in second grade."

"Try them on," Cheyenne said.

"Doesn't one size fit all?" Wyatt said.

"You're so *male*, Wyatt," Cheyenne said.

I slipped the earrings into my pierced holes and felt the beads brush the sides of my face. It was a lightly feminine feeling.

"Cheyenne, thanks," I said.

I hugged her. She hugged me back hard enough to break a rib, and then they all left, still talking louder than the TV. Eduardo glared at them and turned it up.

Norie stopped on the porch as if she had almost forgotten something. "What time are you going out?"

"He's picking me up at seven," I said.

"Okay, will you be done with dinner by six?"

"I should be."

"Good."

"Why?"

Cheyenne elbowed in. "Let me tell her. Brianna's coming over to help you with your hair and makeup."

"Only if you want her," Norie said. "She said to tell you if you hate the idea it won't hurt her feelings."

"I love it!" I said. "I was afraid I was going to look like I didn't belong in Shannon's outfit."

"Right," Norie said dryly. "Come on, gang."

I wore the earrings while I cooked dinner and asked Abuelo to read the summary of *Twelfth Night* to me as I was sautéing. Luisa got confused and disappeared. Anthony came through at one point, stopped, listened, and said, "Haven't you ever read that before?" and walked out in superior disgust. Reney came in at the end and about drooled onto the table as Abuelo described the big gala wedding scene.

"I love weddings," she said.

"Too bad," Eddie remarked to her. "You're never going to have one. Geeks don't get married."

She chased him out screaming, and I serenely put plates on the table. Abuelo smiled at me.

"Estás hermosa, Marissa," he said.

If it had been anybody else, I would have said, "I am not beautiful!" But in our family, you didn't argue with your elders.

I did feel loved though. Especially when Brianna arrived with her makeup case. With Reney, Gabriela, and Luisa all gathered around, she applied a little mascara, a scootch of eye shadow, just the tiniest amount of blush, and some lipstick that seemed to bring my whole face to life.

"Put more on!" Reney said.

"She has enough, girl," Brianna told her. "Face like that, coverin' it up with a bunch of stuff is a crime."

Reney sniffed and left.

Gabriela looked wistfully at the contents of the makeup case. "Can you do mine?" she said.

Brianna twitched an eyebrow at her. "When do you think you'll be going out on your first date?" she said.

Gabriela, bless her heart, had to count on her fingers. She isn't the smartest of my sisters. "Six years," she said.

"I'll be back in six years to do yours," Brianna said. She went after my hair with a brush as Gabriela trailed out.

"Marissa always brushes my hair," Luisa said.

"She does?" Brianna said.

Luisa nodded and then for some reason threw her chubby little arms around my neck. We waited until she was done hugging me.

It was a wonder Brianna ever got me done, but I liked the result. She didn't change my 'do. Heidi would have told her to give me a complete makeover, I was sure. But she made my hair seem fluffier, shinier, and fuller somehow.

"How did you do that?" I said.

But she didn't get to answer because Anthony came in to tell me the phone was for me.

"Hurry up," he said. "I'm expecting a call."

"What are you, the phone police?" I heard Brianna say to him.

It was Tobey.

"Hi," she said. "I bet you look incredible about now. Not that you don't always."

"I don't always," I said. "But I like what Brianna did."

"I wish I could see you," Tobey said. "But listen, I just called to say have a great time. I know you will. And don't let his cool exterior fool you; Jason's excited too."

"You've talked to him?" I said.

"A couple of times," Tobey said. "But that's all I'm going to say. I have the biggest mouth on the planet."

"So you know where he's taking me," I said.

"Yup. Have to go. Have a blast!"

She hung up. I had a suspicion they all knew where we were going. I was about to interrogate Brianna when the doorbell rang. I vaulted a kitchen chair, but I couldn't reach the door before Anthony did.

"Hey," my brother said, when he opened the door to reveal a very cool Jason standing there. "You the paperboy?"

"Yeah," Jason said. "You owe me $25.99."

Anthony stood there for a second then yelled over his shoulder, right into my face, "Romeo's here!"

Everybody but Tipper and Al Gore entered the living room at that point. I thought I was the most embarrassed I knew how to be. Until Papa stepped up to Jason and said, "You're taking my daughter out?"

I wanted to die.

Jason stuck out his hand and said, "Yes sir."

"She has to be home by eleven," Reney said from her perch on her knees in the chair Papa had just vacated. Gabriela punched her and then giggled. Papa stared them both down.

Then he looked back at Jason. "Eleven-thirty," he said. "Where are you going?"

For the first time, Jason looked a little caught off guard.

"Uh, that was going to be a surprise for Marissa, sir," he said. His eyes shifted to me.

"I'll call you when we get there, Papa," I said.

Papa didn't seem to like that idea. In the meantime, I could feel my mother giving me the once-over, assessing my outfit, my hair, my makeup—let's face it, my every pore. I might as well have been in my sweats, as beautiful as I felt about then.

"All right," Papa said finally and gruffly.

I heard a soft grunt behind me and turned to see Brianna doing her own assessment of the situation. I'm sure she didn't miss it when my mother quietly handed me a Kleenex and pressed her lips together. At least she didn't say aloud, *Wipe off some of that lipstick.*

"Then I guess we'll see you at 11:30," Jason said. His confidence seemed to have returned, and he grinned at me. I smiled back, then smiled behind me at Brianna and caught Abuelo in the doorway with his walker. He put two fingers to his lips and kissed them and held them up to me. God love him.

The agony didn't end until we were well out of the driveway. Even as we were pulling out, all the kids from Anthony on down had their faces pressed to one window, and Papa was none-too-subtly peering out of the other one. I had a horrible image of Mama ushering Brianna into the kitchen for questioning.

But Jason was chuckling as we drove off down my street in

what looked, to my surprise, like a very old car all shined up.

"I'm sorry about all that," I said.

"How many brothers and sisters do you have?" he said. "I lost count."

"Four sisters and two brothers. My older sister wasn't there. She's modeling in Italy."

"I thought there were about a hundred," Jason said. "You sure put up with them. I'd have to pop that short guy in the baggy jeans."

"Eddie," I said. My siblings were the last thing I wanted to talk about, but I'd have discussed Yeltsin with Jason Oakman.

"Okay, enough with the family reunion," he said. "Have you guessed where we're going?"

"No!" I said. "Does it have anything to do with Shakespeare?"

The look he gave me was so disappointed I almost bit off my tongue.

"How did you know?" he said.

"Lucky guess?" I said.

"Out of thin air…What are you, clairvoyant?" But he smiled. "That's okay. It's still neat."

"What's still neat?" I said.

He didn't tell me. He just let the evening unfold like the dream it turned out to be.

I WENT BACK AND FORTH BETWEEN LOOKING AT JASON'S better-than-Leonardo-DiCaprio profile and peering out the window to see where we were going. The car was winding through the old Reno neighborhood where I lived—and heaven knows, I'd seen that ten thousand times in sixteen years—so Jason's jaw line won out.

When we came to a stop sign, he ran his hand along his chin and glanced over at me.

"You sure Tobey didn't tell you?"

"No," I said. "She wouldn't say a thing."

He pulled into the intersection and stretched his arm along the back of the seat. "Why don't you scoot a little closer? I can hardly hear you all the way over there. It's a big car."

I inched my way over until I could smell his Polo Sport and feel the warmth of his arm close to my back. At that point, forget it. We could have gone to the Washoe County dump together, and I would have been happy.

But we didn't. Jason pulled into the north parking lot at UNR—that's the University of Nevada, Reno—and grinned.

"You're taking me to college?" I said.

"Yeah, I thought we would sit in on a biochemistry class."

"Oh," I said.

He laughed his silent laugh. "I said you were fun to tease. No. Look." He pointed up at the marquee, which I had missed when we drove in because I had mentally been measuring Jason's eyelashes.

"Nevada Repertory Company Presents," it read, "Shakespeare's *Twelfth Night*."

"Is that…are we seeing a play?" I said. "Shakespeare?"

He was watching me, his green-gold eyes sparkling. "You definitely are different. I *have* to see it for English. Tobey said you would sell your sister to see it."

Actually, it wouldn't take much for me to put Reney on the market, but that wasn't the point. How recently had I said I would love to see a real play and that I would love to study Shakespeare?

He nudged me. "You don't really have to sell your sister. Personally, I'd unload the brother who answered the door."

"No!" I said. "This is wonderful! I've wanted to see a play for so long."

"Tobey said that. Okay, cool."

He climbed out of the "land yacht" and reached down a hand to pull me out. He didn't let go as he led me toward the fine arts building, although he did look back once as if to make sure the car wasn't following us.

"You'll be okay," he said.

"Who are you talking to?" I said.

"My car."

Then he laced his fingers between mine and said, "You're going to keep me awake during this thing, right?"

Nobody needed to keep *me* awake, that was for sure. The theater itself was amazing, with the set lurking up onstage in a sort of blue half-light and the ushers in black and white bustling all around. Jason shared a program with me, his arm slung casually across the back of my seat. He smelled so…guy-ish, and he laughed so softly and he talked so easily, I wasn't sure what to enjoy most.

But when the houselights went down and the stage sprang to life, there was no contest. I was enchanted.

On a background of zany set pieces made out of filmy, colored cloth and to stringed and piped music, people in glittering brocade costumes cavorted on the stage with pure poetry flowing out of their mouths as if they were half singing, half having ordinary conversations. I guess it helped that I had read the summary, but I didn't miss a funny line, a prank, an innuendo. It was so entrancing I felt as if I were part of the story.

When the houselights came up for intermission, I had to blink myself back to reality.

It took me a second to realize Jason was looking at me and grinning.

"What?" I said.

"You're really into this, aren't you?" he said.

"It's incredible!"

"You've never seen a play before?"

"Have you?"

"Yeah. I was in this theater every time somebody did a children's play when I was a kid. My mom wanted me to get my face out of Super Mario World and get some 'culture.'"

"Were they like this?" I said.

"Like in a foreign language?"

"No. Like...I don't know...different. Like magic."

He just grinned. "You're not putting me on. You really like this stuff?"

I nodded.

"Cool," he said. "You want something to drink?"

We spent intermission in the lobby, sipping Cokes, listening to a string quartet, and looking at paint-spattered canvases on the walls.

"These college people can be pretty weird," Jason said. He cocked his head at one piece that had various parts of Barbie doll anatomy popping out of it.

"Students here did these?" I said.

"Yeah. Scary, huh?"

I pondered the Barbie canvas. "Brianna's better than this. She took Cheyenne and me to an art show one time, and that was amazing. I wish I could go back to one."

Jason gave my shoulders a squeeze. "I have a lot to show you, girl."

"You do?" I said. I could be so eloquent sometimes.

"I can tell you don't get out much." He was grinning. "I'm going to change that."

They flashed the lobby lights, which obviously meant we were supposed to go back inside. If the second half of the play hadn't been even better than the first, I would have spent the whole time rolling Jason's words around in my head. You know, the way you make a Jolly Rancher last as long as you can in your mouth. *I have a lot to show you,* he had said. *I'm going to change that.* His words were more delicious than the sour-apple-flavored ones.

When the play was over and I shamelessly joined the shrieking crowd that gave the actors a standing ovation, Jason led me through the lobby mob and out into a silky, late-April night.

"You hungry?" he said.

"Are you?" I said.

"Does a chicken have lips? Come on, let's eat."

We passed Burger King, McDonald's, Wendy's, and Denny's, making our way downtown. Finally we pulled into a parking garage near the river, and Jason made me close my eyes while he opened the trunk. I was clueless and didn't even try to see what he was carrying as we raced, hand in hand, toward Wingfield Park, which ran along the Truckee River in the center of town.

"The trick is to pick the right spot," Jason said.

"For what?" I said.

He didn't answer but bolted toward a spreading cottonwood on a gentle slope by the water. I looked a little nervously over my shoulder. What, exactly, was his plan out here in the dark? I had heard homeless guys slept here.

When I looked back at Jason, he was leaning over his mystery package, which turned out to be a basket, and pulling something out. A blanket. He spread it under the tree with a flourish, sat on it, and stuck a hand up for me. I sank down beside him, and his eyes twinkled into mine.

"You like caviar?" he said.

"I don't think so," I said.

"Good. 'Cause I brought peanut butter sandwiches. Hope you like them with sweet pickles."

I was speechless—big surprise—as he pulled out a pile of sandwiches, a package of Double Stuffed Oreos, two Cokes, and a bag of barbecued potato chips big enough to put Luisa in.

He also produced cloth napkins from the basket. "My mom said you would want cloth napkins." He fluffed one onto my lap, deposited a sandwich, soggy with pickle juice, onto it, and popped open both Cokes.

"What shall we drink to?" he said. Then, because I, of course, didn't make a suggestion, his eyes lit up, and he said, "To us!"

"To us," I said.

We both took a swig, and while the bubbles were still fizzing in my nose, he said, "You know what?"

I shook my head.

"I like you. You're a blast."

"I am?" I said.

He laughed, leaned over, and kissed me on the cheek. That was it. I could hardly eat. Not that I could have gagged down peanut butter and pickle anyway. I know I just sat there starry-eyed and listened to the sparkling stream of words that came out of him. By the time his sandwich was gone and most of the chips and cookies, too, I felt as if I had known Jason Oakman since nursery school.

His favorite dinner was steak and fries, the wedge kind, not like they serve at fast-food places. He played pool when he wanted to relax and sang with his collection of Disney soundtracks when he needed to get psyched. He knew all the words to *Lion King, Little Mermaid*, and *Beauty and the Beast*. He had skipped *Pocahontas* and *Hunchback* and was working on *Hercules*. Arby's was his favorite fast food. *Casablanca* was his favorite movie. He was an only child and had a great relationship with his parents and could finally beat his father in a bike race all the way around McCarran Boulevard, which was about twenty miles.

He had been a Christian all his life and figured Jesus was his best friend. He felt sorry for kids who hadn't figured out that was the only way to go. He said all of that as easily as he told me the only way to eat an Arby's roast beef and cheddar was with hot sauce.

I really hated it when I looked at my watch and realized it was 11:10.

"I have to get home," I said.

"Bummer," he said. "I bet we could talk all night."

"Yeah," I said.

He came up off the elbow he had been leaning on, and with just one finger brushed my hair off my cheek. "I'm not going to take you home unless you promise me we'll have more nights like this."

I wasn't sure I could even breathe, much less answer. I just nodded.

He smiled, right at my mouth, and then kissed it—gingerly, the way you set somebody's grandmother's best china teacup on a saucer. I didn't even think about his smooth-shaven upper lip. That was way too mundane for the moment.

Veronica, I thought as we piled the remains of our picnic into the basket, *I've now been kissed.*

But I knew I wouldn't tell her. I knew I wouldn't tell anybody. It was almost too fragile to even write a poem about. I just wanted to hold the moment gently in my mind, like that teacup.

Forget holding it for too long though. When we climbed back into his car, Jason turned the key in the ignition, and the engine churned for a second like an asthmatic old man trying to breathe and then died.

I held my breath while he tried again and again, three more times. His beautiful jaw line was an accordion of straining muscles.

"Do you know what's wrong?" I said.

He mumbled something about the carburetor and got out of the car. As he raised the hood, I looked at my watch—11:20. If we left this minute, I might make it in by curfew. Obviously we weren't leaving this minute.

I dug in my purse for thirty-five cents and climbed out of the huge car. Jason was studying the engine like a pediatrician examining a sick baby.

"I need to call home," I said. "Do you know if there's a pay phone?"

"Use my cell phone," he said without looking up. "It's in the glove compartment."

I wasn't sure I knew how to use a cell phone, but I'd have learned Morse code if it were the only way to get in touch with Papa. Otherwise, I could be grounded until I qualified for Social Security.

My father answered abruptly after the first ring.

"Hi, Papa," I said. "Jason's car won't start so I'm going to be late."

"Where are you?" he said.

I told him.

"I'll be there. You stay," he said.

So much for the teacup in my brain. I died six, maybe seven

times, before Papa arrived in his work truck and climbed out with his toolbox.

Jason glanced up, and for just a moment I saw an I-can-fix-my-own-car look flicker through his eyes. I was sure he could. I was also sure he could leap tall buildings in a single bound.

But the look faded, and he grinned sheepishly. "I'd shake hands, but I'm a little greasy."

"Is this a '56?" Papa said.

Jason nodded.

Then they started to speak a foreign language that included words like "valve," "fuel line," and "overhead cam." Within ten minutes, "the '56" was once again humming.

"I didn't know about that one valve adjustment," Jason said. "He's cooking now though, isn't he?"

Papa nodded and clanked a wrench into his toolbox. I died for the eighth time.

"I'll have Marissa home in ten minutes," Jason said as he reverently closed the hood.

"I'll take her," Papa said.

I could hardly look at Jason, except to warn him with my eyes not to argue. He twitched his eyebrows at me.

"I'll call you tomorrow," he said.

"After she washes the car," Papa said. He worked at his mustache. "That's your punishment for being late."

What did this make, twice now that I'd been disciplined since I'd known Jason? I didn't die for a ninth time; it wasn't doing me any good. So much for moonlight picnics and china-teacup kisses. Jason, with his superparents, was going to want to stay as far away from my family as possible.

Papa and I rode home in rigid silence, and I barely muttered a good night as I went to bed. Sylvia purred sympathetically in my ear, and I whispered to her, "Be happy you were taken away from your parents when you were a kitten."

I woke up before anybody else except Abuelo the next morning and put on my cutoff jeans and a faded T-shirt. I was in the kitchen filling up a bucket when my grandfather tottered in with his walker and took in the atmosphere with a glance.

"You didn't have a good time last night, *muchacha*?" he said.

"I had a wonderful time—until Jason's car broke down and Papa came and fixed it. It was after 11:30."

"And your punishment is to flood the kitchen," he said.

I yanked the faucet to a stop and looked at the now almost overflowing sink.

"I have to wash the car," I said.

"You couldn't wait until the sun came up?"

I shook my head. I wasn't so eager to do my penance. I just needed to do something physical to get rid of all the anger that was sizzling in me like a pan of fajitas.

Mama's seen-better-days van was in its usual place in the driveway, and I dragged the hose toward it with a vengeance. As I started to scrub, miraculously I didn't rub the paint off, with the thoughts that were raging in my head.

It isn't fair! It wasn't my fault the stupid car wouldn't start.

I called right away. I did what I was supposed to do. And what does Papa do? He embarrasses me. No, he humiliates me in front of the only guy I've ever looked at twice.

Thank you, Papa. Thank…you…so…much…

"You missed a spot," said a voice behind me. "Let me get that for you."

Jason took the rag from me and started to scrub my mother's van.

I HAD BEEN SO WRAPPED UP IN MY MENTAL MUTTERINGS, I hadn't even heard Jason pull up. But he was grinning, washing, and singing, "I Just Can't Wait to Be King."

"What are you doing?" I said stupidly.

"Playing tiddlywinks with manhole covers," he said.

"But you don't have to do this!" I said.

"Sure I do," he said. "Because your father's looking out the front window, and he seems pretty impressed. How else am I going to convince him to let me take you out again?"

I started to look toward the house.

"Don't look!" Jason said. "You'll blow it!" Then he added, "Don't just stand there; grab the hose."

Later, when we were having chips and salsa for breakfast on the front steps, with Luisa, Reney, and Gabriela all hanging around, Papa came out and actually said thank you. Even later, at the dinner table, long after Jason was gone, he said, "That boy that was over here today—"

"Jason," Reney said.

Papa grunted. "He's a good kid."

"*El zorro*," Abuelo said.

"He's Zorro?" Eddie said. He slashed the air with his knife.

"No, idiot," Anthony told him. "He's speaking Spanish."

"What's it mean?" Gabriela said.

"I know," said Luisa. "*El zorro* is 'the fox.'"

Gabriela giggled. "Jason's a fox."

"That's what we used to call good-looking guys back when I was…looking at good-looking guys," Mama said.

"Then Jason is!" Reney said, practically drooling.

"Was Papa a fox?" Luisa said.

"Oh, don't go there," Anthony said.

I looked at Abuelo, but he was busy eating his enchilada casserole. I had a feeling that wasn't the kind of fox he meant.

Now, for me, Jason was more some Shakespearean actor swinging in on a vine and swooping me up off my feet. In the next three weeks, he certainly carried me off to places I'd never been before, just like he had promised. Every day at lunch, a Flagpole Girl or two would be waiting to hear about our latest adventure. I had no trouble talking about it, telling them all the details…well, all the ones that weren't sacred.

One night I cooked Jason's favorite dinner for him—steak and big-wedge fries—in his kitchen while his parents ate TV dinners in the den. I had never cooked a steak before, but he ate it like a ban on beef was about to be declared.

Another night he taught me how to play pool in their rec room. I was awful at it, but he got a big kick out of trying to perfect the way I held the cue stick.

Still another night he shared his CD collection with me, using the big stereo in the den while his parents were repainting their kitchen or something. He sang with every song in his pretty decent voice. I, of course, thought he was right up there with Stephen Curtis Chapman. I even asked him if he was going to be a recording artist when he graduated.

"Minister of music probably," he said. "I guess I could record in there somewhere. But wherever the Lord leads me, that'll be it."

I picked up the case for *Aladdin* and toyed with it.

"How will you know?" I said.

"Know what?"

"Where the Lord's leading you?"

"Same way you do."

I laughed. "I don't!"

"Serious?" His face grew so sober I was almost sorry I had asked.

"Yeah," I said. "The Girls are always talking about hearing God's voice, and, I mean, I pray, I pray a lot, and I go to church, and I read the Bible. But I don't, like, *hear* God. I don't know what

He wants me to do except follow, like, the major rules: Don't kill anybody, love your neighbor as yourself—all that."

I wasn't sure he was staring at me because I'd never heard God speak to me or because that was the most I had ever said to him all at once. But Jason sat there for a good thirty seconds while I stacked the CD cases into a perfectly aligned pile.

"I've prayed that I'll hear," I added faintly. And I had, ever since that day Brianna had prayed that Shannon would hear and know it was God.

"Yeah," Jason said, "but it takes a real commitment and a lot of work to get to that point."

"Is that how you reached it?"

"Well, yeah. See, you've only been a Christian how long?"

"*Really* a Christian? Since I started going to church with Veronica."

"Wow," Jason said. He sat up straight on the floor and reached out to grab my hands. The CDs toppled over.

"What?" I said.

"It's like I just got another whole piece!" he said.

"Of what?"

"Of why I want to be with you so much. I mean, I like you—a lot. You know that, but it's more than that. It's better than that."

I was looking at him like Luisa would look in a calculus class, I'm sure.

"I think I'm in your life to help you get closer to the Lord," he said. "I've had all this experience, and you haven't, and it's like I can show you the way."

"You would do that?" I said.

He put his hands on my face and looked at me with his wonderful eyes. "I'd be in big trouble if I didn't."

"With who?" I said.

He grinned. "With God."

I grinned back, and he hugged me. It felt like God was in that hug. I guess because Jason seemed so connected to Him. I think it might have been about then that I stopped praying to hear God's voice. Jason had that under control. I think that was about when those "sacred" things started to happen—the ones I didn't tell the Girls about.

We were doing a Saturday afternoon Humphrey Bogart movie marathon in his family room, and his parents were working in the yard. Each I-don't-ever-smile Bogart character was starting to pretty much look like the rest, and I guess I dozed off with my head on Jason's shoulder. I woke up feeling his hand running through my hair.

"I think I love you," he whispered.

I didn't know whether I was supposed to hear that or not. I stayed really still and felt him kiss me softly on the top of the head. Then on the forehead. Then on the tip of my nose. I opened my eyes, and that's when he kissed me on the lips, until I almost couldn't breathe.

I had been wrong when I thought I had been kissed that night in the park and every time I had seen Jason since. *This* was a kiss.

After that, he almost always kissed me that way when we were alone. I dreamed about those kisses. They were the first thing I thought about when I woke up in the morning and the last thing that floated through my mind before I went to sleep at night. Sometimes I even wished he were there, next to me, where I actually could kiss him.

But we had plenty of other opportunities. Jason made sure of that, and I didn't complain when he asked me to "help" him change the oil in his car so we could be in the garage alone or when he would locate a spot behind the rosebushes in Wingfield Park during one of our picnics. I waited for those times. That's when I felt grown-up and free and far away from Mama and Papa's strict stares. That's when I thought I might be almost as pretty as my sister Cecilia. When I was kissing Jason, I was somebody I really wanted to be.

Next to those times, I liked it best when we talked. Papa still wouldn't let me go out on weeknights, and two weekend nights weren't enough for all we had to say. Jason usually called me about nine every night, when Mama and Papa were both well settled in front of the TV, Luisa was in bed, and I could curl up on the floor in the kitchen outside Abuelo's door. We could talk for a good forty-five minutes without anybody's noticing, except my brothers, whom I ignored.

During one of those phone conversations, after we had been seeing each other about three weeks, we talked about marriage.

"My aunt says I can bring you to her wedding if you want to come," I said.

"A wedding," Jason said, snickering. "Oh, boy, little mints and cake with too much frosting."

"You've never been to a Latino wedding, have you?" I said.

"Uh, no."

"Forget the finger food," I said. "You'll have so much stuff to eat you'll explode. I'm serious."

"Serious?"

"Serious. We're talking carne asada, paella…"

"Sounds like a par-tee."

"It is."

"That's the kind of wedding I want. I mean, not 'carnal aside' or whatever you said, but a big bash celebration, you know?"

"Uh-huh."

"Because when I get married, it's going to be to the perfect woman, and I want everybody to be there to celebrate it."

I giggled. "You're marrying a Barbie doll?"

"What? No, she won't be *perfect* perfect. I mean, nobody's perfect. But she's going to be perfect for me."

"What's perfect for you?"

He didn't even hesitate. He started in as if he had it written down on a piece of paper in front of him. "She has to be a Christian. I mean, that's a given. And she can have a career and all that, but I want us to come first. My mom's like that. She always has time for my dad and me. And she doesn't have to be drop-dead gorgeous. I think if a woman is really into the Lord, it'll just kind of glow out of her. Besides, I like natural anyway. Oh, and no feminist stuff. Like, who's that one girl in your group?"

I laughed. "Norie?"

"Yeah. I mean, I don't want some ditz. You know I like to have an intelligent conversation, all that stuff, but I don't want her jumping all over me every time I open the door for her. I like to help people. I want to be able to help my own wife. My dad takes care of my mom. That's what I want."

There was a long silence. I wasn't sure what I was supposed to say. I couldn't help but wonder—I mean, come on, I'm human—whether I fit any of those qualifications. I was mulling over whether anything "glowed out of me" when he said, "I want to tell you something."

No, please don't! I wanted to say. *Please don't tell me I'm un-qualified!*

Instead I said, "What?"

"Remember before when I said I wasn't the type to date just one girl?"

"Yeah," I said.

"Well, forget that."

I didn't say anything.

"I don't even want to think about another girl right now," he went on. "I just want to be with you."

"You do?" I said.

"Come on, Marissa, yes, I do. You're all that stuff I just said about the perfect woman. You're like right out of the Bible."

I forced myself not to say, "I am?"

"We just have to work on your Christian education some. And why would I want to run around with a bunch of other girls when I can be doing that with you?"

"I don't know," I said.

"Good answer." I could picture him laughing. "Okay, so now you have to tell me."

"Tell you what?"

"What's your perfect man? I have to know if I fit!"

He didn't sound the least bit concerned, but he definitely was waiting for my answer. And I didn't have one.

"I don't know," I said. "I haven't really thought about it."

"Well, think about it and get back to me," he said, still chuckling.

"I'll talk to Sylvia about it," I said.

"Which one's Sylvia?"

"My cat."

"Oh. I thought it was one of your sisters."

"No, I get along with Sylvia better than I do most of my sisters. Except Luisa, the little one. She hasn't figured out how to smart-mouth me yet."

"Don't let her hang out with your brothers, and she won't learn," Jason said. "You could be a great influence on her, you know."

"How?"

"Do you read the Bible to her?"

"No," I said.

"You ought to. So, anyway, go talk to the...cat." He said it as if he were smelling a litter box, and I laughed.

"You don't like kitties?"

"Nope. They're too arrogant."

"Sylvia doesn't even know what 'arrogant' means!"

"Has she met your brother?"

"Of course!"

"Then she knows about arrogant."

We hung up laughing. I went to my room and sat down with Sylvia, who went immediately to her back to have her stomach rubbed.

"What would be the perfect man for me, Sylvia?" I whispered so I wouldn't wake up Luisa.

She wrapped her front paws around my arm. I think that communicated, "Someone tall and furry who will rub my belly on demand."

That was more than I could come up with myself. I did the only natural thing. I pulled out my notebook and started to write.

> Warm cat on the bed
> stretches her paws out four ways
> then curls in a ball.

I entitled it "Contentment" and went to sleep.

The next morning I saw Shannon at her locker before classes, and I charged right for her. Having any time to talk to her was rarer and rarer these days. I wasn't sure whether it was because of her or because of me.

"Hey, girl!" I said.

She jumped about a foot and pushed her locker door almost closed in the process.

"I'm sorry," I said. "I didn't mean to freak you out."

"I just didn't hear you coming. How *are* you?" she said.

"Great. But you have to help me with something."

"What?" She was pulling notebooks out of her backpack with more concentration than the job required.

"Jason wants to know what I see as the perfect man," I said. "I don't even know where to start! You want to have lunch today, talk about it?"

"He wants you to describe *him*."

We both looked up to see Brianna standing there. "Girl, you're in dangerous territory. When a guy wants to know your perfect-man vision, if you go one inch off his personality profile, his ego is going to deflate like a balloon."

"Nu-uh!" I said.

Brianna grinned at me, and I started to smile back, but my eyes caught the interior of Shannon's locker as she hurriedly slammed the door. I could feel my smile fading, and Brianna turned around to follow my gaze. She saw only Shannon's closed locker.

I myself had seen four packages of Ex-Lax stacked in the bottom next to her math book.

Brianna looked back at me, black eyes narrowed. "What's wrong with you, girl?"

"Nothing," I said.

Shannon knew I had seen because she hitched her backpack up over her shoulder, said, "Bye, guys, I have to get to class," and took off as if she were being chased by a pack of dogs.

"We have to pray for that girl," Brianna said. "She's about as jittery as a parakeet. Hey." She gave me a friendly poke. "You want to go see Ira with me after school today?"

"Sure," I said. And I stared at Shannon's closed locker door.

We did pray for Shannon at lunch that day, in her absence. Then Tobey wanted to know what Jason and I were doing that weekend.

"He says if the weather stays nice we're going to hike up Mount Rose."

"Do you like to hike, Marissa?" Ms. Race said.

"I don't know; I've never been," I said.

"And you're going all the way up Mount Rose your first time?" Wyatt said.

"Jason's been hiking since he was a little boy. He says I'll be fine. He's not going to let anything happen to me."

Norie stopped, spoon poised over her yogurt. "That little piece of reassurance wouldn't be enough for me. I'd want to be sure I could take care of my own sweet self, thank you very much."

That's why I'm his perfect woman, I thought.

"I think it's kind of romantic," Cheyenne said. She gave Fletcher a poke, but he looked clueless.

"You're definitely experiencing a lot of new things with Jason," Ms. Race said. She was toying thoughtfully with her braid.

"I am!" I laughed. "I never ate Arby's so much, that's for sure."

"Gross," Fletcher said.

Cheyenne smacked him.

"Well, it is," Fletcher said. "Every time I eat there I get diarrhea."

"Thanks for sharing, Fletch," Wyatt said.

"I do!"

"Maybe they put Ex-Lax in their sandwiches," Cheyenne said.

"You're serious, aren't you?" Norie said to her.

I didn't hear the rest. Funny they should mention laxatives. Since this morning I hadn't been able to get them out of my mind.

Until after school, when I went with Brianna to see Ira. Then it was Jason I was thinking about.

Ira lived in Norie's neighborhood, only, if possible, his house was even more like a mansion than hers. Brianna said Mrs. Quao, Ira's mother, wanted everybody to know how rich she and her doctor husband were. It was a good thing they were rich now because that meant they could have private nurses and physical therapy equipment for Ira. He was still in a neck brace, still couldn't walk.

But he sure grinned from one side of his handsome face to the other when Brianna walked into their family room. He was sprawled out in sweats on a hospital bed, flipping channels on the biggest TV on the planet. He switched it off and held out his arms to her.

"Hey, baby," he said.

She melted right into him and gave him this big old hug and a kiss on the cheek.

"Hey, Marissa," he said. "You come here and give me some sugar too."

I giggled and gave him a hug. I felt awkward trying to work around the neck brace, but it hadn't seemed to bother Brianna at all. In fact, she seemed comfortable with all the machines, medicine bottles, and weird things on Ira's body. I knew I'd hate it if Jason had all that.

"So what you been up to, girl?" Ira said to me.

"Not much," I said.

"Not much?" Brianna said. "Don't let Jason hear you say that."

Ira's eyebrows went up. "Who's Jason?"

"He's a guy," I said.

Brianna handed Ira a glass of some kind of murky-looking protein drink and rolled her eyes. "He isn't 'a' guy. He is 'the' guy."

"He's your main man then," Ira said.

I squirmed and turned red, I'm sure, and looked at my knees.

"Ooh, baby, she's got it bad," Ira said. "Look at how she's all foldin' up!"

Brianna grunted. I gave her a quick look.

"What does that mean?" Ira said.

"You know what it means."

"If I knew what it meant, I wouldn't have asked."

Good grief. They sounded like married people.

Brianna looked at me. "You *aren't* foldin' up over this boy, are you?"

"I really, really don't know what 'folding up' means," I said. My hands were starting to get clammy.

"It means if he asked you to have a tattoo you would do it," Brianna explained.

"I would not! Jason wouldn't ever ask that anyway."

Once again, Brianna grunted. "You just be careful 'bout what he *does* ask you."

Ira cleared his throat.

"What?" Brianna said to him.

"You know 'what.'"

"If I knew 'what,' I wouldn't have asked you," she said.

Then they wrinkled their noses at each other, and I giggled for no real reason, and we talked about other stuff.

Brianna, I decided, was weirding out. I went back to thinking about Shannon.

Which was the first thing I talked to Jason about when he called that night.

"I'm worried about Shannon," I said.

"She's the sister in Italy."

"No, she's my best friend. You met her; she was in our group at Tobey's church that first night."

"Yeah, gotcha. Skinny—"

"Willowy."

"Whatever. Okay. What's wrong with her?"

"I don't know," I said. "She's been sick for like a month and— I hope this doesn't gross you out…"

"You can say anything to me."

"Today I saw all this Ex-Lax in her locker."

"Sounds like she's constipated."

"Four boxes worth?"

"Oh."

"Yeah. And I don't think she's been to the doctor. She keeps saying she's okay."

"All you can do is pray for her," he said.

"I do, but—"

"If she's not ready for any other kind of help, then all you can do is pray. Prayer's powerful stuff."

"Oh, I know. We've prayed our way through some major things. Last fall, Tobey tried to help this girl who was being—"

"Yeah, I heard about that. But see, that girl was ready for help. Sharon isn't."

"Shannon," I said.

Jason chuckled. "Between your girlfriends, your relatives, and your cats, I can't keep track of all these women's names. I think I'll call them all Henry."

"No!"

"Yeah, so how's Feminist Henry?"

I cackled. "Stop!"

"How about What-Are-*You*-Lookin'-at Henry?"

"Who? You mean Brianna?"

By the time he had finished giving every female I knew a

Henry nickname, my jaws were hurting from laughing. When we were hanging up, he said, "You're feeling better."

"Yeah," I said.

Like always he said, "Good night. I'll pray for you."

CHAPTER ELEVEN

IF IT SOUNDS AS IF ALL I DID WAS SPEND TIME WITH JASON and tell the Girls about most of the time I was spending with Jason, that isn't a true picture. So much was going on in my life, I don't think it had ever been so full.

At Jason's suggestion, I was spending more time reading my Bible and reading it to Luisa, too. When I had made my real commitment to Christ about a year before, Veronica had given me a copy of *The Message*, which is an interpretation of the New Testament, the Psalms, and Proverbs by Eugene Peterson. He, I decided, was a poet, too. He even wrote about it:

> My heart bursts its banks,
>   spilling beauty and goodness.

I read to Luisa from Psalm 45 one night.

> I pour it out in a poem to the king,
>   shaping the river into words.

"Wow," I said to Luisa. "Isn't that beautiful?"

She nodded sleepily and wrapped her chubby arms tight around Sylvia, who mewed an irritated protest.

"It makes my ears happy," Luisa said. "Sylvia's, too."

I read on. "Now listen, daughter, don't miss a word."

But Luisa was already breathing evenly, eyes closed. Sylvia squirmed away and sat on the window sill to bathe herself indignantly.

I was also totally into what we were doing in Mrs. Abbey's class. Concentrating was a little easier than before because the *mocosos* were being icily cold to me. Frosty silence made for easier concentration than the heat of their verbal onslaughts.

We kept on studying haiku, and I was practically bathing in it. I would leave class and still be luxuriating in some little seventeen-syllable bubble like I was in a tub up to my neck. I had a different favorite every day. One day it was "Before the rainstorm / warm breezes turn leaves over / to the silver side."

Another day it was "The cardinal's call / drills a row of scarlet holes / in the summer air."

I decided Luisa was right. It did make my ears happy, and my mind, too.

"You see how there's another layer?" I told Jason on the phone.

"Sounds like it's about a bird," Jason said.

"I think it's about people, too," I said. "Voices do different things."

"Like what?"

"Like, they can drill a hole in the air, or they can hammer at it, or they can make it all soft, like wrapping you in a blanket. Luisa's does that."

"What does mine do?" he said.

I thought about it for so long he had to ask, "Are you still there?"

"I'm thinking," I said. "Your voice clears the air. It makes everything crystal."

"I'm not into crystals. Okay, so are you ready to go hiking on Saturday?"

Okay, moving on.

"I'm planning our picnic," I said, still blinking. Our first date's picnic had been romantic, but I figured I was going to need something other than Oreos and peanut-butter-and-pickle sandwiches to get me up Mount Rose.

"We're going to have a blast," he said. "Some kids from church are coming too. It's more fun when you have a bunch of people."

"I'll pack lots of food," I said.

I was also still worried about Shannon, although she didn't make it easy for me to tell her that. She only came to the theater lobby at lunch on Fridays now, and I could almost never reach her at home on the phone.

"Your line is always busy," I told her the one time I did get her.

"My parents are on the phone with my sister every night," she said.

"Is it still awful with her?" I said.

I could almost see Shannon shrugging. "I really don't want to talk about it."

I didn't press it, and I have to admit that on Friday when Mrs. Abbey made her assignment in English, that kind of pushed a lot of things out of my head.

"I've given you just a taste of one kind of poetry," she said to our only-half-awake class. "Now I want you to explore on your own. Come up with a collection of at least ten poems that you fall in love with."

"Gay," Patrick said sleepily. He kicked my desk for emphasis.

"I want you to put them together in some creative way, with a copy of the poem, an illustration of some kind for each, and a brief explanation of why it turned you on."

Patrick started to pant. Heidi turned around and hit him.

"I'm turned on," he whispered.

"You're obscene," she said.

"Like you would know what it even means to be turned on," Lana said to Patrick.

I honed in on Mrs. Abbey. Her eyes were fluttering like hummingbird wings. "And I don't want to hear anything about this being corny," she was saying. "This is a chance for you to expand yourselves a little."

"Don't expand any more, Lana," Patrick hissed at her. "You'll bust out of your jeans."

It was her turn to hit him. I tuned them out and started to flip through the poetry book.

"Feel free to use other sources besides the text," Mrs. Abbey said.

I looked up at her quickly to find her staring right at me.

"We have a nice collection of poetry in the library," she said.

As soon as she told us to get to work, I asked for a library pass. As Mrs. Abbey was scribbling one out for me, she said, "You could also write your own for this assignment."

Her voice was so low I wasn't even sure she was talking to anyone but herself.

"Excuse me?" I said.

She pressed the pass into my hand. "You understand this all so well, you might want to try writing some poetry of your own for this collection," she said. "I'd like to see that."

I nodded and scurried out of the room. That was all she had to say. The assignment was practically done.

Then, of course, on top of all that, I had Veronica's wedding present to think about. Mama and Papa were buying her and Gerald a travel iron, a portable alarm clock, and a bunch of stuff like that. "For this nomad life you're going to live," Mama had told Veronica. But I wanted to do something on my own. I couldn't just send off one of the closest people in my life with a bunch of impersonal batteries-not-included appliances.

I hadn't gotten too far on it, however. A lot of crinkled-up balls of paper were in the wastebasket in my bedroom, but just the night before I'd decided to write five haiku and put them all on one decorated page. Maybe one for each step of her relationship with Gerald, as I had seen it happen.

There wasn't much to do in the office fifth period that day, and I was sort of playing with Veronica's poem when I felt Ms. Race at my side. I looked up from the counter and closed my notebook.

"Do you have something you want me to do?" I said.

"No," she said. "I was just wondering what had you so engrossed over here. I'm back there at my desk feeling restless, and I look up and you're in another world." She brushed her hand across my shoulders. "I think I was a little envious."

I nodded and shrugged, and because I didn't know quite what to say I started to pull my underneath skin into place. But she was looking so longingly at the notebook, I opened it back up.

"I'm writing a poem for my aunt for a wedding present," I said. "It's probably kind of a lame-sounding idea, but she'll understand."

"I think it's a lovely idea!" Ms. Race said. "She'll have that longer than she'll have her first Mr. Coffee, I can tell you that."

I laughed and then looked down at the page. "Do you want to read what I have so far?"

Her eyes sprang open for a second. "I'd love to. I'd be honored, in fact. But don't just do it because I'm being nosy."

I shook my head and pushed the notebook toward her. My cheeks were already getting red, I could feel them, but it was like pulling curtains open a little or something. Eugene Peterson would have been able to put it better—what I was feeling.

I didn't watch her read, but I listened to her little hmms and oohs. They were so soft none of the other secretaries even looked up. When she was done, she handed it back to me with both hands, like she was passing me the Holy Grail.

"I had no idea," she said. "This is beautiful, Marissa."

"Do you think she'll like it? I mean, I know you've never met her, but she's a lot like you. She always says, when I talk about you, that you're a great role model for us Girls. I know you would like her."

"It's obvious *you* do," Ms. Race said. "You put your heart into that."

"I did?"

"I don't know that much about poetry, but I love song lyrics. That's almost the same, right?"

"I think so."

"I can usually tell when there's real soul in the words to a song, and when they were just looking for something that rhymed."

The phone rang, and she went reluctantly for it. I ran my hand over the poems and sighed to myself.

The next morning I was up at the crack of dawn, carefully filling up the basket Mama had told me I could use for our picnic-hike. I had to dig into the backs of the cabinets and the refrigerator to retrieve the stuff I had hidden so Anthony and Eddie wouldn't devour it. As it was, they had located the jar of hot peppers and polished them off.

But I still had enough homemade guacamole, chips, and salsa, plus pita sandwiches stuffed with meat, cheeses, and lettuce. I wasn't as good at baking cookies as Shannon, but my peanut butter ones hadn't turned out too bad, and I had spent ten minutes at Safeway picking out plenty of gorgeous grapes, bananas, and kiwi. I had found some extra-large paper plates I could arrange all that on.

Papa came in just as I was tucking a cloth napkin over the top of the whole thing. "Where you off to today?" he said. He was obviously off to work. His eyes were still sleep-puffy, but his work shirt was crisp, and he was clean-shaven.

"I'm going on a hike," I said.

"With your boyfriend?" he said.

Something in his tone made my protective skin crawl into place.

"He *is* your boyfriend, isn't he?" Papa said. He poured himself a cup of coffee and looked at me over the top of his mug through the steam.

"I guess so," I said.

"If he isn't, you're spending an awful lot of time with a casual acquaintance."

I nodded.

"Too much time, I think maybe sometimes, huh?" he said.

He reached for the sugar bowl, but he still managed to keep his eyes on me.

"I don't think so," I said. "Only on weekends. He doesn't even go to my school."

"Every weekend, all weekend," Papa said. "That's a lot for sixteen-year-olds."

"Are we talking about Romeo?"

That came from Mama, who was obviously not going to work. She was still in her bathrobe, hair standing on end. She looked as if she could use another eight hours sleep.

I wished she would go back and get it so we didn't have to have this conversation.

"How many hours a week?" Papa said.

"Excuse me?" I said.

"How many hours a week do you spend with him?"

"With Jason?" I said.

Mama reached for the coffeepot. "Who do you think we're talking about, Marissa? Who else do you spend any time with?"

"Luisa," I said. "And Anthony and Eddie—"

"I'd be watching my tone," she said.

I rubbed my cheeks and felt their redness.

"You didn't answer my question," Papa said. He leaned against the counter and sipped his coffee as if it were scalding his lips.

"Four hours every Friday night, four every Saturday night," I said.

"Plus the time you spend on the phone every night," Mama said. She cocked an eyebrow at me. My cheeks grew even redder.

"Less than an hour a night," I said.

"I'm up to thirteen hours," Papa said. "And what about today? How long will this hike take? Six, eight hours?"

"I guess so," I said.

I could see Papa doing a mental calculation. He grunted. "I have part-time laborers who don't put in that many hours a week."

I looked down at the picnic basket. "It isn't a job, Papa," I said almost inaudibly.

I'm not sure he heard me because just then Abuelo pushed his walker in from his bedroom. "*¿Por qué la molestas?*" he said.

I did a quick translation. *Why do you pester her?*

Mama busied herself finding the cream in the refrigerator. Papa looked straight at Abuelo. "I'm not doing anything worse than you ever did to Veronica."

Abuelo dismissed that with a wave of his hand. "I never made Veronica feel as if she was committing a crime because she had *un amante*."

Papa's eyes darted to me. "He had better not be your lover."

Before I could even open my mouth, Abuelo had his hand on my arm. "She's a good girl. She works hard. She deserves to have a good time."

Papa took a long drag on his coffee that had to have burned the inside of his mouth. His eyes didn't even cringe as he swallowed and looked back at me. "What time will you be home today?"

"What time do you want me home?" I said.

Papa held up five fingers.

"Are you going out again tonight?" Mama said.

"I think so," I said.

I held my breath. Mama stirred her coffee intently. Papa looked at Abuelo.

"That's a lot of 'good time,'" he said.

I almost dissolved into a puddle of relief when I heard Jason pull into the driveway and nobody told me I was staying home. I picked up the picnic basket and turned to Abuelo. He kissed me on the cheek and whispered, "You have fun with *el zorro*."

I gave Mama and Papa each a peck and fled.

Jason was psyched for our day, and that made it easy for me to forget the little scene in the kitchen. He sang almost the whole way to Mount Rose. Evidently this was *Aladdin* day, and he could sound just like Robin Williams.

"I'm amazed you can remember all those words," I told him.

"Wait till you hear Bryce and Indy and me get going."

"Indy?" I said.

"Short for Indiana Jones—that's his nickname."

"Why?"

"Because he was into that when he was a kid. He can recite just about all the dialogue from *Raiders of the Lost Ark*."

"You guys must have spent your whole childhood in front of a screen!" I said.

Jason slanted a glance at me. "We weren't allowed to watch whatever we wanted though. We all have Christian parents."

I had to force myself not to shake my head to get *that* sorted out. If I wasn't mistaken, Jason had almost scolded me. But then, I was probably wrong. I shrugged.

"Have you seen all the Disney movies?" he said.

"Not all of them—"

"Okay, tonight—Disney marathon—my place—be there."

He squeezed my knee and turned into Davis Creek Park where the Mount Rose trail began. My little sting went away.

Four people were waiting for us in the parking lot. Two of them I recognized from that first night at the True Love Waits rally. Bonnie was the little blue-eyed, pixie-faced one who hadn't been able to turn loose of Jason's arm for more than seven seconds. Currently, she had her arm linked with a tall, lanky kid whose waist was about up under his armpits. I learned, a few minutes later, that that was Indy.

The other girl I didn't recall as well. Carly was her name; I had that part. I just hadn't remembered her having such gorgeous long hair, or an upper lip that looked like it was smelling something bad. She held that expression as she braided her hair in front of a mirror the other guy was holding for her. That had to be Bryce.

He wore glasses, was stocky, and had a big grin that, I quickly realized, just about never went away.

I grabbed the picnic basket as Jason dragged me out of the car and pushed me along ahead of him. He high-fived both the guys then picked up Bonnie and swung her around while she trilled a giggle up and down the scale like a baby bird. He finished up with a face in Carly's mirror. She stuck out her tongue at him and gave her braid another careful inspection. I remembered her better now. She was the serious one who had Jason up on a pedestal.

Neither of the girls seemed to recollect ever having seen me before, and they both looked from me to Jason and back again until *he* remembered me and slung his arm around my shoulders. "This is Marissa," he said. I was reassured by the trace of pride in his voice. I felt a little strange being with these girls who somehow had missed out on being Jason's girlfriend but obviously wanted to be if he had given them half a chance.

"What's in the basket?" Indy said, peering over Jason's shoulder, which he could easily do since he was about seven inches taller, most of it from the waist down.

"Picnic," Jason said. "Marissa's a great cook."

"You're going to carry a basket up the trail?" Bryce said. He was still grinning, even though his voice sounded a little, shall we say, disdainful?

"Oh yeah. Not a good idea," Jason said.

"I have an extra backpack in my dad's car," Carly said. "Just dump the food in there and carry it that way."

"Cool," Jason said. "Can you guys get it?"

Obviously I was one of the "guys" in question, because he let go of me and turned to high-five Indy again. I followed Carly toward a silver Bronco.

"We brought drinks," Carly said over her shoulder. "I'm making Bryce carry them. He has to be good for something, right?"

I gave a nervous laugh as she handed me a very dusty empty backpack.

"Will it all fit in this?" she said.

"I guess so," I said. I shook out the pack, and Carly laughed. "You can tell you've been dating Jason—Mr. Fastidious. Neither of the other two would notice a little dirt, trust me."

I pulled off the basket napkin and looked for a minute at my carefully arranged array of fruit and sandwiches. Carly squatted beside me and grabbed the container of guacamole and tossed it into the backpack.

"Hurry up, you guys!" Bonnie called to us. "If the wind comes up, it's going to be murder."

"You want us to go without food?" Carly called back.

"No, take your time!" Indy said.

The three guys hooted and high-fived for about the fifteenth time. I didn't remember ever seeing Jason use that particular move before.

Somehow we crammed the food into the backpack, and Jason slung it over his back and tightened the straps while I wondered what was happening to those gorgeous grapes. But I forgot about that as we took off up the trail and the term "charging San Juan Hill" came to mind.

"First one to hear a rattlesnake wins," Bryce said as he led the way with Carly right behind him.

"Wins what?" Bonnie said. She looked at Jason.

"First dibs on Marissa's guacamole," Jason said.

"I hate guacamole," she said.

"Don't worry about it," Indy told her. "You jack your jaws so much, a snake would have its fangs in you before you ever heard it."

Bonnie wrinkled her cute nose at him and passed us with Indy hot on her trail. That left Jason and me bringing up the rear for about three minutes, at which time he grabbed me by the arm and jockeyed us up to the front.

"Hey, what's with this?" Bryce said.

Jason turned and walked backward. I was doing good to navigate the trail facing front with my eyes glued to the dirt.

"Hakuna Matata!" Jason shouted.

Indy and Bryce launched right in like Jason was holding a conducting stick. Bonnie tried to chirp along, although she didn't seem to know the words much better than I did. Carly looked at the scenery.

Okay, I don't have to sing, I thought. *I can pretend I'm looking at stuff, and they'll never suspect it's all I can do to keep from falling off the edge.*

Right. On the second chorus, Bryce lunged ahead to fling his arm around Jason's neck. I had to sidestep to keep from being bowled over. My foot slid on the soft dirt at the edge of the path, and I let out a squeal.

Somebody grabbed my arm. I think it was Indy, who was getting into position with the trio.

"You okay?" Carly said from behind us.

I gave a dizzying glance over the side and nodded. "I'm fine," I said.

I looked at Jason, who was riveting his eyes on me. "What happened?" he said.

I didn't inform him that Bryce had knocked me out of the way so they could do their chorus line. I just shook my head.

"Come back here with us," Carly said. "Those three are out of control. Well, Indy and Bryce are."

I fell into step beside the two girls. Carly smiled her upturned-lip smile and went back to watching the piñon pines go by. Bonnie gave up singing and watched the three guys.

"Okay, you have to admit," she said.

"Admit what?" Carly said.

"There's no contest when it comes to shoulders."

"Shoulders?" I said.

"The shoulders on those three." Bonnie looked at me for about the first time, and I nodded.

"Oh yeah," I said.

"Well, no," Carly said. "Indy isn't even in the running. He doesn't have any shoulders."

"Bryce's are like lumped in with the rest of him," Bonnie said. She grinned her elfish grin. "Guess that leaves Jason."

I decided to turn my attention elsewhere. The girls weren't walking as fast as Jason, and I felt a little better with the trail. I breathed in another big breath of pine and tried to relax.

It took a good four hours to reach the top of the trail. Nobody ever heard a rattlesnake. Who could over the whole soundtrack from *Beauty and the Beast,* complete with Jason performing as Gaston and Bonnie howling because she evidently thought he was hilarious? I ended up walking next to Carly while Bonnie tried to catch up to the guys. If Carly noticed my gasping and foot-dragging, she didn't say so. In fact, she didn't say much of anything, even when I tried to strike up a conversation.

"So you go to Jason's church?" I said.

"He goes to mine," she said: "My dad's the preacher."

"Oh," I said. "What's that like for you? My friend's dad is a minister and—"

She shrugged. "Just like being anybody else's kid, I guess."

I tried again. "Do you have to, like, be perfect all the time—on your best behavior, all that?"

She turned from the trees for a second to look at me. "Why wouldn't I try to do that anyway? I'm a Christian."

"Me, too," I said faintly.

Then I stopped trying. I thought about coming up with some haiku about the mountain bluebirds, the fluffy pines, and the breathtaking span of mountain range you could see from up there, but nothing occurred to me. The only thing I discovered is that you can't create when you're swathed in second skin.

When we reached the top and Jason finally selected the perfect place to picnic, I tried not to sigh too loudly as I flopped to the ground. Jason was suddenly there beside me, pulling off the backpack.

"What's to eat?" Indy said.

"Yeah, open up that baby," Bryce said. "I'm starving."

"When aren't you?" Carly said dryly.

"Are you even hungry when you're sleeping?" Bonnie said.

Bryce let his smile drain for a second as he stared at her blankly. "How would I know? I'm sleeping."

"Oh," she said.

She would have reminded me of Cheyenne, or even Roz, if she hadn't immediately turned to me and said, "Did you really bring guacamole?"

I nodded.

"Won't it be spoiled?" she said. "Did you put sour cream in it?"

"No," I said. "I just use avocados and lemon juice—"

"No sour cream?" Bryce wailed.

Carly eyed his stocky frame. "You don't need sour cream."

Bryce looked indignantly at Jason, who grinned at him and dug into the backpack. He yanked things out in about the same style Carly had crammed them in. I winced when I saw the grapes.

"Yuck," Bonnie said.

"Could you be a little more rude, Bonnie?" Carly said.

"What?" she said. "You like squished grapes?"

"Sure," Bryce said. He grabbed a bunch and stuffed them into his mouth while he watched me spread out the sandwiches. I decided to forget about arranging the rest of the fruit on its platter.

"Got any peanut butter and sweet pickle?" Indy said.

"You better believe it," Jason said. "Rissa knows that's my favorite, right?"

He hugged my shoulders as I stared at him blankly. In the first place, I didn't know my name was now "Rissa," and in the second place, no, I hadn't brought peanut butter and sweet pickle. I hated peanut butter and sweet pickle.

"Didn't you?" he said.

I shook my head.

"Busted!" Bryce said.

"Shut up," Carly said. "You'll eat anything so start doing it."

She smashed a sandwich against his middle amid a chorus of laughter that I only halfheartedly joined in. I nibbled at a sandwich I didn't taste and tried to listen to the conversation, which turned to the time Jason, Indy, and Bryce did this, and the other time they did that…

I gazed off at the mountain. A hawk was sitting on a naked, dead pine nearby, observing.

> Hawk finds a good branch
> then hears the cawing below
> and flaps himself gone.

I was still watching him try to select another tree when Jason nudged me.

"Let's go for a walk," he said.

He stood up, and I stuck up my hand, but he was already walking away. I followed quickly.

"Where are you going?" Bonnie said.

Jason didn't turn around. "We'll be back," he said.

"No, you can't go," I heard Carly say to her. "I think it's a private conversation."

"Why?" Bonnie said.

That was what I wanted to know. I suddenly realized Jason and I hadn't had *any* conversation since we had started up the mountain. What could we have to talk about at this point?

Obviously plenty. Jason led me up over a rise and then finally turned to me, hands on hips. "What's up?"

I was clueless. All I could do was look at him.

"What's up with the silent thing?" he said. "You've hardly said a word all day."

I didn't point out that nobody seemed to care much what I had to say. I didn't feel right about saying that. They were his friends, after all. I shook my head.

"What does that mean?" he said with an edge of irritation in his voice.

"I'm listening," I said.

"That's okay," he said. "But how are they going to know what you and I have together if all you do is listen?"

I was completely flummoxed by that time. I just kept shaking my head.

"What is *that*?" he said again.

"I don't know what you're talking about," I said. "I'm just here, and you're doing your thing, and they're doing theirs, and you guys have all this history. So what am I supposed to do?"

To my surprise, Jason suddenly took my face in both of his hands and got close to me. "Is that what this is about?"

"What?" I said.

"Are you jealous?"

I hadn't used that word in my mind. I wasn't sure it was even the right one. Before I could decide, he gave me one of those kisses and kept his face just inches from mine.

"I want them to be *your* friends too," he said. "They're part of my life. You and I can't be alone all the time."

"I don't want to be," I said.

He kissed me again, even longer this time.

"They take some getting used to, I'll admit," he said. "But they're cool people. They're Christians, just like me. I guess you're just so comfortable when you're around me, I forget how quiet you are when you first meet people."

"Yeah," I said.

His face grew soft, and he kissed me again. He pulled his hands from my face and put his arms tight around me. I could feel the wind swirling around us. I could also feel his hand sliding down to the back pocket of my jeans.

But at the same time, I didn't feel it. No one had ever touched me there, and it made me feel as if it were happening to somebody else.

"I want to be here for you," Jason whispered into my ear. "And I want you here for me. Let's show them what we have, okay?"

Although I had no idea what he was talking about, I nodded, and he kissed my nose and held me, just looking at me. I tried to bring myself back to the mountaintop as his hand went up my back again.

"So what have you been thinking the whole time?" he said.

I looked down. "I made up a poem while we were having lunch."

Jason's shoulders shook in his silent laugh. "No, I mean about Bryce and Bonnie and all them."

I didn't have a chance to answer. Bryce and Indy started to sing, "Can You Feel the Love Tonight?" from below. "In short, our pal is doomed" came up louder than the rest. Jason's full, ripe lips went into a grin.

"We better go," he said. He gave me one more kiss and murmured, "We'll finish this later."

Finish what? I wanted to ask him. *And what is it I'm supposed to be showing them about you and me? And—*

But he was already into a chorus of something that some animated character had sung on some screen at some point. I stuffed the picnic remains back into the dusty backpack.

I CLIMBED DOWN THE MOUNTAIN WITHOUT KILLING MY-self, and Jason and I spent a hilarious evening watching everything from *The Little Mermaid* on up. I was about cross-eyed by the time we came to *Aladdin*—or was it *Beauty and the Beast*? But I had fun listening to Jason recite every line in a perfectly mimicked voice. He was so involved, I think he forgot what we were supposed to have "finished" from up on the mountaintop. That was fine with me. It hadn't felt bad, but I wasn't sure it was good.

Papa wouldn't let me see Jason on Sunday, in spite of Abuelo's dark looks at him across the dinner table. So I spent the day finishing Veronica's poem. I think it was the first piece of poetry I had ever written I was really proud of. I even showed it to Mrs. Abbey before class on Monday.

Big mistake.

"May I keep this for a few minutes?" she said, blinking at me from behind her contacts.

"Sure," I said.

I sank into my seat, cheeks just on the tingling-pink side, and barely noticed the *mocosos* dragging themselves into place. They must have partied hard that weekend. They looked like the people you see lined up at the mission downtown, waiting for free soup.

"What happened to you?" Lana said to Patrick.

"What?"

"You look like you were run over by a truck."

"Did she slug you?" Heidi said.

"Who?" Patrick said. He kicked my desk as he sat up straighter in his seat.

"Whoever the girl was you tried to hit on."

He must have given her some kind of hand signal at that point because she swung around with her lips drawn up all sour. Lana snickered, and Patrick kicked my desk two more times.

"All right, gang," Mrs. Abbey said. "I'm going to send you off to work on your poetry projects independently, but I want to read something to you first."

"Can't wait," Patrick muttered.

"I have you looking for poetry you like," she went on. "But don't forget that there's another option."

"Not doing it?" Heidi said.

Mrs. Abbey ignored her.

"Remember that, if you feel so inclined, you may write your own poetry," she said.

Patrick hissed, and I could feel his feet trailing down the back of my desk as he returned to his on-the-spine position.

"Somebody in here *would* actually write their own poetry," a kid in the back said. He said it the way you might say, "Somebody in here *would* actually bench-press 450 pounds."

"Someone already has," Mrs. Abbey said. "Marissa has written a lovely piece here."

I jerked up in my seat, sending my pencil bouncing to the floor. She picked up my poems from the desk—the ones I'd written for Veronica—blinked at them, and cleared her throat.

"'Seasons of Love,'" she read.

I didn't see it, but I could feel Heidi rolling her eyes at Lana. I stared hard at my desktop.

"Red berries dancing / in the February wind / to winter's cold tune," Mrs. Abbey read. "One leaf at a time / spring comes with aching slowness / to the naked trees."

"Oh, this is *my* idea of love," Lana said under her breath.

Mrs. Abbey looked up from my poem. "What was that, Lana?"

Give it back to me! I wanted to scream.

"Nothing," Lana said.

"I thought you had a comment about Marissa's poem."

Don't! Just let me have it back!

"I don't want to discuss Marissa's poem, okay?" Lana said. She folded her arms over her chest. The class fell into an oh-boy-aconfrontation silence. All I could hear was the screaming in my head. *Don't read any more. Just give it back to me!*

"How about if you and I discuss your attitude out in the hall?" Mrs. Abbey said. She snapped my poem back onto her desk and bolted toward the door. Lana slowly drew herself out of her desk. Patrick kicked the back of mine. The room fell into a buzz.

As soon as the door closed behind Lana and Mrs. Abbey, I went to her desk and retrieved my poems. I was stuffing them back into my notebook, when Heidi leaned over and said, "What you know about love could obviously fill a thimble."

I didn't answer her. My face was so hot I knew it would explode if I said a word. I pulled my second skin around me and stared at the top of my notebook.

If I hadn't had my surprise at lunch, I think I would have been one big pincushion all day. But when I appeared in the theater lobby, Tobey was standing there grinning—and Jason was standing next to her.

"Look who I found loitering in the foyer!" she said. Her smile sparkled from ear to ear.

"Hey," Jason said softly to me. I went up to him, and he pulled me right into his arms. I could feel the gathering Girls watching from behind me. I wriggled free and looked up at him. He was looking pleased with his little self.

"What are you doing here?" I said.

"I had a dentist appointment this morning, and then it was lunchtime, so I thought I would drop by here before I went back to school."

"Hey, Jason," Wyatt said. He dropped his stuff on the floor and stuck out a hand, which Jason grabbed and did some kind of guy thing with. Wyatt looked a little confused, but he pulled it off. Jason then high-fived Fletcher, which no longer surprised me since I'd seen him do it at least a hundred times on Saturday.

When we all finally sat down, he put his arm around me, pulled me into him, and kissed the top of my head. I could feel my cheeks going magenta.

"Do you want some lunch?" I said, reaching for my backpack.

Jason grinned at the circle. "She's always trying to feed me."

"She can feed me anytime," Tobey said. "She's a great cook."

"I didn't cook this sandwich," I said, "but I'll share it with you."

Jason looked at it, shook his head, and kissed my forehead. I found myself looking nervously at the Girls, but the minute I did, they all focused on their chips and apples.

"Where's Brianna?" Norie said. "I need to talk to that girl."

"And what about Shannon?" Cheyenne said. "Has she, like, dropped out or something?"

"You can't 'drop out,'" Norie said. "I mean, you can't, right?"

"I'm worried about her," I said.

"Yeah, me, too," Tobey said. "I mean, it's one thing to pray for her, but if we don't *do* anything—"

Jason squeezed me closer to him and put his lips near my ear. "Remember what I told you," he whispered.

I looked at him.

"About Sharon—'"

"Shannon."

"Skinny Henry. Just pray for her. You need to concentrate on your own walk with the Lord right now."

I was about to answer—and say what, I'm not sure—when out of the corner of my eye I caught Brianna and Ms. Race coming toward the group. Instinctively I inched away from Jason a little. At least I tried to, but he kept his arm around my shoulders like a steel band. I nibbled at the edges of my sandwich.

"You sure it isn't too late?" Brianna was saying to Ms. Race.

"They said not," Ms. Race said. "I think it's an incredible opportunity."

"What is?" Cheyenne said.

But Ms. Race and Brianna had both caught sight of Jason and me, and their eyes took on two totally different gleams. Brianna's were instantly suspicious—but, then, that was Brianna. Ms. Race's lit up with recognition.

"I'm assuming this is Jason," she said. She smiled her wonderful smile and came toward us with her hand extended. Jason let go of me long enough to start to get up, but she waved him back down.

"Keep eating," she said. "I wouldn't miss one of Marissa's lunches to shake hands with anybody!"

She wrinkled her nose, the way she did a lot, and waited just a millisecond for Jason to say something. But he looked back at me and gave me another squeeze.

"Brianna," Norie said, "are we going shopping this afternoon?"

"We are, girl," Brianna said. "If we don't find you a prom dress, you're going to be pinning your corsage on naked skin."

Wyatt looked up abruptly. "Corsage?" he said. "Oh, man, I forgot all about that."

"You need Ira to keep you straight," Tobey said.

"Don't worry about it, Wyatt," Norie said. "If I don't have a corsage, it isn't going to be the end of the world."

I had a hard time imagining our feisty Norie with a big ol' flower attached to her bodice anyway. But Ms. Race and Wyatt were whispering, and I thought it was kind of cute.

"Next year," Jason whispered to me.

"What?" I said.

"Next year we'll go the prom. I didn't meet you soon enough to take you this year. You wouldn't have had time to buy a dress and all that."

I laughed. "That isn't bothering Norie!"

"Yeah, well, you're not Feminist Henry," Jason said. He looked pretty glad of that, too. It stung me somehow. But he gave me yet another squeeze and whispered into my hair. "Next year. I'll make it really special."

I just nodded. The idea of going to the prom at Jason's school hadn't really occurred to me. After Saturday, I wasn't champing at the bit to spend more time with his friends. *Our* friends, they were supposed to be.

I looked around at the Girls. Well, now we were with *my* friends, and I was proud. They were all going back and forth between talking to each other and watching us like they were waiting for a chance to say something. The minute I looked up, Norie jumped right in.

"So how was the hike, you guys?" she said.

"Great," Jason said. "Great day."

"How was it, Marissa?" Cheyenne said.

"Rissa did great," Jason said. "Made it all the way to the top, no problem."

"I slipped once," I said.

"You did?" Jason said.

"Yeah, when Indy—"

"That was no big deal. She did great." Jason nodded at the group as if to say "End of discussion," put both arms around me, and kissed the side of my head. Ms. Race chose that moment to look up from her conversation with Wyatt. I pulled away.

"Did you get him checked out on the corsage?" Tobey said.

Ms. Race peeled her eyes from me and grinned. "He's set."

"Are you still not going to the prom, Tobey?" Cheyenne said.

There was a general throwing of hard looks at Cheyenne, who missed the point completely.

But it didn't seem to bother Tobey. "Nah, and you know what? I mean, not that it isn't cool for you and Wyatt, Nor, but I'm not even into it that much. I'm okay with it."

"You are *so* okay, Tobey," Ms. Race said.

I heard Jason grunt softly beside me. I gave him a quick look, but he just kissed my nose. I was beginning to feel a little slobbery—and more than a little uncomfortable. Fletcher and Cheyenne were always holding hands as if they were attached at the fingers, and Wyatt gave Norie the occasional peck on the cheek during lunch—just to get mayonnaise on her face and make her mad. But nobody was all over each other, not even Brianna and Ira when he wasn't in a body cast, and they had been going together forever.

Jason glanced at his watch. "I have to jam," he said.

"Too bad," Wyatt said. "I'd always rather peanut butter."

Norie groaned. Jason looked at him and then gave a weak smile.

"Nice meeting you, Jason," Ms. Race said.

"Bye, Jason," Tobey said.

A chorus of good-byes followed us as we headed for the outside door. Jason took my arm and slowed me down so he could get his hand around my waist.

"You in a hurry to get rid of me?" he said.

"No!"

He grinned as he pushed open the door. "I'm just teasing. You're still fun to tease."

He flung his arm around my neck so his elbow crooked right

into it. I could barely walk at that point. It's amazing that I saw Shannon hurrying across the parking lot.

"There's Shannon!" I said, breaking away.

"Okay," Jason said.

"I really need to talk to her," I said.

"Okay, well, walk me to the car, and then you can grab her."

"I can't just 'grab her.' She's like a fish lately."

"Hey, listen to me," he said. His voice clear and calm like usual, but a force was behind it that made me tear my eyes away from the disappearing Shannon and look right at him. His green-gold ones were intense.

"Remember what I told you," he said. "You can't rescue her, and definitely not until you're steady in your own walk with the Lord."

I cocked my head at him. "I do have a walk with the Lord."

"I know you do, but are you hearing His voice? Are you sure you know exactly where you're going?"

"Well, do you all the time?" I said.

He put his hands on the sides of my face, the way he had on Saturday. "We're not talking about me. We're talking about you. And you know what, speaking of you?"

I shook my head, as much as I could with him holding it in his hands.

He leaned in and kissed me hard. When he pulled away, he looked at me and said, "I love you."

I opened my mouth—to say what, who knows—and he put his finger up to my lips.

"Tell me later," he said. "I have to go."

With one more kiss on the cheek, he slid into his car, revved up the engine—making a half-dozen people look up through their windshields—and took off. I waited until he was out of sight, and then I went to find Shannon.

I couldn't, of course. And I'm not sure I should have. My mind was way too confused to say anything to her that would have made any sense.

The conversation I had the next day with Tobey didn't help much.

Just she and I showed up for lunch in the theater lobby. I

could tell she had something on her mind, just by the way she was talking about stuff she never talked about, like how cute my shoes were and how her pen had run out of ink during fourth period. Finally she sighed, rolled her eyes, and said, "Can we talk?"

I immediately felt nervous, but I nodded. She could talk. I would listen.

"Brianna and I were talking about this—and I don't want you to think we sit around and discuss your life behind your back, but it just kind of came up…"

"What did?" I said.

"Well, Jason," she said.

"What about him?"

She shrugged, although I knew she knew *exactly* what she was going to say next.

"Are you okay with the way he treats you?"

I wouldn't have been more surprised if she had asked me if I planned to try out for the Pittsburgh Steelers.

"Yeah," I said. "He treats me just fine. I don't understand—"

"You don't ever feel that he, like, smothers you or something?"

I shook my head. I was too dumbfounded to speak.

She looked relieved. "I told Brianna if you had a problem with it, you would deal with it."

"A problem with what?"

She stopped and miserably studied her cuticles. "Look," she said finally. "I'm no authority on guys. What have I had? One boyfriend? And he was no prize."

"Damon was cute," I said.

"And a liar," she said. "He was the worst. If you'll recall, he pretended to be a Christian just so I would go out with him."

"But Jason *is* a Christian!"

"I'm not comparing them. Honest, Marissa," she said. "I know Jason's a Christian, and he's respected, and that's all wonderful. That doesn't automatically make him the perfect boyfriend though."

I stared at the tops of my socks. "I think he's pretty perfect."

She didn't answer for a minute. Then she sat up really straight and said, "Good. That's all I need to hear. If Brianna wants to hear more, she can ask you herself, right?"

"Sure," I said.

Then I made a vow to avoid conversations alone with Brianna for a while. I was confused enough as it was.

I didn't see her much the rest of the week either, except on Friday at our usual meeting. By then my thoughts were pretty much centered around Veronica's wedding the next day.

"You get to dress up even if you *aren't* going to the prom," Cheyenne said.

"You really want to get yourself into a ball gown, don't you, girl?" Brianna said to her.

Cheyenne started to protest, but then she grinned. "Yeah," she said.

"Nothing wrong with that," Ms. Race said. "I get the itch to put on something long and elegant once in a while myself."

"Does your boyfriend take you out to fancy places?" Tobey said.

I thought I saw Ms. Race blush. It made *me* turn red. Call me an empathetic blusher.

"Let's not go there," Norie said.

"Let's pray," Tobey said. "Who has needs?'

I waited for Shannon to say something, but she just looked around the circle expectantly, like she always did. When I caught her eyes, she smiled, like a wisp, and looked down at her sandals.

"My decision about art school," Brianna said. "I want to pray about that."

"What's going on?" Norie said.

Brianna glanced at Ms. Race. "We found out that the Seattle Art Institute is still taking applications. They have scholarship openings they haven't filled."

"No way!" Norie said.

"It's unusual," Ms. Race said. "But we're trying to get in on it."

"You go, girl!" Cheyenne said.

Brianna threw back her head and laughed—something you seldom see.

"We'll definitely pray for that," Tobey said. "Who else?"

As people put in their requests, I slipped for a minute inside my second skin and thought. I wanted prayer for certain things. Veronica's marriage, of course, but something else was stinging at me and had been since Monday. It was Jason saying "I love you."

What, you may ask, was the problem with that? Didn't that sound like something sent right from God Himself?

It could have. It should have.

But it was Jason saying I love you after Saturday—and after being there Monday. I couldn't put my finger on it, but something was different, something was changing. And it wasn't just because of what Tobey had said to me.

Whatever was happening wasn't bringing me closer to God. If anything, I was feeling further away—

"Marissa, are you with us?" Tobey said.

I looked up, turned red, and laughed at my knees. Nobody said anything. They were all waiting.

"Something going on with you, girl?" Brianna said. "This is the place to spill it, you know that."

Tell that to Shannon! I wanted to say. *She's the one who needs it. I'm just being stupid.*

But when I looked up at Shannon, she was watching me with that if-you'll-do-it-I-will look on her face. I took a deep breath.

"I want to hear God's voice," I said. "I know that sounds stupid…"

"Doesn't sound stupid at all," Norie said. "Saying that it sounds stupid, sounds stupid. I mean, well, not stupid—"

"We get the idea," Ms Race said. Her voice was soft. "We definitely will pray for that, Marissa, although I think you would be surprised."

"About what?" Cheyenne said.

Ms. Race wrinkled her nose at me. "I think you might be hearing it already, and you don't even know it."

Not according to Jason, I thought. But I nodded and reached out for the hands on either side of me and bowed my head. We started to pray.

ONE OF MY PERSONAL PRAYERS WAS DEFINITELY OFF TO a good start. The wedding was gorgeous.

I dressed at home since Jason was driving me to the church. The look on his face when I came out in the teal silk dress with the V-back was one of those things you dream about when you're eleven. Reney would have killed for it at age eight.

"Whoa," he said. "You look…incredible!"

"Thanks," I said.

"You make that thing look pretty sensational."

"Thanks."

He narrowed his eyes playfully. "Who's walking you back down the aisle?"

"The groom's brother," I said.

"How old is he?"

I laughed. "He's thirty-five, and he's married."

"Yeah, but does he have buck teeth?"

"What?"

"I want him to be ugly, too."

"Stop!" I said.

He gave me one of his shoulder-shaking silent laughs and practically carried me to the car so I wouldn't get dirty. I was feeling like the teacup again.

"What's in the bag?" he said when we were on our way.

"My present for Veronica," I said. "Want to see it?"

"Not if it's an electric knife or something," he said. "I can't get too excited about stuff like that."

"No, it's a poem. Well, a bunch of poems. I had Brianna do some artwork on them, and I framed them."

I pulled my creation out of the gift bag and swept it over onto my lap so he could glance down when we were at the stoplight. He took it from me and gazed at it for a minute, and I smiled. He was a far cry from Patrick and those guys. I still wanted to scream at Mrs. Abbey every time I thought about her reading the poems in class.

Jason smiled and handed it back to me. "Cool," he said. "Which way, left or right?"

"Um, left," I said.

I put the poetry back into its bag, and I could feel my smile fading.

No, I'm being too sensitive, I thought. *He didn't say it like that.* I had been thinking of how Mama would look at one of Luisa's drawings and say, "How cute."

No, I was being overly sensitive. And besides, Ms. Race had read it yesterday and said it was "exquisite." And besides *that*, who needed anybody else's approval?

I startled myself with that last thought. Where it had come from, I wasn't sure. It slipped away as soon as it came, and I looked at the bag and wondered if the poetry was ever going to be hung on any wall anywhere.

The wedding was the lavish affair Veronica and Gerald had hoped for. Calla lilies were in abundance, and the smell of about fifty candles and the sound of music trumpeting from the pipe organ announced that two more people had become one in God's eyes and were starting a life together. Until then I always had wondered why people cried at weddings. One look at Veronica's glowing face, and I knew.

Walking back down the aisle on Gerald's brother's arm, I caught Jason's eye and smiled. He formed his mouth into buckteeth and then grinned at me.

When we were finally through taking thousands of pictures and throwing the first round of birdseed from little net bags, we piled into cars and drove to Rancho San Rafael. Every kind of Hispanic dish, from paella to swordfish in cilantro and lime, was piled onto platters, and mariachi music was rocking the park.

Before I knew it, we were all dancing, howling with laughter, and proposing ginger ale toasts one after another.

Gerald and I found out we could do a pretty mean tango together, and while I stood one out with Abuelo, Jason danced with Mama.

"*El zorro*," Abuelo said to me. His eyes were twinkling.

"Why do you always say that about Jason, Abuelo?" I said.

He pulled his crusty old hand across his face, and to my surprise, it looked as if he were wiping the smile off of it.

"You are a smart girl, *muchacha*," he said. "I thought you had figured that out long ago."

"No," I said. "I know it means 'the fox…'"

"And what is a fox?"

"Um, a little red animal with a tail."

Abuelo held up a finger. "A sly little animal."

"You think Jason is sly?" I said.

He chuckled. "Sly enough to get exactly what he wants. Not a bad thing always. You'll watch yourself, I know. I have no doubt about you. I tell your father that all the time."

"Thanks," I said.

"Marissa," said a voice at my elbow.

I looked up into Papa's face. He held out his arm. It took me a minute to realize he wanted me to dance with him.

I had never danced with my father before. It was a little funky at first, my putting my arm stiffly around his neck and placing my hand into his brick-hardened one. But once we started to move, I was surprised at his rhythm, and at the little smile that cracked around the corners of his mouth.

"Where did you learn to dance, Marissa?" he said.

"Just…around," I said. "Mostly Cecilia."

"Too bad she couldn't be here for the wedding," he said.

I nodded. He looked at me, and for a moment, his brown eyes took on a soft sheen. "But you are every bit as beautiful today, *mi hija*," he said.

Our eyes met, and he smiled at me. Teacup doesn't even describe how I felt. Try crystal goblet, precious to its owner. It came to me as he took a tighter hold and spun me around the room…

Thin crystal goblet
kept in a polished glass case—

"May I cut in?"

Papa and I both looked up to find Jason tapping my father on the shoulder. Papa's eyebrows gave a quick twitch, and then he let go of me. Jason put both arms around me, grinned down at me, and danced me toward the door.

"Where are we going?" I said.

"For a walk," he said.

It was that soft, brink-of-evening time that's one of my favorites of the day. The air was May-gentle, and Jason put his arm around me as he steered us down a flower-lined path away from the reception's happy sounds.

The gardens of Rancho San Rafael were dotted with benches in hedge-hidden nooks, and Jason pulled me toward one of them. His shoulders were already laugh-shaking as he sat on a bench and pulled me onto his lap. He was kissing me before I could even untangle my arms.

"I thought we were taking a walk," I said when I could come up for air.

He smiled at my mouth. "*Now* who's doing the teasing?"

I felt my forehead furrowing, but Jason tucked my head against his chest and held on to me. "Vanessa and Jerry look really happy," he said.

"Veronica," I said. "And Gerald."

"Don't you wish we were about to spend *our* first honeymoon night together?"

It took me the usual fifteen seconds to get it, and longer than that to think of a reply. This time Jason waited.

"Well, sure," I said finally. "But we can't. So why even talk about it?"

"We can't," Jason said.

It wasn't a question. It was more like a restatement of *my* statement. I wriggled away enough to sit up straight on his lap.

"Well, no," I said. "You said that yourself at the True Love Waits thing."

"Did you sign a pledge card?" he said.

I nodded.

"Did you read it first?"

"Of course."

"What did it say?"

I could feel my face reddening and my protective skin sliding in. Everything told me, *Don't get into this conversation!*

He squeezed me. "What did it say?"

"I don't remember exactly…"

"'I make a commitment to God, myself, my family—blah, blah, blah—to be sexually abstinent from this day until the day I enter a biblical marriage relationship.'"

"Right," I said. "I guess."

"'A biblical marriage relationship.'"

At that point, something started to come up my backbone, a feeling I couldn't identify.

"Yeah," I said. "A biblical marriage relationship." I tried to stand up. "We should go back."

"Okay, just hear me out," he said. His arms wouldn't let me budge. "What does that mean, 'a biblical—'"

"It's a marriage in God's eyes," I said. "Just like Veronica and Gerald's."

"And your mother and father's?"

"What?"

"Are they Christians? They're not, are they?"

I stared at him. "They haven't been to church in a long time, if that's what you mean, but—"

"If you haven't made a commitment to Jesus Christ, then you aren't—"

"Are you saying my parents aren't really married?" I tried to laugh. "That isn't what you're saying!"

"What I'm saying is that when you think about it, we're as married as they are."

I couldn't answer. Even my mouth was in shock.

Jason buried his face in my neck for a minute while I stared at the gardens. They looked as unreal as something out of one of his animated movies.

"Sometimes I just wonder," he said. His voice sounded…sleepy. "I wonder if Jesus meant marriage really is based on a ceremony and a license, or if it has more to do with the commitment two people make with their hearts."

"Don't you think it's both?" I managed to say.

"I'm not so sure," he said. "Rissa, nobody could love another person the way I love you. I mean that. I know I picked a lame time to tell you the first time, but it just came out the other day when I was at your school. I do love you. I do."

I still couldn't say anything. Suddenly, he just let go of me and set me aside on the bench and took off. I sat there like a statue until he came back, fiddling with something with his fingers. Going down on one knee, he took hold of my hand.

"What are you doing?" I said.

He didn't answer but slipped something onto my finger. It was a tiny flower bud, still attached to its stem that he had worked into a circle. He snuggled it onto my finger like a ring.

"I'd have bought you a real one for tonight if I'd known this was going to happen," he said. "But maybe we don't need a real ring. Maybe we don't need a ceremony or a license or anything. Maybe we just need God's blessing."

"For what?" I said.

He sat on the bench and put both arms around me. "To be one," he said.

Pulling me tight up against him, he kissed me—long and hard. One hand slid down the V in the back of my dress. The other crept around, under my arm. I could hear the party sparkling and tinkling beyond us. I could smell Jason's Polo Sport. I could feel him pressing insistently against me.

But I couldn't feel me.

Where the vision came from, I don't know. But suddenly, behind my closed eyes, I could see Daniela, sitting coldly at a table in the mall food court, saying, "I didn't even feel like I was in my own body. It was like it was happening to somebody else."

I pulled my arms away and tried to push Jason off, but that wasn't what got him away from me. It was Papa's hands, yanking Jason back and pulling him to his feet by the back of his suit jacket.

I slapped my hand over my mouth and stared at my father. His eyes were smoldering, first at me, then at Jason. I refused to look at Jason myself. I stared down at my rumpled bridesmaid's dress in horror.

"Go home," Papa said.

"Mr. Martinez—"

"Go home. Go now, before I say something we both gonna regret." Papa was slipping into his accent. He was losing his layers of control.

"You better go, Jason," I said through my fingers.

I heard him go off down the path, gravel popping under his dress shoes. Tears blurred the sight of my teal skirt.

"Go back to the party," Papa said to me.

"I can't," I said. "It wasn't what you think—"

"I will not discuss this right now, and you will not ruin your aunt's wedding. You understand?"

I nodded.

"Go. Wash your face, whatever you have to do. And you go back to the party."

I nodded and stood up, dabbing under my eyes where I was sure mascara and eye shadow were already running down my cheeks. I swallowed it back—all of it—because I wouldn't have ruined Veronica's day for anything. I felt like Mrs. Abbey, blinking back my tears. I plastered a smile on my face and grabbed Anthony and made him dance with me.

"Where's lover boy?" he said.

"He had to go," I said stiffly.

"I'm dancing with my sister," he said. "I feel like an idiot."

"I know the feeling," I said. "Keep dancing."

I thought the reception was never going to end. People kept eating, toasting, and dancing, and Veronica took ten hours to throw her bouquet, which Reney caught, and another twenty to change her clothes. I kept a smile glued to my lips—until Mama poked her head out the door to where we were all waiting with our second round of birdseed bags and said, "Marissa, Veronica wants to say good-bye to you."

That was my undoing. The minute I walked into that room and she was there with her overnight bag and her newlywed smile, I couldn't hold it back any longer. I threw my arms around her neck and burst into tears.

"Mi sobrina, mi sobrina," she said. "I'll miss you, too, but we promised we would write. You remember?" She pulled me away to look at me, and the smile zipped right off her face.

"What is it?" she said.

I shook my head. "You have to go; it's all right."

"It's not all right! Something is bad. You tell me."

"Not tonight! You have to go on your honeymoon!" I tried to smile through all the stuff that was coming out of my eyes and my nose.

She held up her finger just the way Abuelo always did. "You promise me, Marissa, you promise me you will talk to someone about this. Go to that Ms. Race. Go to her."

"Okay," I said. I was sobbing by now. I would have agreed to anything. "Go. They're all waiting for you out there."

"With those miserable birdseed bags?" she said. She smiled at me and hugged my shoulders. "You stay in here. Collect yourself before my brother sees you."

I nodded.

She kissed me soundly on the cheek and whispered in my ear. "You promise me?"

I nodded, and she was gone. I pulled the flower-ring off my finger and threw it across the room.

The next day, because Veronica was gone, I didn't get up to go to church. Luisa crawled into bed with me before dawn and asked me if we were going. I shook my head and held on to her and waited until she went back to sleep to start to cry again. She still had some wedding cake frosting in her hair, and somehow that made me sad.

Everything made me sad that day. The silence of the telephone. Every poem I tried to write. Even the prayers I tried to pray.

That was the worst. I felt so horrible, so ashamed, so confused, I couldn't even pray or read *The Message*. Jesus' words just kept getting all mixed up.

"What does He really mean?" Jason had said.

"If He would only talk to me, I would know," I whispered.

Anthony, of course, chose that moment to pass my room. "She's lost it," he said loudly into the hall. "She's in there talking to herself."

At least Papa wasn't in there talking to me. He hadn't said a word to me since he had found Jason and me on the bench. He just kept giving me smoldering-charcoal looks and turning away. I was sure he hadn't told Mama, or she would have been in my room, telling me more than I really wanted to know about what kind of person I was. She wasn't the one I wanted to talk to. But who? Veronica had said Ms. Race, but now, wouldn't *that* just be a conversation? I could picture the disappointment in her eyes.

Around five o'clock, Mama did come into my room and close the door behind her. I tried to pull into myself, but it was already too late. Papa had told her.

"I know why you're here," I said to the bedspread.

"Look at me," Mama said.

I did. Her face was tight, almost gray. She looked older than I had ever seen her.

"Don't you have any respect for yourself?" she said.

"Yes," I said.

"That isn't what your papa told me. He said that boy had his hands all over you."

"It wasn't like he thinks," I said. "I was trying to get away—"

"How did you get yourself there in the first place, Marissa?" Mama said. "That's what I want to know."

"I didn't know that was what was going to happen—"

"He was right; your father was right," Mama said. "You spend too much time with this boy. That's where it leads, Marissa."

"It doesn't always!" I said.

Her face flickered surprise. I pulled right back into myself.

She sank down onto my bed and put a stiff hand over one of mine. "You don't know. This is your first experience with a boy. You have no idea."

It's not like anybody's taken the time to tell me, I wanted to say.

My face must have said it. She drew back and folded her arms across her chest. The weariness of her busy life pinched hard between her eyebrows, and I was even more confused.

"But you do know right from wrong, Marissa," she said. "You had better remember what's right. Until you do, I think you had better stay away from that boy."

I didn't answer. She walked out, leaving the door cracked

halfway open. It didn't take five seconds for Reney to appear.

"That is so unfair," Reney said. She came to the bed and put her skinny arms around me. I shrugged them off.

"Were you listening?" I said.

"I heard," she said. "I would have told her—"

"Just leave," I said. My voice came out dull, but the one inside my head was screaming.

"I just wanted to help," she said.

"Help by getting out," I said.

She flounced herself to the doorway, lanky arms dangling resentfully at her sides.

"Close the door," I said.

She didn't. Eddie appeared, and he took hold of the doorknob.

"Busted!" he said and then slammed the door behind him. I fumbled on the bedside table and picked up the first thing my hand came to and hurled it in his direction. It splashed against the wood in a flurry of paper and fell, ineffective, to the floor. I went for it, all set to kick it out of the way. Until I saw what it was.

All the stuff I had brought home from the True Love Waits rally. I sat down on top of it and sobbed. Even Sylvia couldn't comfort me.

Nobody came and got me for dinner. It was dark by the time I stood up and listened at the door. Mama was giving Luisa her bath. Everybody else seemed to be in their corners, doing their thing. The TV was murmuring down the hall in the living room with Papa undoubtedly in front of it.

I crept out and made my way unseen to the kitchen. Anthony was on the floor on the phone, his back to me. I knocked softly on Abuelo's door and heard his "Come in."

He was propped up on his bed with a book on his lap. He set it aside, took off his glasses, and patted the mattress. I went to him and leaned against his frail body.

"You're a good girl, *muchacha*," he said.

"I don't feel like one," I said.

"But you are."

I shook my head against his chest. "You don't know."

"I do. Your papa told me I was steering you in the wrong direction and that I should mind my own business."

I sat up straight and stared at him.

"Of course, I told him he was wrong." Abuelo's eyes were twinkling. Tired, but still twinkling.

"Maybe he isn't," I said. "Maybe I don't know anything about love."

Abuelo pushed air impatiently out between his lips. "You know more about love than anyone else in this house—anyone," he said. "You haven't figured out the details yet. That's what I say."

"I've had enough details," I said. "Just ask Papa."

Abuelo waved that off. "He's talking about sex; I'm talking about love."

I looked down at the blanket and giggled. "I don't want to talk about sex with you, Abuelo."

"Neither do I. But if you look at the details of love, you won't have to worry about what to do about sex." His eyes drifted closed, and I started to get up.

"Sit here awhile, Marissa," he said.

"Okay," I said. I pulled a chair closer to the bed and sat on the chair's edge. With his eyes still closed, Abuelo reached out his hand, and I put mine in it. It made me think of putting my hand in Papa's to dance, and I wanted to cry again. Instead, I curled my fingers around Abuelo's.

"Good," he said. "You hold on."

I sat there for a long time in the dark, listening to him breathe so gently and peacefully, and it made me feel a little better. When I was sure he was asleep, I kissed his forehead and left.

He never woke up.

ABUELO DIED OF A STROKE, THEY SAID. A MASSIVE ONE. He probably never felt it.

Like that was supposed to comfort Mama, Papa, and me as we stood in the kitchen, staring at each other in shock. When the coroner left, Mama's face started to crumple, and she put her hands up to hide it. Papa pulled her against his chest, and that's when I cried. Papa held out his arm to me, and I ran to him. He held us both. We were still standing there when the kids started emerging, one by one, rubbing eyes, scratching chests, and looking pasty-faced. It was probably the first time in two years that I hugged Reney.

She, Gabriela, and Luisa clung to me like baby monkeys as they cried. Anthony and Eddie each gave Papa a hug and then went off to hide their tears someplace. Papa himself didn't have any tears. He just stood in the middle of the kitchen floor, holding Mama and nodding as she sobbed out what needed to be done next.

"Call Veronica. Call the church. Call the funeral home."

Papa just nodded and rocked her and stroked her hair.

It was eight o'clock before Mama was able to wash her face and start to make arrangements. We all understood without anybody saying anything that I would deal with the younger kids and tend to the meals. Actually, casseroles started to pour in about noon, and Reney and Gabriela managed to go back to bed and sleep. Luisa followed me around like a bewildered puppy somebody had left out in the rain.

"But where did he *go*?" she said to me at one point when I was trying to find a place in the refrigerator for yet another dish of chile rellenos. I looked up to find her standing wistfully in Abuelo's doorway.

"He's just gone," I said. "Gone to heaven."

"Can't he come back?"

I abandoned the casserole on the table and went to her. "No," I said. "He's with us inside ourselves though."

I put my hand on her chest, but she brushed it away, eyes flaming, looking like Papa. "I don't want him inside here! I want him inside *here!*" She flung a chubby finger toward Abuelo's room and stomped her foot and then threw herself out of the kitchen. It was the ultimate frustration. I sat down on the floor and put my face in my hands and cried.

Above me, the phone jangled, and I could hear Anthony lunging for it. No matter what the situation, the phone was still his domain.

I was surprised at how shaky his voice sounded when he said hello, and when I looked at him, how puffy his eyes were. Who knew Anthony had any feelings left in him besides sarcasm?

When I put the phone to my ear, a smooth voice eased into it. "Hi, Marissa," Ms. Race said. "Are you all right?"

I leaned back against the wall then and let out the first real breath I think I had taken since I had heard Mama calling for Papa at six that morning.

"Hi," I said.

"Oh, honey, you sound terrible. Are you sick? When you didn't show up this morning without calling, I knew something was really wrong…"

"My *abuelo* died," I said. "My grandfather."

"The one who lives with you?" she said.

For some stupid reason, I said, "He doesn't live with us anymore." And then I just sobbed into the phone.

By that afternoon, all the Flagpole Girls knew about Abuelo's death. I knew they knew because they responded with their usual wonderfulness.

Tobey and Cheyenne and, to my delight, Shannon, appeared at four o'clock, arms full of food.

"Tassie says she can't do Mexican," Cheyenne said as she set a big pot of beef stew soundly on the table. "But she figures at a time like this, food is food."

It obviously didn't bother Eddie and Anthony. They came out from their hiding places and sniffed around like hounds.

Tobey laughed. "Do all brothers go to some school to learn how to be obnoxious? Fletcher would be doing the same thing."

I just shrugged, and she hugged me hard. The best part was that the Girls were just there. I didn't have to say anything.

Shannon didn't say anything either, although she had outdone herself with the cookies. There were piles of them, which the boys stood there and grazed over. When the four of us were deep in conversation, the boys absconded with the whole two plates.

"Hey," Cheyenne called after them, "bring those back!"

"Come on, Chey," Tobey said. "I know how to handle brothers."

They took off after the boys, leaving Shannon and me standing like two little waifs in the kitchen. She rearranged a few casseroles on the table, and then she looked up at me with a jerk, and I saw her eyes were about to spill over.

"I'm so sorry, Marissa," she said.

"Thanks," I said. "They keep telling me he was old, he lived a good life—"

"That isn't what I mean." She gripped the back of a kitchen chair, and her face worked miserably. "I mean, I just haven't been there for you lately. It's like I've been in some other world, and now I feel awful about it."

At the same instant she burst into tears, I held out my arms. Tobey and Cheyenne found us by the table, slobbering all over each other, dangerously close to a large bowl of salsa.

From that point on, Shannon wouldn't leave my side. The feel of her arm linked through mine, skinny and bony as it was, was comforting, and I clung back.

Ironically, the day was beautiful, and we sat on the front steps in the sun. Tobey plucked uneasily at the grass, and then she said, "Jason has been calling me since Saturday afternoon—about every two hours."

I looked down at my hands, which clenched themselves in my lap.

"He thinks he's blown it forever with your father," she said.

"How come?" Cheyenne said. "What did he do?"

Tobey's eyes flashed quickly to mine. "After school I called him and told him about your grandfather, and now he's all upset about that and wants to see you. Do you think your father would let him come over?"

I shook my head then I nodded it; I didn't know what to think. Right now, I wanted to run into Abuelo's room and ask him, ask him about those details…

"I don't understand what's going on," Cheyenne said.

Bless Norie's heart. She arrived just then in her Jeep with Wyatt and strode up the walkway as if she were about to change everything because Norie always could. But the look on her face was as sad and helpless as anybody else's.

"Hi," she said to me. "I didn't know what else to do so I brought you a book."

She thrust a slim volume toward me, and I took it gratefully in my hands.

"*A Grief Observed*," Cheyenne read over my shoulder. "By C. S. Lewis."

"Is that the Chronicles of Narnia guy?" Shannon said.

"Yeah," Norie said. "How many times did you read those books as a kid? Let's have a contest—"

I stood up and hugged Norie. When I pulled away, Wyatt was right there, and he pulled me gently against him and held on for a second.

It was sweet, that's all I can say. I wanted to hold on, and not because I had any romantic feelings for Wyatt. Even in my almost-smothering blanket of sadness, I could just feel a difference between the way he hugged me and the way Jason had tightened his arms around me and didn't let go until he was ready.

"Here comes Brianna," somebody said.

I went from Wyatt to her in a blur, and she held me the way I had held Gabriela and Reney that morning. "I been there, girl," she whispered to me. "I know what you're feelin'." She put a big, flat, brown envelope on the step and told me to open it later.

Shannon and Cheyenne went inside to retrieve what was left of the cookies, and Brianna went in as backup. Tobey pulled me down onto the step beside her.

"I want you to know," she whispered, "that Jason told me your father caught the two of you—uh—kissing at the wedding reception."

I felt my face redden, and I fastened my eyes on my knees.

"Look, you don't need to be embarrassed in front of me," Tobey said. "It's not like I never kissed anybody before."

Not like that, I thought. But I just nodded.

"Anyway, I haven't told anybody, and I'm not going to. I wouldn't have said that much in front of Cheyenne and Shannon, but I didn't know if I would get to talk to you alone. Anyway, I figure if you want any of the other Girls to know, you will tell them yourself."

"Thank you," I said.

We sat on the porch, all of us, eating cookies, while family and friends picked their way past us as they arrived to comfort my parents. Later Papa, Reney, and Gabriela left to pick up Veronica at the airport.

"So much for her honeymoon," Norie said. "What did she have, like one whole day?"

"I hope this doesn't sound bad," Tobey said. "But don't you wonder sometimes about God's timing? I mean, really?"

"Are we supposed to wonder about that?" Cheyenne said.

"I do," Wyatt said.

Next to me, Shannon put her arm through mine, and I smiled at her. I wasn't sure who was comforting whom, but it felt good to have her there.

"Here's the way I look at it," Norie said. But her sharp, eyes-like-a-bird gaze settled on something in the street, and she stopped. We all craned to see what she was looking at.

"Is that Jason?" Cheyenne said.

"Well, it's about time the boy got here," Brianna said. She swept her eyes over me. "Sorry, Marissa, but it just seems to me that your boyfriend should have been the first one—"

"Go meet him, Marissa," Tobey said. She was looking at me with almost panic in her eyes.

But I stayed there with Shannon on my arm, mind racing like a mouse maze. *Do I tell him to go home before Papa gets back? What if there's a scene? Should I even want him here? This is about Abuelo.*

One look at Jason, coming up the walk clutching a casserole like a little boy, and most of that disappeared. He stopped short of the steps, nodded at everybody, and then looked at me. His eyes were—there is no other way to describe it—they were soulful. I heard Brianna give a soft grunt.

"Hi," he said. "I know I'm not, like, supposed to be here, but my mom wanted your family to have this."

He held out a foil-wrapped Pyrex dish until his wrist shook, and Norie took it from him. She scoped out the situation with a glance and said, "Come on, guys, let's go see if we can fit this on the table."

Brianna, Cheyenne, and Wyatt followed her, with some prodding from Tobey. Only Shannon stayed there, as if she herself might fall down if she let go of my arm.

"Thank you," I said to Jason.

"It's okay. I liked your grandfather."

It occurred to me that I'd never even seen him look at Abuelo twice, but I nodded.

Behind us, I heard the screen door creak, and Jason looked over my head. I actually watched his face turn pale.

"Hi, Mrs. Martinez," he said. "I'm sorry about your loss."

I looked up quickly at Mama. I expected to see her staring Jason down with a piercing gaze, but her face looked too tired for piercing—or much of anything else, for that matter.

"Thank you," she said.

Jason cleared his throat and looked uneasily at my mom. "I know I'm not exactly the person you want to see right now, but do you think it's all right if I just talk to Marissa for a few minutes?"

Mama sighed, and to my surprise, I felt her fingers brush the top of my shoulder. "Stay as long as you want. Marissa needs all the help she can get. It's a sad time."

Jason waited until she had gone back into the house to let his face break into a smile. He was on the other side of me before I could even register what had just happened. His arm went softly around me, and he tugged at me until I put my head on his shoulder. My other arm stretched awkwardly through Shannon's.

"Do you mind if I talk to Marissa for a couple of minutes alone?" Jason said.

I could feel Shannon stiffening, but she stood up. I had to twist myself around to see her.

"Come back in a minute," I said.

She nodded vaguely and went in the house. Jason put his other arm around me and held me against him.

"I am so sorry," he said.

I didn't ask him about which thing. I just nodded against his shirt and his Polo Sport and his compact chest.

"God's with you," he said.

"I know."

"I know you were crazy about him. You talked about him all the time."

"He was the best," I said.

"But he's with God now."

"I know."

"If you get to hurting, just tell me, and I'll remind you of that."

The Girls and Wyatt reappeared with canned drinks for everybody then. I shook my head at the offer of a can and slid my arm back into Shannon's.

"I'm not having one either," she said to me.

It was an almost lame thing to say, and yet it didn't matter. It was a *real* thing to say.

"Can I say something?" Cheyenne said, as they all settled onto the grass in front of us.

"Who's going to stop you?" Norie said.

"No, seriously, everybody talks around it like we're all pretending nothing bad happened," Cheyenne said. "Is that what you do when somebody dies?"

Everybody looked at each other, their inexperience hanging out like tongues.

Brianna was the only one to nod. "Some people do. I myself would rather just get it out in the open. You can't be walking around with a bunch of grief knotted up in your chest, or worse things start to happen."

"Then I'm going to say it," Cheyenne said. "This is really sad. Your mother looks like *she's* going to die, Marissa."

"And it wasn't even her father, right?" Tobey said.

"Her father died before she left Mexico," I said. "Abuelo was like her real father. She was as close to him as my Aunt Veronica is."

"It's so *sad*," Cheyenne said again.

"It isn't really, though, when you think about it," Jason said.

"I'm thinking about it," Norie said. "And it's still sad."

"For us, maybe," Jason said. "Not for him. He's with Jesus now. What could be happier than that?"

A sort of uncomfortable silence folded around us. It was true—I knew that—but it didn't exactly settle over us like a warm blanket.

"I think we all know that," Tobey said. "But that doesn't mean—"

"He was a Christian, right?" Jason said to me.

"Of course!" I said. "He just didn't go to church because he couldn't really get out, but he—"

"Then there you go," Jason said.

Brianna, I could tell, was bristling. "So you're saying Marissa shouldn't grieve because her grandfather has gone to a better place? Even though she's left here with this big ol' honkin' *hole* in her life that is going take a while to fill?"

"But if she's thinking about where he is now, won't the hole be smaller?" Jason said.

Shannon tightened her arm on mine, and I held on to it. Jason looked over at me and pulled me back to him. "That's what I'm telling her anyway," Jason said. "It only makes sense, if we're actually practicing what we believe."

"Boy, you ever had anybody close to you die?" Brianna said. She was sitting up straight, her neck extended E.T.-style. Shannon's hold on me tightened.

Jason shook his head.

"Well, I have, and I can tell you, that all sounds real good, but it isn't going to help Marissa one bit today. It's going to be weeks before that even starts to sink in."

"I don't think so," Jason said. "I'm going to keep reminding her."

Brianna gave him a long look, and then she stood up. "You do that," she said. "I have to go."

"Me, too," Tobey said. "You ready, guys?"

Cheyenne scrambled up, but Shannon still held on to my arm. "Can somebody else take me home later?" she said.

"We could," Norie said, "but I think we have to go too."

Wyatt nodded, and Shannon reluctantly untangled herself.

"Maybe Jason could take you when he leaves," I said to her. "Could you?"

I turned around to look at Jason, just in time to catch something going through his eyes. He glanced down at me, and it was gone.

"I could," he said, "but can we talk for a minute?"

"We'll come by tomorrow," Norie said to me. They all wandered toward the cars, with Shannon following at a distance and looking back uncertainly. I put a hand up for her to wait, but Jason got in my ear.

"You want her to stay?" he whispered.

"Yes," I said. "I'm worried about her, and this is the first chance I've even had to be with her, and—"

"This is not the time for you to be worrying about her," he said. "You have your own stuff to deal with."

It didn't occur to me to point out that he had just said not two minutes before that I pretty much shouldn't even be grieving. I just looked at him.

"She's sick," I said. "She won't eat. She throws up all the time—"

"Get a clue, Rissa. She's anorexic or maybe bulimic. You don't need that right now."

My head snapped up toward Shannon, who was all the way out to the curb by now. A gust blew her flowy skirt against her, and I could see her hipbones protruding from her sunken-in belly.

"I guess I'll go on with Tobey," she called to me. Even her voice was thin as it reached me and then went off on the wind.

"Do you think that, really?" I said to Jason.

He put his arms around me and pulled me to his chest, face hard against his shirt front. "That's what I love about you," he said. "You're always thinking about everybody else. Come on, let's think about you."

Just then Luisa came to the door and looked out longingly

through the screen. I went in to her, with Jason at my heels.

"I put Sylvia in Abuelo's room," she said.

"Why?" I said.

"So somebody will be there, just in case he comes back."

I crouched down and explained it to her one more time. Then I had to give her a bath and make sure she had something to eat and a quiet place to curl up as the voices, the weeping, and the rest of the grieving went on around her.

"Come sit with me now," Jason said when her eyes finally closed. "You need to rest."

But Veronica arrived then, and my tears started all over again. I was still holding her in the hallway when Jason said from somewhere, "I have to go home."

I nodded to him over her shoulder and said, "Thank you."

By about eight o'clock Veronica was calmed down enough to sit with Mama and Papa in the living room and discuss the "arrangements." Everyone else filtered out, and I went into the kitchen to try to organize the food. The first thing I did was let poor Sylvia out of Abuelo's room. She put her paws up on me and meowed a protest. I picked her up and held her against my face, but I was all cried out.

"Hi," said a voice from the doorway. I turned around, and Ms. Race was standing there, holding a Crockpot.

"Hi!" I said. I put down Sylvia to hug Ms. Race and smelled the incredible aroma of vegetable soup.

"For tomorrow's lunch," she said. She looked at the table and grinned. "Although it doesn't look like you'll need more food for a week."

"You forget, I have two brothers," I said.

Ms. Race added her Crockpot to the array and held on to my arm. "How are you doing, sweetie?"

"I'm okay."

"You don't have to be. It's okay to fall apart, you know."

"Not according to Jason," I said.

Ms. Race's eyebrows went up, but I shrugged. "Never mind. Do you want some tea while I clean up?"

"I want to help you clean up," she said. "I'm here to do whatever you need."

I didn't argue with her. It felt good to have someone there emptying the dishwasher and clinking the forks and spoons in companionable silence. It felt good not to have to think of anything to say.

We were almost finished when she said, "I think I'll have that tea now, Marissa. Join me?"

I didn't even drink tea, but I nodded and put on the kettle. She beckoned me to the chair beside her. The house was quiet now, except for the murmuring of voices in the living room. I rested my elbow on the table and put my face in my hand.

"There you go," Ms. Race said. "Relax a minute. You're a mainstay in this family, aren't you?"

"Am I?" I said.

"I think it's obvious. But don't let that keep you from getting what you need."

"You came," I said. "And the Girls were here before—and Jason. I'm okay."

She nodded, like she didn't believe it for a minute. "I know how close you were to your grandfather. This has to be incredibly hard, no matter how old he was or how sick or any of those things. I know when my grandmother died, all I could think about was when she was younger and stronger and we used to do the malls together until I dropped—not her, mind you—me!"

I laughed for the first time that day.

"But there's more to it than that, isn't there?" she said. "Something else is really on your mind, and it's making things worse. Am I right?"

I looked down at the table.

"You don't have to tell me," she said. "But I'm going to make a suggestion."

"Okay."

"I think you need to go to a place where you can meet yourself, Marissa. I know you're needed here, but tonight find a few minutes to be alone and talk to God."

"I'll be the one doing all the talking," I said.

She cocked her head, her clear eyes searching me. "You've said that before. But I think you're wrong. I think you're waiting for some voice that sounds different from yours to come down like the angel Gabriel or something and speak into your ear. It doesn't work that way for me. But, then, we all have our own way of communicating with God."

"We do?" I said.

"We all have our own way of communicating with each *other,* don't we?" she said. "You certainly don't chatter the way Cheyenne does or give a commentary like Norie."

"I couldn't if I tried!"

"Exactly. Cheyenne keeps a gratitude journal. That's how she talks to God. Norie does what I do, which is more a contemplative type of prayer. Brianna paints. We're all different."

"Jason says it takes years of commitment and work to reach that point. He's been trying to help me."

Ms. Race's eyebrows went up. "Why are you asking Jason? Why don't you ask God?"

She put her hand at once on my arm and squeezed it. "Don't let me get into that. I'm sorry. You just think about it, okay?" Then, to my relief, she pointed the conversation in another direction.

She left after we had tea. Mama and Papa kissed me good night and went to bed, leaving Veronica asleep exhausted on the couch in the living room. Only Sylvia and I were awake, and when she jumped up into my lap, I carried her into Abuelo's room and sat on his bed with her.

Go to a place where you can meet yourself, Ms. Race had said. This was as close as I was going to get, if it could ever happen.

"I don't even feel like me," I whispered to Sylvia. She didn't answer. Nobody answered. All I had were questions, which I whispered into the dark. "Why did Abuelo have to die just when I needed him the most? And why does Veronica have to leave now just when I need her the most? And what about Shannon? She just came back. I felt close to her again and then—"

Jason. Jason had come and all but chased her off the porch.

"But he just cares about me," I said to Abuelo's empty room. "He feels like I'm his wife. He wants to take care of me. He said I was his ideal woman, somebody he could take care of. I don't understand!"

The details, Abuelo had said. *The details of love are what you don't understand.*

"Then somebody help me!" I said in a tiny voice. "God, why don't you find some way to talk to me?"

I sound like Cheyenne, I thought. *And Roz, and that Bonnie girl. They're never quiet long enough for anybody to tell them anything.*

I squeezed my lips together and shut my eyes. I held Sylvia and tried to calm down.

Get quiet.

Just get quiet, even though I was never going to hear anything. That was all I could think to do. I lay down and got quiet.

All I heard were some syllables in my head—you know, those last thoughts before you drift off to sleep, that sometimes make sense and most of the time don't. But you think they do.

> *A virgin hears it,*
> *a gentle whisper from one*
> *she never thought would speak*
> *to her.*

"That's not a haiku, God," I heard myself mutter.

I turned over, Sylvia curled up against me. She purred and my syllables did, too.

> *The virgin knows it,*
> *knows the Voice believes in her,*
> *but she shies away.*

"Why?" I thought sleepily.

> *It's too beautiful*
> *to be her.*

"Not enough syllables," I mumbled to Sylvia.

And then I fell asleep.

THE FUNERAL WAS ON THURSDAY, AND IT HAD TO BE THE longest day of my life. Even Anthony and Eddie hung on me all through the church service, all through the endless droning on at the cemetery. My two little, macho, smart-mouthed brothers acted as if they were scared to death Abuelo was going to rise up out of the coffin and drag them in with him.

I was pretty sure they picked me for "protection" because I was the available one. Papa and Mama had their hands full with Veronica, who took it harder than anybody. She had already lost her mother when she was little, before Cecilia and I were even born.

By the time we reached the reception at our house after all the ceremonies, I was like a ball of fraying string. I was never so happy to see anybody as I was Ms. Race and Shannon when they slipped in the front door and found me standing there like a robot with the coffeepot, waiting for someone to ask for a cup of French roast.

"How you doing, sweetie?" Ms. Race said.

I handed the pot to Gabriela and flung my arms around both of them.

Take me off somewhere, I wanted to say.

But, of course, we stayed there and talked for a while. I held on to them the way my brothers and sisters had been clinging to me all day. Shannon seemed distant again though. The one thing I could pull myself together to do was to try to shorten that distance.

"I'll be back at school tomorrow," I said to her. "Can we sit together at lunch?"

"Sure," she said. But she wouldn't meet my eyes.

You didn't have to be a nuclear physicist to figure out why, but it wasn't really clear to me until Jason arrived. Then she stood up and said to Ms. Race, "I have to get home."

Shannon didn't even look in Jason's direction as she hurried out the door.

Jason folded my hand between his. "You didn't get into her stuff with her, did you? Not today."

"No," I said. That uncomfortable feeling nagged at my backbone like when Jason and I took our "walk" at Veronica's reception.

"Come on," he said. "You look stressed. Let's take a walk."

I felt myself go rigid.

What happened next was what I think they call uncanny. At just that moment, Papa kind of melted out of the crowd and looked at Jason and me.

"Hello, Mr. Martinez," Jason said. He put out his hand. "You weren't here the other night when I came by. I'd like to say how sorry I am about your father."

Papa nodded and brushed at his mustache as he looked at me, not Jason.

"Mama said it was all right," I said.

My father did something then that…well, it would have surprised me less if he had gotten up on the coffee table and tap-danced. He leaned over and kissed me on the forehead.

"Your Abuelo said you were a good girl," he said to me. "I believe him."

He turned to somebody else then, and Jason tugged gently at my hand. We were out the door and down the street before I stopped running the scene over in my mind.

"It's good to be out of there," Jason said. "You look better already."

"Where are we going?"

"To the park. I think they have swings there."

Then he broke into a run, dragging me along behind him. There were swings in the park, and Jason lifted me onto one and stood behind me. "How high do you want to go?"

"I don't care," I said. I curled my fingers uneasily around the chain. This was weird. It didn't feel right to jump back in where we had left off when this wasn't where we had left off.

Jason swung me up until I could almost see our house. I could see Brianna's apartment, too, which was just across the street from the park. I wondered what she would think of this whole scene. She had made it obvious she wasn't all that crazy about Jason.

He let me slow down, and then he grabbed the chain to stop the swing. I couldn't look at him, but he lifted my chin with his finger.

"I want to apologize to you," he said.

"For what?" I said.

"For the other day at the reception."

The words were like that first taste of Coke when you're about dying of thirst. I gulped at them. "I'm so glad you said that!"

"I would have said it sooner, but it's not like I've had a chance. I was afraid to call you Sunday."

"Papa wouldn't have let me talk to you anyway."

"He was pretty mad. I'm surprised he didn't take me out."

"I wasn't really mad at you—"

"I didn't think you were—"

"I was just confused."

Jason squatted down and looked up at me, still perched on the swing. "I don't want you to be confused."

I didn't say anything, but I could feel a smile coming back to the corners of my mouth. There were things about him I really loved. I didn't want to lose that. And he did care about me. Maybe he just didn't have his details straight either.

But it looked like he did now, and when he saw my smile, he pulled me off the swing and twirled me around in a hug, the way he had Bonnie.

"Okay, look," he said. "Tomorrow's Friday, right?"

"Right."

"Let's go out. You need to have some fun."

"Okay," I said. "We can do that."

"Yes!" he said.

He squeezed me tight. I held my breath. But he let go and took my hand, and we skipped—seriously, we really did skip—most of the way back to the house. He stopped in front of his car and put his hands on my shoulders.

"I love you," he said.

I nodded.

"I want to hear you say you love me, too," he said. "Only I know you; you aren't going to say it until you've practiced it in your head a thousand times. That's okay; that's you." He kissed my forehead, in about the same spot Papa had kissed me.

"I didn't get to finish what I was saying before," he said.

"What?"

"I'm sorry your dad had to catch us. That put you in a bad place with him. I didn't mean for that to happen."

"It's okay. He understands," I said.

But I wasn't sure I did. As I watched him pull away, something nagged at my backbone again. I think it was doubt.

Still, it felt as if maybe things were going to be all right. I did get to talk to Veronica that night, which was good since she was leaving the next day to rejoin Gerald.

"How are you?" she said to me as she sat on the edge of my bed. With Luisa already asleep, we were both whispering.

"I'm good," I said. "Things are better."

She looked hard at my face. "You wouldn't lie to me."

"Never."

She sighed. "I am going to miss you so much. More than ever now. Gerald is wonderful, but I don't think he can know what this is like for me to lose my father. He understands that he can't know. At least he isn't trying to tell me to cheer up, you know?"

I nodded.

"You understand though, *mi sobrina*. In your quiet little way, you just know." She curled her hands around both my wrists. "Those poems you wrote for me, I didn't have a chance to tell you, but they are beautiful, Marissa. I'm going to treasure them."

"You liked them?"

"'Like' doesn't even come close. Neither does 'love.' They just touched me. The little details…they went straight to my heart."

"Details?" I said.

"You used so few words, but I could see what you were saying. How can you write like that? It must be God, huh?"

"Must be," I said, grinning. "I didn't even know that I was doing it!"

Although I cried again when I said good-bye to her the next morning before I left for school, I felt stronger. Strong enough, in fact, that I was determined to find Shannon and talk to her about what Jason had said to me, about her being anorexic. In spite of everything, it had hardly left my mind since the night he had said it.

I decided that was God too, because I found her right away, standing at her locker. I caught a glimpse of the Ex-Lax again as she slammed the door, but they made sense now. Just another way to lose weight.

"We need to talk," I said to her.

Her eyes darted away from me, and she hiked her backpack onto her back. "I have to go to class."

"You have time," I said. "The first bell hasn't even rung yet. Come on, let's go out to the courtyard."

"Talk about what?" she said. Her mouth looked all trembly, like it was as weak as the rest of her.

How could I have missed it before? I wondered. Her cheekbones were sticking out. Her eyes looked sunken in. I could even see the bones in her wrists as she nervously brushed her hair back off her face.

"Not here," I said. "Come on."

I led her out to the courtyard by the arm. It felt unfamiliar to me; I didn't usually force people to do things they didn't want to do. It just seemed like the only way.

I insisted she sit on one of the cement benches, and I sat beside her. Then I got right in her face.

"I know, Shannon," I said.

She blinked. "Know what?"

"I know about…that you're starving yourself."

Real fear jumped into her eyes. If I could have pushed a button and reversed the whole thing, I would have. I shook my head.

"I'm sorry. I shouldn't have come at you like that, but I'm worried about you."

"Are you saying I'm anorexic?" she said.

"Yes. But I'm not judging you or anything—"

"Don't even think about it," she said, "because I'm not!'

"Then you're sick, and I—"

"Just don't worry about it, okay?"

The fear was gone, and in its place was something I never dreamed I would see in Shannon D'Angelo's pale eyes. It was anger.

She stood up. "I'm going to class," she said.

I didn't try to stop her.

I only sat there for about a second before I hightailed it to the office. It wasn't my morning to work, but I had to talk to Ms. Race. Shannon could deny it all she wanted, but she might as well have signed a confession. Jason had been right.

But Ms. Race looked busy. No, more than busy. Preoccupied, like she was stamping admit slips with her hands and thinking about an African safari or something. It got that way in the office sometimes. Reluctantly, I went to first period.

The morning dragged. I played around with some drawings for my poetry collection, but they were all lame. I absolutely could not draw. Everything came out stick figures, and they all looked like Shannon.

We had a Flagpole meeting at lunch, but she didn't come. Neither did Ms. Race, which was strange. I could only hope they were together somewhere. The rest of us prayed for Abuelo and our family and some other things, but I wasn't with it. When Brianna asked me if I was still dating Jason, I jumped back to the present like a startled rabbit.

"Sure," I said. "We're going out tonight."

Tobey looked at me over the top of her PB&J.

"We had a long talk," I said.

She nodded. "I'm glad you worked it out."

"Worked what out?" Cheyenne said. "How come I never know what's going on?"

"Everything is on a need-to-know basis," Norie said. "I guess we don't need to know."

Sometimes I really loved Norie. Even if she *was* Feminist Henry.

I was eager then to get to fifth period so I could finally talk to Ms. Race about Shannon. She was at her desk, doing nothing in particular that I could see so I went right over to her.

"Hi," I said.

She looked up and smiled like she was coming back from someplace. Maybe that African safari. It obviously hadn't gone well. "Hi, sweetie," she said. "How are you holding up?"

"Fine," I said. "I really am. I'm doing better."

"Good," she said. She reached out and squeezed my hand. "We'll talk soon," she said. And then she went back to doing nothing.

I was a little stung. It wasn't like Ms. Race to pull herself away. It probably wouldn't have affected me so much if Shannon hadn't slammed a door in my face that morning, if Veronica hadn't just left for six months, if Abuelo hadn't left forever. Life felt black, lonely all of a sudden. It would be good to see Jason that night.

I concentrated on wondering where we would go. Actually, I had a few suggestions. Norie had talked at lunch about a poetry reading they were having at one of the coffee shops. I had never been to one.

But I had a hard time imagining Jason listening to rhymed lines while sipping cappuccino. Maybe I could do that with Brianna sometime.

I ran into Francesca, Roz, and Daniela after school, and they were all sympathetic about Abuelo. They had been at the funeral, but we hadn't had a chance to talk.

"Are you okay?" Daniela said.

"Want to go to the mall?" Roz said. "That would cheer you up."

"I can't," I said. "But thanks."

"We're going to look at the puppies at the pet store," Francesca said. It was like she was dangling a candy bar in front of my face. I laughed.

"We always loved to do that!" I said.

"Remember, we would take every one out and hold it until the manager chased us off," Daniela said.

"Let's do that sometime," I said. "Just not today. Things are still…" I waved a hand in the air, and they all nodded knowingly.

"My mother was a mess for weeks after my grandfather died," Roz said. "I know what you're talking about."

"You do not," Francesca said. She popped Roz softly on the head and pushed her toward the door. "We're going to miss our bus."

I watched them go, and for a minute I wanted to run after them. I still felt so lonely. I wanted to go back to someplace safe, where things weren't so confusing.

I wished Jason would take me to the pet shop and let me hold the puppies. I grunted to myself. Nope. Couldn't see that either.

Besides, as I knew he would, Jason had a plan when he came by to pick me up that night. "First, we have to go by my house," he said. "I want to show you something."

"What?" I said.

"Just wait. You'll see."

When we pulled into his driveway, the first thing I saw was that no other cars were there.

"Where are your parents?" I said.

"The 'rents are out for the evening," he said. "Come on."

"Should I go in if they aren't there?" I said.

He laughed his no-sound laugh. "It's not like when we were ten, and they were afraid we would burn the place down or something. I just want to show you this."

I climbed slowly out of the car, and for a second I felt strange. Like we were breaking into someone's house. I shook that off and followed him in. He was right; we were just going in to see "something," and we would be right out. It was fine.

"So what are you going to show me?" I said.

"It's up here," he said. He took my hand and led me up the short set of steps that we usually took to the rec room to play pool. I was a little disappointed. I had trouble getting real worked up about new cue sticks.

But we turned in a different direction, and he took me down a hall where he pushed open a door and turned on a light. I saw a blur of posters.

"What?" I said.

"My room," he said. "I wanted to show it to you."

"Why?" I said.

"Because you never saw it before, and I was so freaked out over that thing with your father I spent the whole day Sunday cleaning it up." He grinned down at me. "I wanted you to see what you made me do."

I looked around. The room was nice and definitely bigger and better decorated than Anthony and Eddie's. Some Christian posters were on the wall, a stereo system almost as big as the one in the den stood against a wall, and a big futon on the floor was piled with plaid cushions. It was nice.

"Sit down for a sec," he said.

Like I had a choice. He nudged me toward the futon, and I sat on it like a folded stick. I really wanted to leave.

Jason pushed several buttons on the stereo, and some music started. It wasn't, surprisingly enough, Disney. I think it was DC Talk.

"Check out this lamp," he said. He turned on a brass lamp on the desk and snapped off the overhead light. The room had a golden glow I almost couldn't see through.

"Neat," I said. "So where are we going tonight?"

"Can we talk about something else first?" he said.

He sat beside me and inched with his legs, with me in tow, toward the pile of cushions. He cuddled up beside me with his arm around my shoulders, but he didn't kiss me. I tried to relax.

"Talk about what?" I said.

"I want to make sure you know something," he said. "I mean, after the other day—"

"We already talked about this," I said.

"But I just want to make this really clear. I have never slept with a girl."

"I knew that," I said.

"And I wasn't lying at the True Love Waits thing or putting on an act."

I relaxed some more. "I know. I believe you."

"And here's what else—when I was there with you the day your grandfather died and all, I loved helping you through that."

I nodded.

"It made me feel even more like we're married people. I mean, that's what they do for each other. I *feel* like that."

I stopped relaxing.

"We share everything married people do," he went on. "Our problems…"

My thoughts stirred. *We don't exactly share our problems, Jason,* one of them said. *I tell you things, and you fix them.*

I wanted to say it out loud. I wanted to set that straight. I even opened my mouth, but he didn't give me a chance.

He put his hand on my cheek and turned it to him and kissed me. One of "our" kisses. I started to melt into him for the free and adult and beautiful way those kisses always made me feel.

Slowly, Jason pushed me back and pressed his chest against mine until I couldn't tell where he stopped and I started. The music cupped itself around us, and the room filled with the smell of his cologne—the room we were in all by ourselves.

Jason pulled away just enough to look at me, and I smiled at him. He lunged for my mouth again and pulled me up from the small of my back. I could feel one hipbone pressing into me, one hand sliding down to the seat of my jeans. I stiffened. The beautiful feeling froze in me, but I didn't pull away.

Maybe this isn't me, I thought crazily. *I can't feel my feet. I can hardly breathe. Maybe this isn't me. Maybe Daniela was right.*

There were definitely too many syllables in there.

But a few managed to untangle themselves from the rest.

The virgin knows the Voice believes in her, one said.

Abuelo said you were a good girl, and I believe him, said another.

I pulled my mouth away. "No, Jason," I said.

He didn't seem to hear me as he just slipped his lips on down to my neck and pulled a hand around to my stomach.

"Stop!" I said.

I put my hands on his chest and pushed. He jolted away from me and stared.

"What?" he said.

"Stop," I said.

"Why?"

"Because...I can't do this."

Jason nodded. "Okay, I'm rushing you. I'm sorry."

"We should go," I said.

I started to get up, but he held on to my arm. "Okay, but just a minute. Just tell me why."

"I'm not ready," I said.

"Okay." He seemed to like that answer. He ran his hand over his hair and then along my arm. I felt chills.

"Tell me why," he said. "Please. I want to know."

So I started through my litany, the one I had given Veronica that day. Jason had an answer for every one.

"I'm in love with you," he said. "And I think you're in love with me, aren't you?"

"I love—"

"Okay, and I'm not just going to respect you tomorrow, I'm going to respect you always. It doesn't get any better than that. Plus, you don't need to be embarrassed with me. I mean, shoot, I don't know what I'm doing either!" He smiled. I didn't. His face turned serious. "I even have protection."

I pulled back from him, and he at least knew enough not to grab me right then.

"You had this planned?" I said.

He looked down at his knee for a minute. "I'm not going to lie to you. Because I never have. I've always told you the truth."

"You must have known you were going to do this, or you wouldn't have bought…whatever!" I said.

"I've been thinking about it. But I'm taking care of things, Rissa. I'm being responsible about it."

I shook my head, but he kept talking.

"And what was your other thing? Oh, like I'm really going to tell anybody about this. This is a private thing between two people who want to be one," he said. "Two Christian people."

I didn't answer right away. He took that opportunity to cup my face in his hands and kiss me. I didn't even feel it. All I could sense was Aunt Veronica saying to me, "If those reasons ever stop being enough, come see me."

Only I couldn't see her. And I couldn't see Abuelo. And Ms. Race was off somewhere in her own world, and Shannon—

The sound of a car brought me back to the moment. Jason heard it too, because he pulled away from me and half rose from the futon.

"What was that?" I said.

"I don't know," he said.

He jumped up and went for the door. "It's okay. It's all right for us to be here," he said. And then contradicted himself by bolting out into the hall and down the stairs.

I only had one thought as I stood up, smoothed out my

clothes, snatched up my purse, and headed off after him. *If it's okay for us to be here, doing this, then why are you so scared somebody is going to find out?*

By the time he was headed back up the steps with a relieved smile on his face, I was on my way down.

"It was just somebody turning around," he said.

"Good," I said.

He looked at my purse over my shoulder. "You're ready to go, I guess."

"Yes," I said.

He gave me one long look. Even as I watched, his green-gold eyes went cold.

We went to a movie. Through the whole thing, let's just say he was a lot further away than an African safari. I didn't sit close to him in the car, and he didn't even mention it. When he took me home, he kissed me, coolly, on the cheek.

I opened my mouth, just to say good night, but he put his finger to my lips.

"I don't want to talk about it," he said. "I just thought you were together enough to handle this, that's all." Then he walked back toward his car.

CHAPTER SIXTEEN

I COULD HEAR THE TELEVISION IN THE LIVING ROOM AS I stood on the porch, watching Jason's car disappear and wondering what had just happened.

On the surface, it was obvious. I had been dumped.

Part of me felt relieved, and I knew why in about two seconds. That's how long it took to ask myself, *What would have happened if that car hadn't turned around in the driveway?* I didn't know how to fight him off. I didn't know how to argue the way he did.

It hit me like a slap. How could I? I had never been allowed to argue.

I leaned against the front door, still hearing the TV droning on. The last thing I wanted to do was go inside and face my parents with my feelings smeared across my face. Relief was only one of them—a very small one.

Try "ashamed" for another one. After all, I liked being in Jason's arms, kissing him back. Nobody had warned me it was going to feel that good. Was I just as guilty as he was?

And try "humiliated" for an even bigger feeling. "I thought you were together enough to handle this," Jason had said.

Now where in the world would he have gotten that idea? I felt about as together as a puzzle still in the box. One minute I was so perfect I was practically his wife, and the next I was so immature and childish I wasn't even worth speaking to.

That's where the humiliation came in. Because the only difference between one minute and the next was that in one he thought I was going to have sex with him, and in the next, he knew I wasn't.

Behind me, the door opened, leaving me leaning against only the screen. The living room was quiet now, and I turned to see Papa silhouetted in the doorway.

"You coming in?" he said.

"Yeah," I said.

I opened the screen door, and he looked curiously out into the street.

"Where is he?" he said.

"He left."

I stepped inside the room, and the light from the lamp on the end table hit my face. It hit Papa's, too. His eyes were red and puffy.

"Are you all right, Papa?" I said.

But he was looking hard at my face. "Are *you*?" he said.

Then, because I could never lie to my father, I started to cry. He pulled me against his chest, and I could feel his brick-hard hand tentatively touching my hair.

"Mi niña buena," he said.

I didn't feel like a good girl. I felt like a stupid one.

When I was finished crying, neither one of us said anything. I just went off to bed. Papa turned off the light in the living room, and I think he sat down in the dark.

For some reason, the first thing I thought about when I opened my eyes the next morning was that it was prom day. It had never entered my mind to go until Jason had mentioned it. *Next year,* he had said. Huh. Now there wasn't even going to be a next week.

I tried to think about Norie preparing to go, and Wyatt coming to the door with a corsage and fumbling all around trying to pin it on her. I could see it all too plainly, and I didn't want to.

The only thing I could think to do was try to write. I pulled out my notebook while Luisa was still curled up asleep and Sylvia was bathing nearby. I scratched down whatever came into my head. There were haiku—plenty of them.

> It's still too early
> for the wind to blow so hard,
> but it does.

Crows are waking up
making obnoxious crying
in the empty air.

You are like my wife
he said as he pushed me down
like a toy he owned.

"You're writing noisy," said a sleepy little voice.

I looked over at the tousle of curls that was coming up from under the blankets on Luisa's bed.

"What?" I said.

"You're writing noisy. I can hear your pencil scratching."

I looked down at my notebook. The words were not so much written on the page as they were carved into it. Engraved at the end of my angry pen.

"I'm sorry," I said. "It's too early. Go back to sleep."

The room was still gray, and she did. Apparently it wasn't too early for somebody to call, though, because I heard the phone ring in the kitchen. Even Anthony wouldn't answer it at this hour.

"Hello?" I said breathlessly when I got to it.

"Hi."

It was Jason. Sounding brittle.

"Hi," I said.

A strange, unusual silence fell, as if he were actually waiting for *me* to say something. I didn't.

"Um, I think we should get together to talk," he said.

I bit back a "You do?"

"Tonight?" he said.

I still didn't answer.

"Look, I know taking you to my place was a bad idea. We'll go out somewhere. We'll talk, okay?"

"Talk," I said.

"Well, we can't just leave it like this. I mean, I can't. Can you?"

"I guess not," I said.

Another silence followed. He snapped into it with his next question. "Do you want to work this out or don't you?"

"Do *you*?" I said.

"I wouldn't have called you if I didn't. This is important to me, Marissa."

"Okay," I said. The edge in his voice was cutting at me. Maybe I owed him that much. Maybe I was being childish by wanting to just close back in under my protective skin.

"What time?" I said.

"Seven," he said.

When he hung up, I must have stood there for a good minute before I realized my hand was still on the receiver on its hook. When I pulled it away, my palm was clammy.

One thought was in my head: I didn't know what to do next. I needed somebody to help me.

Names ran through my head. Veronica. Shannon. Abuelo.

I looked longingly at the door to his room, and something overwhelming sank over me. Not sadness. Fear.

Okay, call somebody. I clawed around in my brain as I went back to my room.

Ms. Race.

That stung. She obviously had her own stuff going.

Francesca, Roz, Daniela...

Daniela and I did have more in common now. Right. And she knew about as much as I did about how to handle it.

I thought of Tobey. But she was Jason's friend, too. I felt as if I would be betraying him or something.

Maybe Norie? She always made good sense. She had a boyfriend; she had experience.

I pawed around on my desk for my list of Flagpole Girls' phone numbers, but even as I did, I knew Norie wasn't the right person. She would just say, "Marissa, do this," and that wasn't what I needed. I at least knew that much.

Besides, I couldn't find the list. I had been adding to this big mess on the desktop, especially during that upside-down week, but I never had managed to clean up any of it. There was still the True Love Waits stuff, and a big brown envelope I hadn't even opened. It was what Brianna had given me the night Abuelo died.

She probably thinks I'm real nice, I thought as I undid the clasp. *I haven't even mentioned it to her.*

The truth was, with all that had been going on, I had forgotten about it. I felt like I always did about three days after Christmas when Mama asked me if I had written my thank-you notes yet. But the guilt stopped when I pulled a black sheet of paper out of the envelope. On it was a simple drawing, done in blue lines that flowed across the black surface. A girl was on her knees, curved over backward so that she formed a perfect circle with her head over her feet behind her. The girl didn't even have a face, but somehow I knew it was me. Where her body almost touched itself at her head and heels, was something gold. It was small, but it stood out in bright contrast to the quiet black and blue. I had to look closely to see that it was a tiny, gold cross with a long, curved top. The cross was drawn so that when I really inspected it, I discovered it was also an *A* with the crossbar not quite completed. Like this:

I sank onto my bed with the drawing and gazed at it for I don't know how long. I was lost in it, I think. I couldn't even tell you in words what it told me. I was just with it, and it was telling me about itself.

That's me, I thought. *I'm praying. I'm reaching. I'm reaching for Abuelo, and he's there.*

When I finally put down the drawing, I knew whom I wanted to call.

Brianna still looked pretty sleepy-eyed when I met her at the park, and she was clutching a steaming mug of something with both hands. She sat cross-legged on a picnic table, a long sweater pulled down around her knees.

"You don't drink coffee, do you, girl?" she said.

I shook my head.

"I'll bring some from the apartment if you want. You look like you need something."

"I think I just need some advice," I said.

She shook her head. "I don't give advice. You want me to help you work something through, I can do that. But this sister doesn't give advice."

"That's what I mean," I said. I was feeling better already. I shed my second skin, climbed up beside her, and poured out my story, beginning to end.

She put in the punctuation—nods, grunts, and rolling eyes at all the right places. She didn't say much until I was through.

When she did start to talk, she said every word as if she were measuring it out. "Okay, now first of all, we're not going to talk about sex just yet, all right?"

"But that's what this is about!" I said. "I *want* to talk about it."

"We will. But not yet. 'Cause that *isn't* what this is about."

"It isn't?"

"No. Now let me ask you something."

"Okay."

"All us Girls, we're your friends, right?"

"You're my best friends."

"All right. Would you put up with the same stuff from any of us that Jason dishes out to you?"

"What stuff?" I said.

"You just told me what stuff—and I've been watching it the whole time. Now if you don't want to hear the truth, just stop me right now."

"No," I said. My voice was small, but I was sure.

"Number one," Brianna said, stretching out a long finger. "He never wants to do any of the things you like to do, does he?"

I slowly shook my head. "No, but then, that isn't really fair to him. I haven't even mentioned most of the things I like to do."

"Has he ever asked?"

I considered that. "I guess not."

"He shouldn't even have to," Brianna went on. "Does he see the things in you that you want him to see?"

"Like what?"

"Does he know what a fine Christian you are?"

"I'm not as fine a one as he is," I said.

Brianna put up both hands. "Don't take me there, girl. Let's just move on. Does he admire how responsible you are? How you take care of all those kids running around your house while your mama works? How you always have paper and pencil in your purse, for Pete's sake?"

"I don't know."

"Does he give a hang what a great cook you are?"

"Yes. I cook for him all the time."

"Steak and french fries? Uh-huh. I bet he never put one of your fajitas into his mouth."

"No."

"Does he think you're a wonderful poet?"

"I don't know."

"Why don't you know?"

"Because he hasn't said. Not in so many words."

"How many words has he said about your poetry?"

I looked back at the day of Veronica's wedding. "He thinks it's nice," I said.

She just looked at me. One eyebrow went up about a quarter of an inch. "Now, I'm going to go on," she said. "And this could hurt so you have the right to stop me anytime."

"Okay," I said.

"You remember my saying to you one day, 'Girl, when are you going to start believing in yourself?'"

I nodded.

"I don't think being with Jason has brought you any closer to doing that. If anything, he's taken you further away."

"Are you sure?" I said. "I mean, I thought I was more confident because I had a boyfriend."

Brianna snapped her fingers over her head. "Temporary fix, girl. Let's get to something permanent. Do you still feel like people who come from homes where everybody goes to church together are better Christians than you are?"

I felt myself sitting straight up. "How did you know that?"

"You don't think I felt like that around Tobey and Shannon at first?"

"No!"

"Guess again, girl. Do you talk to Jason about your poetry?"

"Not that much."

"Why?"

"Because I think he thinks it's kind of…childish."

"Uh-huh. And why was he upset when your daddy ran him off from the wedding?"

"Because he pushed me too much."

Brianna brought her face close to mine. "You really believe that? What did he say?"

"He said he was sorry that…" I stopped. Brianna waited.

"He said he was sorry Papa caught us," I said.

"Not he was sorry he did it."

"No."

Dawn was coming up in my head. Brianna could see it. Her eyes were on fire.

"You see what I'm sayin', girl?" she said. "He has you thinking that your mama and daddy are too strict and old-fashioned and that your talents are like some little girl's and that you just aren't as mature and Christian as he is, and he's going to show you the way." She did the E.T. thing with her neck. "He's going to show you the way, all right, girl. Right into his bed!"

"I can't believe he really planned it that way from the beginning!" I said. "You heard him at the True Love Waits rally."

"I heard him. I believed him. I still believe him. But he took so much charge over you, I think he's about talked himself into thinking this is right."

I heard that hanging in the air. I closed my eyes for a second and listened to it again.

"But it isn't," I said. "I don't even want to do it."

"Well, at least you have that going for you."

I cocked my head at her.

"Make no mistake about it, girl," she said. "If you really love somebody—the way I love Ira—it's real hard not to get into bed with him, because you want to do it. Girl, sometimes it's hard even if you *don't* love him! Sex was designed to feel good, or nobody would ever do it, and then no babies would be born. Thing is, I'm glad you don't think you're in love with this boy because he doesn't respect you for who you really are. I watched him the day he came over to King and had lunch with you. He resented every one of us for being important to you, and the same the night your granddaddy died. There you are grieving, and he wants to show us all that he is the only one who can take care of you. I should have said more to you then, but since you asked, I'm sayin' it to you now."

She did the neck thing one more time, and I laughed. I laughed so hard that pretty soon I was sobbing, my face on her knee, with her hand running across my hair.

"I know, girl. I know you're hurtin'."

"I'm disappointed," I said through my tears.

"You better not be disappointed in yourself, or we aren't done talkin'," she said.

I pulled my head up and smeared my face with the back of my hand. "I *am* talking about me."

"That's the whole root to this problem then," Brianna said. "Forget about Jason. He has his own stuff to work out. The boy thinks he's the dad-gum Newsboys or somebody, and he's going to have to come down a notch or two. But it's you I'm worried about."

"Why?"

"Because you have to believe in yourself. Where do you get off *not* believing in yourself, when God Himself does?"

"You feel that?" I said. "That God believes in you?"

"Girl, that is the reason I haven't slept with Ira. It doesn't have anything to do with that other stuff you were talking about—getting pregnant or whatever. It has to do with God saying, 'If you do this, Brianna, girl, no matter how much you want it and how much you love him, you are going to get hurt. That's why I'm tellin' you, it's wrong. I don't want you gettin' hurt. You have to take My word for it.'"

"At the rally, it sounded like they were just saying, 'Don't do it.'"

"You weren't even half-listening," Brianna said dryly. "That's where this whole thing started. You were so focused on that boy, you couldn't even hear God. And you know what?"

I shook my head.

"I think that's exactly the way Jason wanted it."

"No way!"

"Not consciously. But deep down, he thought he was saving you. And girl, you know only one person can save you."

I folded my arms across my knees and put down my head. "I just don't even know where to start."

"With yourself."

"But how?"

"Do what my mama has taught me to do—and she doesn't take any credit for it. She learned it when she was seeing a counselor. Anyway, she says you have to do two things. One, every time somebody pays you a compliment, you have to accept it like God told that person to say it to you. You're not going to throw back something in God's face, are you?"

I lifted my head and said, "No."

"And two, you have to give at least one compliment a day to another person and at least one to yourself. My mama says words heal, and she's right. I know she is."

"Okay," I said.

"I'm going to test you now," she said. "Girl, you are about the most unselfish person I have ever known."

I looked down at my knees. "I'm not really," I said. "You haven't seen me with my brothers and sisters—"

She grabbed hold of my arm. "Did you just hear yourself?"

I stopped. Then I nodded.

"You've always been a little bit like that, but nothing like since you started going out with that boy. I'm not saying it's all his fault, but he sure has had something to do with it. You have to admit that."

I felt that feeling in my tailbone again, and it wasn't about Brianna.

"I guess so," I said. "No, I know so."

"And that doesn't make you mad?" she said.

I nodded.

"Then why don't you just come out and say it?" Brianna said. "Yell at the boy like he was standing right here!"

I giggled. She didn't.

"Okay," I said. "When he looked at my poem that I wrote for Veronica…"

"Uh-huh."

"He handed it back to me like, 'How cute.'"

"Did that make you mad?"

"A little."

"A lot!"

"Okay, a lot. I worked hard on that. I wrote it from my heart. Even Veronica said that."

"Then where does that boy get off making you feel as if you're some kind of kindergarten kid?"

"And you know what? He hurt Shannon's feelings that night when you were all over there—and after the funeral, too. And you should have seen him 'performing' when we went up to Mount Rose. It was like I wasn't even there!"

"Show-off."

"Brianna, he even had…a condom…last night. He was all ready."

"I think we just made a quantum leap, girl," she said. Anger was smoldering in her eyes the way I knew it was burning in mine.

"So what are you going to do tonight?" she said. "You still going to see him?"

"Ooh."

"Yeah."

"I think I have to."

"You don't 'have' to do anything."

"I want to. I want to, like, tell him some of this stuff. Just to close it out. I don't want to leave it hanging."

"You want me to go with you? I have nothing to do after I go with Ira to physical therapy at three."

I shook my head. "No, I'll be all right."

"He isn't going to be happy about this."

"I know, but he's not a bad person, Brianna. He isn't going to do anything to hurt me."

"I think he's already done plenty of that," Brianna said, "and you didn't even know it."

"I'll be okay," I said.

Then we prayed together, and I spent the rest of the afternoon doing the same thing, and writing poetry and thinking. I kept running my conversation with Brianna over and over in my head, and one thing stuck with me more than anything. Her mama had said to think of every compliment as being inspired by God. I was thinking everything Brianna had said had come right from Him. Maybe that was the way God spoke to me.

I was a little sad when I started to dress to go out with Jason, and I remembered the big deal we had all made out of my getting ready for my first date with him. I just put on some jeans and a red pullover top for this outing. It was probably going to be short anyway.

"Aren't you going to put on lipstick to go out with Jason?" Luisa said to me as I was brushing my hair.

I was saved from having to answer by Anthony yelling from the kitchen that the phone was for me. Half hoping it was Jason calling to cancel and half hoping it wasn't, I took the receiver from Anthony and said, "Hello?"

The voice on the other end was barely audible.

"Marissa?" the girl said.

"Shannon?" I said.

"I need help," she said.

Then I heard a bunch of choking sounds.

"What's wrong?" I said. "Shannon, where are you?"

"I'm at a pay phone down by the college," she said. "I walked from Rancho San Rafael. Could you meet me?"

"Of course," I said. "Where?"

"The gate at Rancho."

"Okay, just go there," I said. "I'll be there in fifteen minutes, I promise."

She was still sobbing when I hung up. Fingers shaking, I dialed Jason's number. His mother answered.

"Hi, Marissa!" she said. It was a cinch she didn't know anything about our problems. "Jason just went out to do a little errand for me. He said he would be back in time to leave to pick you up at seven."

"Please tell him something came up," I said. "It's going to have to be later. Would you tell him I'll call him in maybe an hour or two? It's important—really."

"Everything all right at home?" she said.

"Yes, fine. It's something else." I glanced anxiously at the kitchen clock. "Would you please tell him?"

"You bet I will," she said.

I was out the door, Jason forgotten, before she even hung up on her end, I'm sure. I ran all the way to Rancho San Rafael, which was a good half-mile from my house. I was gasping when I reached the gate, but I could still breathe a major sigh of relief. Shannon was standing there.

She looked horrible, mind you, but she was there. She was leaning against a pole, hugging herself so that her hands almost met behind her. She was still crying, but all the tears were gone. There is nothing more empty than the sound of dry crying.

"Hey," I said.

She turned her face to me, and it cracked like the shell of an egg. The inside of Shannon came running out.

"Oh, Marissa," she said, "my whole family is falling apart. I can't stand it anymore!"

I nodded.

"Can we talk?" she said.

"As long as you want," I said.

Then I put my arm around her, and we walked.

CHAPTER
SEVENTEEN

SHANNON AND I WALKED THROUGH THE GARDENS, across every bridge, and along every path three times. It was almost dark before she wound down.

The Christian boarding school, Shannon told me, wasn't going to let her sister come back next year. Caitlin was out of there. "Incorrigible," they had called her. She needed more intense counseling than they could give her.

"She's already had so much counseling my parents had to take out a second mortgage on our house," she said. "Colleen, my older sister, might not get to go back to William and Mary next year unless she finds a student loan."

"So, no counseling," I said.

"Oh, they'll get her some," Shannon said. "They have to. The judge gave a court order."

"Judge?" I said. I was trying not to sound too shocked, but it was hard.

"When they picked her up after she ran away," Shannon said. "The judge said if my parents got her counseling, he wouldn't put her in Wittenberg."

"Cheyenne used to talk about Wittenberg."

"It's an awful place," Shannon threw back her head. "But I've even thought maybe they ought to let her go there. Maybe it would shake some sense into her." She sagged. "Then I listen to Cheyenne, and I feel awful about myself. I must be the worst sister on the planet."

"You're not."

"The situation is just so out of control. My parents don't know what they're going to do with Caitlin all summer. Colleen says she's not coming home from Virginia. She's going to try to find a job there to help pay for her books and stuff. But I know she's staying away because she doesn't want to come back to all the yelling and screaming and crying."

Shannon covered her ears with her hands, as if she were hearing it right now. "The doctor told my mother she should take an antidepressant before *she* falls apart. But she won't do it because she says if she just had enough faith she wouldn't need that stuff. My father isn't saying it, but I know he's thinking they can't afford the medication. Those pills cost sixty dollars a month!"

"I feel so bad for you," I said. It sounded lame, but what else could I say? My measly little problems were like one of Reney's tantrums next to all this.

"I just feel like I'm going to explode, Marissa," Shannon said. "I had to leave the house, but I can't be alone, you know?"

"No, you shouldn't be," I said. "Do you want to come to my house and spend the night?"

Her face lit up for the first time since I couldn't remember when.

"Could I do that?" she said.

"If you can stand my brothers."

"Are you sure it's okay, with your grandfather just passing on and everything?"

"Everybody's trying to get back to normal," I said. "Please come. Luisa can sleep in Reney and Gabriela's room. They will squawk, but then, when don't they?"

"Okay," she said.

While we were making all the arrangements and going back and forth from her house to mine with pajamas and toothbrush, I took a minute to call Jason. I don't know what I was expecting from him, but what I got wasn't it.

"Can we talk tomorrow?" I said to him. "I can't leave Shannon."

"Oh, so that was the 'emergency,'" he said.

"I never said it was an emergency!" I glanced over my shoulder to make sure Shannon was out of earshot.

"You go ahead and get involved then," Jason said. "But don't say I didn't warn you."

"Warn me about what?" I whispered. "You're the one who always says you like to help people. So do I."

"What are you going to do for Sharon?" he said.

"Shannon," I said through my teeth.

"Whatever. Skinny Henry."

"No, it's *Shannon*."

"Okay. What are you going to do for her?"

"Listen. Pray with her."

"Are you going to tell her what to do about her anorexia? Do you know anything about it?"

"We haven't even talked about that," I said. "I don't know."

A funky sound came from his end of the line, almost like a hiss. Whatever it was, it wasn't a happy sound. It wasn't a sound that said, "You go, girl. Do what you have to do." It sounded more like "Okay, be childish. I'll fix it later."

And it made me mad.

"Call me if you want to talk tomorrow," I said. "I have to go."

"Well, wait a minute—"

"No. I have to go. Bye."

Then I hung up.

I thought about him off and on during the evening. I couldn't help it. I half expected him to show up on our doorstep and demand I work this out. It occurred to me that Jason really liked to "work things out."

But mostly I concentrated on Shannon. We had a great talk that night while we were making cookies in my kitchen. She said baking was therapeutic for her. Eating evidently wasn't, because she didn't even taste the dough, but I didn't mention it. I just let her steer the conversation where she wanted it to go.

While we were dumping in chocolate chips and chopping nuts, we rediscovered how much alike we were. How we both hated crowds and being in front of people, and how we loved just having a few friends we could really depend on and share things with. It was funny, even though we talked about what we might want to do when we were out of school and what kind of lifestyles we wanted to have, we never once mentioned boys.

I kept away from the subject of anorexia, too. I was really tempted when we were getting ready for bed. As Shannon pulled her nightshirt over her head, I could see her ribs sticking out. It reminded me of pictures I'd seen of prisoners in German concentration camps.

"You want a snack before we go to bed?" I said.

She shook her head without even thinking about it.

"Are you too upset to eat?" I said.

"Yeah. But I'm better. You've really helped me a lot."

"You helped me, too," I said. "When Abuelo died, I loved it that you came and just sat there next to me and didn't try to say something to make me feel better."

"Did that help, really?" she said. "I kind of thought—"

"Take the compliment," I said suddenly.

"What?" she said.

"Just pretend it's coming through me from God," I said. "You were the most comforting person there."

"Oh," she said.

Brianna would be proud of me, I thought. *Now, what else am I supposed to do?*

I couldn't think of it. I fell asleep coming up with a poem for Shannon. I woke up at 5:00 A.M. with it all formed in my head. I went to the window sill where Sylvia gave a disgruntled mew and let me join her in the glow from the streetlight. I tried not to "write noisy."

> Fire in her pale eyes
> but her body is so frail
> it won't hold the flame.

I tucked it into Shannon's overnight bag and went back to bed. I drifted off wondering if God had put the poem there while I was sleeping. It was one of those last thoughts that really doesn't make sense, but then again, it does.

I went to Shannon's church with her the next day, and during the service I couldn't help watching her parents. Her mother, delicate and wispy like Shannon, and her father, a robust chunk of a man with thick wavy hair, acted as if their world were perfectly fine. If Shannon hadn't shared all that with me, I would never have known it was falling apart.

When I arrived back home, Anthony told me, with a mouthful

of tortilla and cheese, that Jason had just called for me.

"Call him," he said.

"Is that what he said?"

"You want an exact quote? He said, 'Have her call me.'"

"I bet he said, '*Please* have her call me,'" Reney said.

"What do you know?" Anthony said to her. "He didn't say please. He didn't even say good-bye." Anthony wiggled his eyebrows at me. "What did you do to tick him off?"

"Breathed," Eddie said.

They were starting to remind me of the *mocosos*. They pushed my buttons.

But I took a deep breath, ignored them all, and went for the phone. I took it into Abuelo's room to get away from their trespassing eyes.

Jason answered on the first ring.

"Hi," I said.

"We have to talk," he said.

"So, let's talk," I said.

"I'll come pick you up."

I didn't say anything.

"I'll come pick you up," he said.

"No," I said. "Why don't we just talk now?"

"This isn't the kind of thing you discuss on the phone."

"What kind of thing?" I said.

"Do you do that on purpose?" he said.

"What?"

"Act dumb?"

I was stunned. Too stunned to even feel a sting.

"I didn't mean it like that," he said. "It's just sometimes, it's like I have to spell everything out for you."

"Maybe I just don't know what you're talking about," I said.

He gave a big sigh, as if he were forcing himself to be patient. "I'm talking about Friday night when we started to make love."

"When *you* started to make love," I said.

"Are you saying you didn't want to?"

I clenched my hands. "Yeah," I said. "That's what I'm saying."

"I told you you didn't have to be embarrassed."

"That isn't why."

"Okay, what were your other reasons? Oh, you would have to be in love with the guy." He sounded a little stunned himself. "Are you saying you aren't in love with me?"

"Yeah," I said in my tiny voice. "That's what I'm saying."

"Who told you that?" he said.

"What?" I said.

"Who told you you weren't in love with me?"

"What makes you think somebody—"

"Because I've seen love in your eyes, Rissa. And I can feel it when you kiss me. It isn't just me kissing you, you know. You kiss me back. You hug me back—"

"That doesn't mean—"

"Really? I don't think you even know what it means."

"What, love?"

"Yeah. Have you ever been in love before?"

"Have you?"

"I asked you."

My head was spinning. I noticed for the second time in a few days that I was holding the phone so hard my hand was sweating. But I couldn't hang up. Because Jason's words when he was angry were as powerful as Jason's words when he was godly. I just switched hands and wiped my palm on my jeans.

"Are you still there?" he said.

"Yes."

"We have to talk about this face-to-face, and we have to do it soon."

"I just don't—"

"We *do*. See if you can convince your father to let you out some night this week. I'm going now. Pray about this, Marissa. It's important."

He hung up. And then I slammed down the phone.

"Save the pieces," Anthony said as I marched through the kitchen on my way to my bedroom.

"Leave me alone," I said.

"Ooh!" Eddie said. "Trouble in paradise."

"What are you talking about?" Gabriela said.

I slammed my bedroom door, ripped a piece of paper out of my notebook, and started "engraving."

Girls,

   I need to meet with you all at lunch today if
you can. It isn't a really big thing like Tobey's or
Norie's. Anyway, I need to talk to you all. I just
need some support for what I have to do.

Marissa

I copied it over five times, and the next morning I stuck one
in everybody's locker. Then I chewed on pencils all morning and
waited for lunch.

They were there in full force, all five girls and Ms. Race.

"We didn't know if you wanted boys," Tobey said, "so we didn't
tell them."

"She doesn't want boys, trust me," Brianna said. "Spill it, girl."

I did. As I talked, the circle around me grew smaller and
smaller, until by the time I was through, Shannon was holding
one hand and Tobey was holding the other.

"You never said a word about this the other night," Shannon
murmured to me.

"It was your turn," I said.

"Now it's yours," Norie said. "How can we help?"

"I think I should break up with him," I said. "But I'm scared."

"You think he's going to hit you or something?" Cheyenne
said.

I shook my head. "No, but he can turn everything I say
around. I just want to get out, and I can't seem to say the right
things."

Tobey was nibbling at her nail. "I don't want to be pushy or
anything, but do you want, like, a Plan of Action?"

"That's exactly what I want," I said. "Is that lame for this? I
mean—"

"Negative," Norie said. "This is, like, so not lame I can't even
stand it."

Her voice was adamant, even for Norie.

"Do I detect some baggage in there, Norie?" Ms. Race said.

It was the first time she had spoken, but she seemed a little bit
more with us today.

"Just a little," Norie said. "Wyatt and I had to work through something kind of like this. I mean, we started to talk about it before it could happen. We came up with this, like, set of guidelines."

"I'm fascinated," Ms. Race said. "You'll have to tell us sometime."

"Right. Let's focus on Marissa," Norie said. "I'm in. I'll do whatever you want. I hope you don't mind my saying this, but lately I haven't been that crazy about Jason anyway. And I got the feeling he wasn't wild about me either."

I didn't answer, but I could feel my cheeks turning pink.

"You know what?" Tobey said. She was looking at the toes of her Nikes. "When we see one of us getting hurt, only that person doesn't realize it, we ought to say something. 'Cause I'm guilty too. We're close enough now we can do that, right?"

"Sure," Cheyenne said. "If somebody goes too far, I'll just tell them to back off."

"I believe that," Norie said.

Heads, guilty heads, nodded around the circle. I nodded with them.

"All right," Tobey said. "So, moving on. Shannon, would you take notes?"

Shannon willingly pulled out some paper and a pen, and we all hunkered down over it.

It was slow going.

"This one's hard," Tobey said about halfway through.

"Yeah, it's not like setting up bodyguards and stuff," Cheyenne said.

"I suggest we stop to pray," Ms. Race said.

We nodded, and we let her start.

"Lord," she said, "does it amaze You as much as it amazes me how eager we are to complicate our lives?"

We all giggled, and I could feel myself relaxing.

I felt even better when we finally had a Plan of Action in place. It seemed weird, having five of my friends help me break up with a guy. But, hey, they had helped me with my first date with him, why not get me through my last?

I was feeling so much better I was even able to go up to Ms. Race during a lull in fifth period and say, "Are you all right?"

She pulled a stack of files off the chair by her desk and patted it for me to sit down. "Did it show?" she said.

I nodded.

"I was going through some things of my own," she said.

"Can we help?"

She looked a little surprised.

"You know what?" she said. "I think you already have, and none of you even knew it. But right now, I'm concerned about you."

"I think the Plan is going to work—"

"No, I'm thinking about your self-esteem. Well, your God-esteem, I would rather call it."

"I'm okay, really," I said.

"Then will you do something for me?"

"Sure."

"Take this piece of paper and write a letter to yourself. Compliment yourself on everything you like about you or the things you think God likes about you. Then give it to me, and I'm going to send it to you."

I giggled. "You're going to send me a letter I wrote to myself?"

"You'll love it. Try it."

"Now?"

"Sure. There's nothing big going on in here. Go ahead."

Feeling more than a little ridiculous, I went over to my corner and sat down with the paper she gave me. I poised my pen over it, waited for the words to flow like they usually did, and then stared at the wall.

For five minutes.

Then I felt the first tear splash down on my arm.

"You okay, sweetie?" Ms. Race said at my elbow.

I shook my head.

"What's wrong?" She squatted down beside me.

"I can't think of anything to write," I said. "Not one single thing."

I expected her to list things for me in the impatient tone I knew I probably deserved. Instead, she put her hand on my arm and brushed away the tear.

"I bet you didn't even know how torn down you were," she said. "I know exactly how you feel."

I couldn't imagine that she did.

"You know the guy who sent me the flowers awhile back? Curtis?"

I nodded.

"I had to break off our relationship this weekend. I just realized one day last week how codependent he was, and I couldn't do it anymore. He was bringing me down, and that isn't what relationships are supposed to do. They're supposed to bring out the best in us." She rubbed my arm. "But that doesn't mean it isn't hard. And the hardest part is getting ourselves back."

"I don't think I even knew I had a self," I said.

"Oh, sweetie," Ms. Race said. "Maybe it's about time you wrote a poem for *you*, huh?"

I didn't do it, not right then. But I did write more poetry that night, the last two for my collection. The assignment was due the next day, and I had it all done except for the illustrations. I had no clue what I was going to do about those, and I was searching my disaster of a desk for some plain paper, when I came across Brianna's drawing again. I tacked it up on my wall, next to the poster Norie had made for me for Christmas and Brianna's painting *Voices of Violence* Norie's mother had bought for me.

I don't have Brianna's art talent, I thought. *I don't have Norie's vocabulary.*

I looked down at the sheaf of poems in my hand. They seemed to shout back at me in protest, "What are we, chopped liver?"

I picked up my pen and, looking at Brianna's drawing, I made a circle on a piece of paper. Something could come out of that. I could do this. It wouldn't be art like Brianna's, but I was the only one who knew the second layer of my poems.

The Girls prayed with me Tuesday. I told them maybe it was all for nothing, that Jason maybe wasn't going to call me again. They didn't look convinced, and they were right. He called that night.

"We are too good together to break up like this," he said. "We have to talk."

"Okay," I said.

I think it surprised him. It took him a second to say, "When?"

"Friday."

"You didn't talk to your father, did you? I'd rather do it to-morrow."

"I can't go out on weeknights, period," I said. I didn't add that the Girls and I had decided I should hold off until Friday.

"No wonder," he said, as if he were talking to himself.

"What?" I said.

"I was just saying no wonder you're still so…young. Your parents put all these limits on you."

"They're doing what they think is right," I said. It came out of nowhere, a pretty solid nowhere. And it felt more grown-up than kissing Jason ever had.

"Yeah, but good grief, you can't even come out on a Wednesday night for an hour?"

"If that's the way my father wants it, then that's the way it is," I said.

"Hey, I'm not saying you should argue with him. You're honoring your 'rents. That's what we're supposed to do."

"I would argue with him—no, I would *discuss* it with him, if I thought I needed to. I've done that before."

"Like when?"

"What time Friday?" I said.

My heart was pounding, but I was following the Plan. "Don't let him get you off the subject," the Girls had advised me. "When you start to feel confused, just get back on the track."

"Seven o'clock," he said stiffly.

I stayed up late that night finishing my poetry collection. Before I tucked it into my backpack, I wrote one more thing, on a piece of notepaper.

"Dear Mrs. Abbey," it said. "Please don't read this out loud to the class. Thank you, Marissa."

It felt just about as good as any of the poetry in the notebook did. And nobody had told me to do that. I just needed to.

The next three days, the Girls prayed with me every lunch. Once I whispered to Shannon before we started, "Don't you want prayer too? You have it a lot harder than I do right now." But she shook her head firmly, and I didn't push it. I also tried to share my chips with her, but she only nibbled at one and pressed it into a napkin when she thought I wasn't looking.

I prayed a lot on my own, too, and when I did, something really different started to happen. Every time I finished reading *The Message* and saying my prayers, I just wanted to write more haiku. They popped out of me like little kernels of popcorn bursting to life.

> I'm always surprised
> at just how big the ears are
> on the fragile deer.

> A rabbit dashes
> through the glare of our headlights
> on his way somewhere.

> Some weeds really do
> look wicked at their edges
> when you lean to see.

I was reading them over on Thursday night when I realized they all had that second layer of meaning, and I hadn't even known it when I had written them.

Is that God? I thought. *Is this how He is talking to me? How He is telling me…Telling me what?*

That everybody has weaknesses, just like me—and strengths, too. That I can't just dash around in somebody else's headlights, but I need to go my own way. That you have to look close at people before you know who they really are.

It couldn't be God yet, I decided. Jason had said it took a long time…

I snapped straight up on my bed. Jason said. Jason said.

What about what Marissa said?

Like it mattered.

But Ms. Race had said it did matter.

I looked back down at my notebook and slowly turned to a blank page.

Write a letter to yourself…Maybe it's time you wrote a poem for you…

So I did. And the next morning, I gave it to Ms. Race to mail to me. I also gave her one I had written for her.

    Cheekbones shimmering
    skin still the color of God
    after her prayers

When she finished reading it, her eyes were shimmering too.

Funny how somebody else's grateful tears can make you feel strong. I was ready for Jason. I was ready to get out of this thing and go on. I was strong.

Until I reached English class and saw all the poetry notebooks on display on the table—and the one Patrick was holding in his hand.

"Fallen leaves don't move," he was reading in a high-pitched falsetto voice, "for the periwinkle blues / poking through sunward."

He looked up, leering out of his freckled lips, and his eyes met mine as I stood in the doorway. "Hey, Marissa," he called out, "what does that mean?"

CHAPTER EIGHTEEN

AT FIRST I HAD THIS EERIE SENSE I WAS IN THE WRONG room. That couldn't be my poetry notebook Patrick was reading out of and then tossing over Heidi's head to Lana, who snatched it up and picked up where Patrick had left off, reading in her loud voice, flat as her face.

This had to be the wrong place. Mrs. Abbey was nowhere to be seen to shout them down. No bell chased the rest of the class to the desks. Just a scene that went on and on with nobody to stop it.

Nobody but me.

I won't lie. My second skin wanted to come out bad. It wanted to pull me right out of the room. But I couldn't run this time. And I couldn't curl up in my seat and wait for Mrs. Abbey to finish blinking her eyes at some journalism student and come rescue me. And I couldn't let them throw my work around like a joke.

I crossed the room. Everything seemed to go into slow mo. Heidi had my notebook by then and was gaping at it with a crooked sneer on her lips.

"Listen to this!" she said.

But no one had a chance because I snatched it out of her hand.

"Thank you," I said.

Then I sat down in my seat, spread the notebook open on my desk, and smoothed out the wrinkled page.

After about an inch of silence, Patrick recovered and said, "Ooh, tough girl!"

Lana reached out to grab it again, and I looked up at her. Her big, hazel eyes met mine, and for a second I know I saw surprise in them. In the next second, she pulled her hand back, flattened her wide face into a hard smile, and said, "Be afraid. Be very afraid."

The bell finally rang, and Mrs. Abbey rushed in like a tardy student, blinking for all she was worth. People scrambled to their seats, and she looked up at the class. For a moment there was a hesitation. Did she see anything? Did she know what had just happened? Then everyone slid back into their eyes-at-half-mast apathy and took up buzzing at each other.

I yanked a piece of paper out of my backpack and grabbed a pen. I could feel my pulse in my throat as I started to write.

> Dear Mrs. Abbey,
>   I really wish you hadn't...

I stared up at the wall for some words. Mrs. Abbey flitted across my vision, searching for her grade book, trying to locate a pen, blinking her eyes, jerking her perm, and looking confused.

"What's she looking for?" Lana hissed to Patrick.

"Probably her mind," Patrick said.

"Nah, she'll never find that," Heidi said.

I set down my pen. Anything I wrote was liable to get lost in that mess. And I wanted Mrs. Abbey to know what she had opened me up for. I really wanted her to know.

She gave up the attempt to unearth her grade book and jerked her head toward the class. "Why don't you take a few minutes to look at each other's notebooks?" she said, motioning with her perm toward the display table.

Patrick snorted.

"We already did," Lana said.

"Good," Mrs. Abbey said. As she opened and closed desk drawers, about half the class shuffled over to the table. I waited until the *mocosos* had gotten up, then I pulled myself out of my desk with my poetry notebook plastered to my chest and went up to her.

"Can you give me just a minute, Marissa?" she said.

"Did you read the note I put in my poetry collection?" I said.

She stopped digging to look at me.

"I did," she said. "I won't read any of your work aloud, although I think you'll find—"

"It's already been read aloud," I said. "I didn't know you were going to let people read them at all."

"Beautiful poetry is meant to be read," she said. I had her full attention now. Even her eyes had slowed down.

"I just don't like being made fun of."

"By whom?" she said.

I shook my head. "It doesn't matter." I pulled my notebook away from my chest and handed it to her. "Could you just not put it out on the table?"

I guess I had underestimated Mrs. Abbey. She stopped blinking, and her hair seemed to settle with a sag. Taking me lightly by the arm, she nudged me out into the hall. When she closed the door behind her, her face was soft and sad.

"Did Patrick and the girls get ahold of this before I came in?" she said.

I nodded.

Her eyelids closed down over her eyes. "I can only imagine what they did with it. Do you want me to—"

"No," I said. "I just don't want my work out there where they can dis it."

"Marissa, I am so sorry."

"It's okay."

"It isn't okay! I wasn't even thinking...I have so much going on—too much." She sighed as if she were collecting her jumbled chaos of thoughts and squeezed my wrist. Her hand was clammy. "The point is, I wasn't sensitive to how much your work means to you, and I'm really sorry. It won't happen again."

I nodded.

"I hope they weren't too evil, those three."

"No," I said.

She looked as if she didn't believe that for a second and gave my wrist another little squeeze. "This is the wrong audience. I should have realized that. They just don't have the ears to hear it. But Marissa, your poetry should be shared. It's beautifully detailed."

"Thank you," I said.

"I'm serious. It touched my heart, and it would touch other people's." Her mouth twitched. "If they *had* hearts."

My mouth twitched too, and suddenly we were smiling at each other. She pressed my poetry collection back into my hands.

"This is a treasure," she said. "You hold on to it."

I nodded and started for the room. Before she opened the door, though, she said, "I'm impressed, by the way." She gave a soft sniff. "You got this away from them?"

"Yes," I said.

She sniffed again. "Then it must really mean something to you. Don't lose sight of that."

Once we were back in the room, she went back to blinking and resumed her archaeological dig for her grade book. But I had a new insight into Mrs. Abbey. I decided that at some point she would be a good subject for a poem.

But from then on, for the rest of the day, poetry was about the last thing on my mind. I had to, as Norie put it, "get psyched" for that night with Jason. It was a good thing I had a lot of help.

All five of the Girls were at my house by six. I had bribed Gabriela to do my kitchen cleanup so I would have time to let Brianna dress me. Shannon, Cheyenne, Norie, and Tobey sat on Luisa's and my beds, with Luisa firmly ensconced among them, watching it happen.

"This top," Brianna said, pulling a dark green, short-sleeved turtleneck out of my drawer.

"She'll be too hot in that," Cheyenne said.

"Yeah, but the point is," Norie said, "we don't want Jason to be hot, if you get my drift."

She didn't. Tobey had to explain it to her.

While I pulled the top over my head, Brianna produced a pair of her baggiest cargo pants out of her backpack.

"Now, she'll swim in those," Tobey said.

"That's the point," Cheyenne said proudly.

I had a twinge then, and as Brianna sat me down to do my hair, I took a deep breath. "Luisa, honey," I said, "could you sit by the window and tell us when Jason gets here?"

She nodded happily and ran out. I made sure the door was shut before I went on.

"You guys," I said, "did I give Jason the wrong idea by always dressing up for him, with the makeup and everything?"

After a chorus of protests, Brianna stopped them all with a hand in the air. "Did you ever once dress like a tramp, girl?"

"No."

"No low-cut blouses with your cleavage showing?"

"What cleavage?" I said.

"No little short shorts? No navel exposed?"

"No! My mother wouldn't let me out of the house like that. Not that I would want to anyway."

"All right then; there you have it," Norie said.

"Have what?" I asked.

"You have a right to look your best," Brianna said. "And if you aren't advertising something, then where does he get off thinking he can take it for free?"

"I am so confused," Cheyenne said.

But I wasn't. I exchanged looks with Brianna in the mirror, and I felt better.

When I was toned down enough to keep a *pack* of wolf-boys away, we went over the plan one more time.

"Diesel says it should work with a '56 Chevrolet," Cheyenne said to Shannon.

Brianna cocked an eyebrow at Shannon. "It would work with a Toyota," she said. "You need to gain some weight, girl."

"Not till after tonight," Tobey said.

"You have the cell phone?" Norie said. "You know my car phone number?"

I patted my purse and nodded.

"You set?" Tobey said.

I nodded but too slowly. They all jumped right on it.

"What's wrong?" Brianna said.

"Come on, Marissa," Norie said. "If you have any doubts at all, get them out now."

I looked at Tobey. "I just need to hear it one more time; just so I have it straight."

"Sure," Tobey said. She crossed her legs Indian-style on the bed. "True Love Waits isn't just about not having sex. A lot of kids who aren't Christians are still virgins."

"That's true," Norie said. "I did some research."

"Of course you did," Brianna said. She nodded Tobey on.

"It's about honoring Christ in your heart and your mind, not just your body. If you're concentrating on what He's saying you need to do with your life, if you're growing and all that, you'll realize sex doesn't fit in. It gets in the way. It's like a barrier between God and you." She scooped up her hair in her hands for a second. "It isn't about what you *aren't* doing; it's about what you *are* doing."

"What *are* you doing?" Cheyenne said. She was entranced.

"Living with a different kind of passion," Tobey said. "It's a whole lot freer to throw yourself into your real life than to throw yourself after some guy."

I drank that in for about the fifth time. Tobey had been coaching me all week.

"I didn't tell you this part," Tobey said to me. She glanced around at the group. "But I want to."

"Go for it," Norie said.

"You know how everybody was all concerned that I wasn't going to prom?"

We all nodded.

"I meant it when I said it was no big deal to me. I watched all these people spend tons of money and get themselves all worked up, and Monday after the prom, I think I talked to about two people who actually had a good time."

Norie raised her hand.

"And that was because you weren't having to perform in some way, you know what I'm saying? So much of that goes on in dating. I'm not saying people shouldn't date or they ought to abolish proms or anything." Tobey took a second to put it together. "It's just...it isn't for me right now. I like guys, I like to be around them, but my life is about something else. When I first got into True Love Waits, I thought it was about sexual purity, but it only, like, opened the door to all this other stuff. People think I'm nuts, but I could care less about having a boyfriend when there's so much else for me."

"Wow," Cheyenne said. She looked a little pale. "Should I break up with Fletcher?"

"Uh, Cheyenne, no," Norie said.

"No!" Tobey said. "You do what's right for you. I'm just telling my story."

"That's what we always do, right?" Norie said. She narrowed her eyes at me. "We haven't talked you into anything, have we, Marissa?"

I shook my head. No, they hadn't talked me into anything. But I was more sure than ever that what I was about to do was absolutely right—for me.

Norie glanced at her watch. "We have to go, guys. You okay, Marissa?"

I nodded and followed them out to the living room where they exited single file to Norie's Jeep. Watching all five of them squeeze in, giggling and snorting, I wanted to go with them.

No sooner had they disappeared down the street than Jason drove up from the other direction. I shouted good-bye to my parents and bolted out the front door as he pulled up to the curb.

"Don't let him think it's a date," the girls had advised me. "Meet him at the car, and don't let him open any doors or anything."

I jumped into the car before Jason could even open his door. He looked startled and then irritated.

"Okay," he said. "You in a hurry?"

"No," I said.

He put the car in gear. "I didn't plan anything for tonight. We're just going to talk."

"I know," I said. "I think that coffee shop on California Street would be a good place."

I think he choked.

"Why there?" he said.

"I've always wanted to go there," I said.

At the stop sign, he stared at me as if I had just said, "I've always wanted to march nude down Virginia Street."

"What's up with this all of a sudden?" he said.

"It isn't all of a sudden," I said. I could feel my heart hammering, but it was okay. I had promised the Girls, I had promised myself, I had even promised God. "I just never said anything before," I said. "We just always went where you wanted to go and did what you wanted to do. I figure I should get a turn."

"Like you ever spoke up," he said. "Like I knew what you wanted to do—"

"Do you want to take me to the coffee shop?" I said.

"I would rather go someplace else, if that's what you mean," he said.

"That's my point," I said.

The words surprised even me. I guess five girls praying in a car in a coffee shop parking lot is powerful stuff.

"So you're saying I don't even think about what you want?" he said.

"That's what I'm saying," I said. "Am I wrong?"

He didn't answer. We drove to the coffee shop in silence.

That was okay because I had the next step to think about. When we pulled into the lot, I concentrated on not looking for the Jeep and put my hand on the door handle. The minute Jason turned off the ignition and started to get out, I was out on my side too, carefully leaving the door unlocked.

I darted over to Jason and pretty much ran to the coffee shop entrance. It worked. Jason was too bewildered to look back for his usual are-you-all-right-boy? car check.

I made sure we sat at a table in the back, away from the window. I ordered an Italian soda and then tried to get comfortable in the chair. Jason ordered a hot chocolate. When the waitress had disappeared, he almost glared at me.

"So what's an Italian soda?" he said.

"They're good," I said. "You ought to try one."

"No thanks." His close-shaven jaw line looked tight.

I felt a twinge when I thought of how handsome that jaw line had always been to me, how it was the first thing I really had noticed about him. This wasn't going to be the piece of cake I had thought it might be in one of my weaker moments. I sat up straight in the chair.

"So, we need to talk," I said.

"Yeah, and I'm going to start," Jason said. "I know I've been acting weird, but you surprised me the other night."

I groaned inwardly. They said he would keep trying to steer it all back to the sexual thing. Man, those girls were smart.

"You thought I would do whatever you wanted me to," I said.

"I just thought you trusted me."

"I did," I said. "But I guess I was wrong."

"Why, because I love you so much I feel like I'm married to you?"

I shook my head.

"Then what?"

"I don't think you love me that much," I said.

"Oh, you don't."

"No, because if you loved me, you wouldn't try to force me to have sex with you."

"Force you!"

"Yes."

Jason's face slackened into a disgusted smirk. "What are you saying, I tried to rape you?"

"Not exactly," I said. "But you didn't stop when I said no. "

"Not on the first no."

"Why not?"

"Because you didn't really mean it."

"How do you know I didn't mean it?" I said. I didn't need to be coached on that one. I could feel my face turning red, my pulse beating in my neck.

"I know you, Rissa."

"*Ma*-rissa," I said.

"Whatever."

"No, not whatever. I have a name, I have a personality, I have a self…" I ran out of words and stopped. He didn't wait for me to start again.

"Like I don't know that," he said.

"Whatever," I said.

"Not whatever! I treated you like a little queen. But that isn't the point. The point is you were scared because I was ready for sex and you weren't, and now you're looking for excuses to run away. But I'm not going to let you do that, okay? I'll back off—"

"You're not going to 'let me'?" I said.

"No, I'm not. You can't just throw away something like we have—"

"What you don't 'let me' do is be the person I am without worrying about whether you're going to think it's lame."

"I made you feel lame?"

For the first time, a shadow of doubt appeared in his eyes. The

Girls hadn't even entertained that possibility. They said he would be hard-nosed the whole way. But I couldn't ignore it. I wanted to chase after it because it was my last hope that maybe Jason and I could fix this.

"Is that what you're saying?" he said again. "I made you feel lame?"

"Sometimes. Like when I showed you my poems for my aunt's wedding present and when we went up to Mount Rose and, like, when I would talk about God and you would say I didn't have the kind of relationship with Him that you did."

"You don't."

He said it as if it were a matter of fact. My heart took a dive that would have put Greg Louganis to shame. I knew it was over. I knew it was time to, as Norie had put it, pull the plug. I took a deep breath.

"That's why I can't be with you anymore," I said. This was the part I had rehearsed. "Because you don't know me, you don't respect me, you just want to rescue me, and I don't need to be rescued—not by you."

There. I had said it. I was sure it hadn't come out *sounding* like I had practiced it because his lower lip was hanging, and his eyes were searching my face like a pair of flashlights on high beam.

"You are so wrong, Marissa," he said finally.

The waitress appeared with our drinks, but Jason slapped some money on the table and pushed back his chair.

"Come on," he said. "I have to get out of here."

That was it. He headed for the door, and I grabbed my purse, heavy with the cell phone, and went after him.

I won't be needing that now, I thought. Suddenly our Plan of Action seemed unnecessary. It was over. Jason was going to take me home, and that was going to be it. I was so relieved I had to force myself to walk out the door instead of sagging into a corner.

Jason was waiting by his car, arms crossed over his chest. I started for the passenger door, but he reached out and softly took my arm in his fingers.

"I just want to know one thing," he said.

"What?"

"Who put you up to this?" he said.

I could feel my eyes popping open.

"Who told you that you ought to break up with me? Who knows anything about our relationship that they can fill your head with a bunch of stuff about how I don't let you be your own person? Was it that Norie chick?"

I fully expected Norie to fly out of her Jeep in the corner of the lot and come stomping over to us. I shook my head.

"Nobody put me up to anything," I said. "This is my decision."

"But I don't think you've really decided," he said. "It's all over your face, Rissa. You're just scared." He held on to my arm. "Come on. Let's go."

I didn't pull back because he was leading me to the driver's side. Just in case Shannon had forgotten to lock the door behind her, I didn't want him noticing that I had left it open. Still, as I crawled in and Jason fired up the engine and practically peeled out of the parking lot, my pulse started to race again. I willed myself not to look behind us. It was almost over anyway. I scooted over toward the door.

"Come back over here," Jason said. "Please."

"I don't want to," I said. "I just want you to take me home."

But he didn't turn down my street. He roared into a parking space at the park, turned off the key, and swiveled to look at me.

"I'm not going to let you do this," he said. "You know that, don't you?"

He was smiling, but I wasn't. It was like he was trying a different approach, groping for some way to lure me back.

"It isn't up to you," I said. "I've already decided."

"Even if I changed?" he said.

Now that was a surprise. Enough of one that I must have blinked, shifted my eyes, or shown some other glimmer of hesitation. Jason took it as an all-out reconciliation.

"Come here," he said. Without waiting for me to, he somehow got me into his arms and put his mouth against mine.

I pushed with the heels of my hands. "Stop!" I said when I could tear my lips free. "I...don't...want...to."

He grabbed my face with both hands and kissed me hard. I was struggling, and I was scared, but I still knew it wasn't a kiss of passion. It was a kiss of anger and wounded pride. Where it would have gone, I don't know. But I didn't wait to find out. I banged my hand against the car seat.

"She wants you to stop," said a thin little voice from the back. "So stop."

CHAPTER NINETEEN

I CAUGHT ONLY A GLIMPSE OF JASON'S ASTOUNDED FACE. I stuck my hand in my purse and pulled out the cell phone.

"742-2195," Shannon said, as she peeked over the car seat.

I poked the number with trembling fingers.

Jason, in the meantime, had retreated to his side of the car and was staring from Shannon to me with his jaw unhinged. It only took until I had finished dialing for him to recover. Then he was just about as mad as I've ever seen anybody.

"What's going on?" he spat out.

Norie's voice snapped crisply at the other end of the line. "Marissa?"

"Yeah. We're at the park on my street. Would you come pick us up?"

"We're right around the corner," she said.

Jason slammed his palms on the steering wheel. I expected to hear the car yelp.

"What are you doing?" he said.

"My friends are coming to pick us up."

"What is *she* doing here?"

He looked at Shannon, who looked at me.

"Helping me," I said.

"Do what?"

I didn't even hesitate. "Get away from you. Come on, Shannon."

I went for the door handle.

"I can't believe you did this," he said. "You didn't have to do this."

"I thought I did," I said. And I still thought I was right. As humiliated as he looked, as confused and bewildered, I still thought I had been right.

Norie's Jeep pulled up beside us, and the passenger door flew open. Shannon was out of Jason's car and in Norie's backseat almost before I could get out. She had done her thing, and she wasn't hanging around.

"Bye," I said to Jason.

He turned to stare straight through the windshield and didn't say a word. I climbed out and went to Brianna's waiting arms.

She pushed me into the backseat where Cheyenne, Shannon, and Tobey were already crammed.

"You all right?" Norie said from the driver's seat.

I could hear Jason's car squealing away, and for the tiniest second I wasn't all right. But Tobey put her hand on my leg and gave it a warm squeeze.

"She will be," she said.

That's when I started to cry. I buried my face in Tobey's shoulder and just sobbed, which was why I didn't see where we were going until Norie stopped the Jeep and I looked up.

"Where are we?" I said.

"Ira's house," Brianna said.

I slapped at the tears on my cheeks. "I really don't want to go in."

"I think you'll be glad you did," Tobey said.

"But this wasn't part of the Plan."

Norie grinned at me in the rearview mirror. "Not the part you knew about anyway."

"Come on," Cheyenne said, tugging at my sleeve. "It'll be okay; I promise."

I even believed little Cheyenne at that point. If somebody would just tell me what to do next, I would be fine.

I trailed into the close-to-a-mansion house behind the rest, with Shannon at my side, arm crooked through mine. She hadn't said a word since she had spewed out Norie's car phone number, but just having her there was comforting.

To my surprise, Wyatt opened the front door.

"How did it go?" he said.

"Great," Norie said. "The little jackal ran off with his tail between his legs."

Tobey poked her.

Brianna took over then and led us to the family room where Ira, as always, was propped up on his bed. Seeing him really wasn't on my list of things to do after breaking up with Jason.

"Sit here, girl," Brianna said. She motioned to a chair right next to Ira's bed. Wyatt sat on the other side, right across from me, and the Girls lined up at the foot of the bed as if they were about to have an audience with the Pope. I looked around blankly.

"What's going on?" I said.

"I haven't been in on a Plan in a long time," Ira said. "So they're going to let me help."

"I don't get it," I said.

Wyatt rubbed his hands together. He obviously had been quiet long enough. "We just wanted to make sure you got the whole picture."

"Of what?"

"Of what you just did."

"Wyatt, would you quit beating around the bush?" Norie said.

Ira, however, was the one who got to the point. "Don't be thinkin' this boy was your last chance or something."

I looked down at the still sweaty palms of my hands.

"Don't *think* it, Marissa," Wyatt said.

Ira couldn't shake his head in his neck brace, but his eyes were all "no." "Not all guys are jerks like he—"

"I wouldn't go that far," Tobey said. "I just think he got a little full of himself."

"A little?" Norie said. But she pressed her lips together and nodded at Ira.

"Here's the thing, girl," Ira said. "Well, two things. Any guy who can't deal with your decision is a guy you don't want."

"Okay," I said.

"What's the other thing?" Cheyenne said.

"Some people might tell you that every guy wants only one thing," Wyatt said.

"I hate that expression," Norie said.

"But it isn't true," Wyatt went on. "There are still some guys who aren't out there just to get you into bed. Some of us are pretty decent."

"But you're both taken," Cheyenne said.

"Cheyenne, zip it," Norie said.

"We aren't the only ones," Ira said. "Somebody is going to come along who is going to love you *because* you want to wait, not in spite of it." His brown eyes grew soft, and he smiled until I could see almost every one of his teeth. I wanted to hug him.

I felt so much better I even ate some of the pizza they had ordered. It wasn't until the next day that I started to feel empty and even a little bit dirty. I was on my second bath when I realized I was trying to wash Jason off of me.

But he was gone; I knew that. The phone didn't ring, and I didn't expect it to. I didn't want it to, and yet I was so incredibly lonely.

I would have called Tobey or Norie, but they were taking their SATs. Brianna was with her art teacher, finishing up the last of her paperwork for the Art Institute. Cheyenne had to do chores every Saturday morning. That left Shannon.

I wasn't sure whether to call her. We were better, the two of us. But the question of her illness still hung between us. I had put it aside when I was getting ready to break up with Jason, but now it was back again. I didn't see how we could go much further before it came up again. She hadn't touched a bite of pizza last night. She had taken maybe two sips of water, and that was it.

I was thinking longingly of how good it would be to have Veronica there when the phone rang. Anthony told me it was "some lady."

"Hi," Ms. Race said when I took the receiver from him. "How did it go last night?"

I took the phone into Abuelo's room and told her. When I got to where I was now, she stopped just saying uh-huh and said, "I have a suggestion for you."

"Anything," I said.

"Well, now, if it doesn't work for you, you won't hurt my feelings," she said. "But it helped me when I went through my breakup."

"Okay," I said.

"Try to find some things that symbolize what's really important to you. You know, your poetry and your family, things like that."

"Okay."

"Put them all around you on the floor, and just listen to God. I don't know, being surrounded by what you love, being with the One you love the most restores you to yourself."

"Is that why I feel so empty?" I said.

"Absolutely. I think that's what loneliness is, missing yourself and missing God."

When we hung up, I slipped off to my room, leaving the shrieking of Saturday morning cartoons and the bantering of my brothers over the breakfast dishes. With any luck, Luisa would be glued to the screen for another hour at least.

I looked around our room and surveyed my things. Slowly, I picked up a few.

My poetry collection.

The notebook I always wrote in.

A photo of my family.

My drawing from Brianna, my poster from Norie.

The Message.

I formed a circle with them on the floor, and I didn't feel idiotic at all the way I thought I would as I stepped into the center and sat down.

All around me were the reminders of what was important to me. My writing—not just what I had done, but the whole process of doing it. My family—infuriating as they could be sometimes. My Girls. My God.

I didn't want to close my eyes to it so I just looked around as I listened. I didn't have much luck at that—too many syllables crowded my head.

From now on, God, I thought, *will You just let me hear who You want me to be—and no one else?*

How are you going to know that, Marissa? I scolded myself.

But the evidence was all there. I would know it through my poetry, wouldn't I? And my family…some of them like Luisa, Veronica, and sometimes even Papa? And my Girls. I would never forget what they had done for me last night. It hadn't been life and death like it had been for Brianna, or my whole reputation like it had been for Norie and Tobey, or even my immediate future, the way it had been for Cheyenne. But it had been so real.

And it all could have turned out so differently.

I did close my eyes then and leaned my chin on my knees. Fifteen seconds later, the door flew open. I startled out of my position, but not soon enough. Eddie stood there with a crooked smirk on his face, and his mouth flew open. "She's finally lost it! All the icing has slid off her cupcakes!"

Anthony materialized beside him, with Reney close behind. They all gaped in the doorway like hyenas slobbering over a kill.

"Could you close the door please?" I said.

"What are you doing in here?" Anthony said. He pushed past the other two and invited himself in. His eyes glittered over my circle.

"What is this, some kind of female ritual or something?"

"She's trying to lure her boyfriend back," Eddie said.

"Did you guys break up?" Reney said. Her face went into a trance, like she was about to tune into *Days of Our Lives*.

"Please get out," I said. I was trying to keep my voice even.

"I'll tell you how to get him back," Eddie said.

"Like you really know," Anthony said.

Eddie flopped himself down on my bed. "What's to know? You just give him what he wants."

"What does he want?" Reney said, and then her eyes took on a spark. "Oh," she said. "That."

"What 'that,' nerd?" Anthony said. "You know even less than he does."

"I know!" Reney said indignantly. She flipped her thin hair over her shoulder. "You're talking about sex."

That was it. I came up off the floor and closed the door myself, with the three of them still in there.

"Sit down," I said.

"For what?" Anthony said.

I gave his lanky body a shove, and he stumbled toward the bed. Reney scrambled for a position between them. Eddie looked at Anthony and shrugged.

"Listen to me, all three of you," I said.

"What, you're going to give us a lecture?" Anthony said.

"No, I'm just going to give you some facts."

"Yikes!" Anthony said in mock shock. "The sex talk!"

"No," I said. "Not the sex talk."

Reney looked disappointed.

"All I want to say is that it's time you guys respected yourselves and the opposite sex. Because someday sex *is* going to come up, and it isn't going to be a joke."

I watched them. Reney looked ready to hear every detail. Eddie looked at Anthony so he would know what to do. Anthony rolled his eyes so Eddie did it, too.

"Okay, fine," I said. "But you need to start thinking about it."

"That's all I do think about," Eddie said, wiggling his eyebrows.

"That's not what I mean," I said. "You guys need to come to Sunday school with me tomorrow."

"Sunday school?" Eddie said. He didn't need Anthony's lead for that one.

"Yeah," I said. "Be ready at nine."

"Who died and left you in charge?" he said.

I looked at him, and he mumbled. "Sorry."

"And Veronica left," I said. "So now it's up to me."

"We don't have to go," Eddie said. "I'm going to ask Papa."

Anthony followed him out. Reney stayed on the bed.

"This Sunday school," she said. "Are cute boys there?"

I started to sigh and order her out of the room, but I stopped. "Yeah," I said. "Lots of them."

Her little beady eyes gleamed. "What should I wear?"

Later, as I was picking up my circle and putting things away, I realized something. I hadn't had anything on the floor to remind me of the *zonsas*—Roz, Francesca, and Daniela.

They weren't like the *mocosos*, I thought as I settled back down on my bed. They were good girls; I still loved them. The *mocosos* thought they had it all figured out. My *zonzas*, they were still ramming around.

As Abuelo would have said, they didn't understand the details. Me, I was starting to think that maybe I did.

I went to the kitchen and called Daniela.

"Hey, girl," she said. "What are you up to?"

"Want to do something this afternoon?" I said.

"Sure. You want me to call Fran and Roz?"

"No," I said. "Let's just you and me have a Coke. I want to tell you about something."

We had a great afternoon. Daniela, to my surprise, cried when I told her what had happened, what the Girls did for me.

"I wish I had had that," she said. "I feel so…trampy now."

I told her she wasn't a tramp, and we shopped some, and I bought her an ice cream. We promised to spend more time together over the summer.

When I arrived home, I had a message from Shannon. Anthony had scrawled it on a piece of paper. He wasn't speaking to me since Papa had said, "Yes, I think it's a good idea you go to church with your sister."

Mama wasn't much happier. He had told her she should take us all.

"You want them to go, you take them yourself," I heard her say to him. "I have things to do too."

What he told her, I wasn't sure. They closed their door. If I really had wanted to know, I could have asked Reney.

Anyway, when I called Shannon, she said, "Meet me at Rancho, would you?"

This time when I found her, she wasn't hugging herself and crying. But she did look white-faced and stiff as a pole.

"What happened?" I said. "Did your sister come home?"

"Monday," she said. "Before she does, I think I have to tell my parents."

"Tell them what?" I said.

She looked down at the toe of her sandal. "That I'm anorexic."

I'm sure I couldn't have looked more shocked if I had never suspected. I tried to recover fast and grabbed hold of one of her little bird-hands.

"What made you decide?" I said.

"Your poem," she said.

I shook my head.

"Yes, the one you put in my bag the night I spent at your house."

"I don't understand," I said.

"I didn't either at first. But what you said, after a while it dawned on me. It's like you listen to a song a lot, and then one day the words make sense."

I tried to remember the poem, but Shannon recited it.

"'Fire in her pale eyes / but her body is so frail / it won't hold the flame.' I think I know what it means," she said. "It's, like, I have so much, but if I keep staying sick, I won't be able to do anything with it."

"Yeah," I said. "That's what I meant. But why do you have to tell your parents? Can't you just start eating again? I'll fix you a whole meal—"

She shook her head, pale hair blowing in the Nevada wind. "I've tried," she said. "Now I can't make myself eat. It's like the food just won't go in, and if it does, I throw it up. I can't stop this by myself. I feel like I don't deserve to eat or something."

I put my arms around her, and she held on like a skeleton. Jason had been right about one thing: I didn't know anything about this. I couldn't really help.

Except to be her friend, the way she had been to me.

"You're the best," she whispered to me. "I don't know what I would do without you."

Monday, when I came home from school, I had two letters in the mail. One was from Jason.

"I've been doing a lot of thinking," he wrote. "I really did push you too hard, and I'm sorry, and I hope you'll forgive me. The Bible says we're supposed to forgive, seventy times seven if we have to. I'm willing to admit I was wrong, see? But I'm not asking you to come back. I don't think it would work. You wouldn't even give me a chance to change. I didn't even know until tonight that you felt the way you did. All I wanted to do was share my world with you and help you. But I can't ask you to forgive me unless I forgive you, and I do. You're still a great girl, and I hope you find somebody who wants to do it your way. Jason."

I didn't even wait for it to sink in. I called Tobey and read it to her over the phone.

"Did I give up too easily?" I said.

"Uh, no," Tobey said. "He has a long way to go before he figures out he's trying to do God's job. Everybody comes off obnoxious when they do that."

"I didn't think he was obnoxious at first," I said. "I guess I'm just naive."

"No, he wasn't obnoxious at first. It changed. He's not really a user; he's just...what's the word? 'Misguided' right now. I just wish I had warned you when I first saw it happening."

I was shaking my head. "You know what, Tobey? It isn't like letting me drive drunk or something. I learned a lot. I'm never going to let this happen again."

"Well, I'm glad you didn't have to learn it the hard way," she said. "A lot of girls do."

"I know," I said. "I have this friend. Do you think you could talk to her about True Love Waits?"

When we hung up, I opened the other letter. It was from myself.

It wasn't a letter exactly. More like a couple of poems I had written just for me. It was funny how I hadn't known exactly what they had meant at the time. But I did now. Especially one.

> The silver spider
> works her web of sticky lace
> without looking back.

A second layer of meaning rested underneath the words, and I'm pretty sure it came from God.

Join millions of other students in praying for your school! See You at the Pole, a global day of student prayer, is the third Wednesday of September each year. For more information, contact:

See You at the Pole
P.O. Box 60134
Fort Worth, TX 76115
24-hour SYATP Hotline: 619/592-9200
Internet: www.syatp.com
e-mail: pray@syatp.com